Dear Reader,

Moving can be heart-wrenching. For much of my life, I lived in a rural south-central Pennsylvania town not far from Gettysburg. I attended college in Virginia but soon made my way back to my roots, where I stayed for more than twenty-five years, until my children were grown. Then my husband and I decided to pursue something we'd always talked about: living in a university town. We moved several hours north to State College, Pennsylvania, a bustling, vibrant little community nestled in the heart of the state among the mountains.

We thoroughly enjoyed settling in, becoming part of the community and making new friends...but we sure did miss our old pals, our home church, and having extended family so close. And, as we soon discovered, it's never quite the same when you go back to visit.

Leaving *Miracles of Marble Cove* behind has been a similarly bittersweet experience. During the creation of the series, each author and editor involved helped shape the characters, the plots, the ultimate direction of the entire series, in ways large and small. Now that the final chapter has been written, it's a bit heart-rending to leave it all behind. Each of us has new projects, new paths to follow, but saying good-bye to Diane, Shelley, Margaret, and Beverly saddens us. We know our readers feel the same. Good friends are hard to find and even harder to leave behind.

Blessings,
Anne Marie Rodgers

For my über-awesome son-in-law
Captain Robert A. Walters, U.S. Army,
currently flying missions in
Operation Enduring Freedom, Afghanistan.
Your presence in our lives (beagles, Blackhawks,
LotR, cutthroat games and all) is such a blessing, and
your devotion to our daughter is a joy to witness.
Love you, Bob. We pray many times daily
for your safe return.

I also must mention two very special kittens who
graced my life during the writing of this story.
This is in memory of Xylo, who died at just
seventeen weeks of age, but who left tiny paw prints
on our hearts that will last a lifetime;
and in honor of Yodel, our little one-eyed wonder,
who overcame the odds.

MIRACLES *of*
MARBLE COVE

TIME TO REMEMBER

ANNE MARIE RODGERS

Guideposts
New York

Miracles of Marble Cove is a trademark of Guideposts.

Published by Guideposts Books & Inspirational Media
110 William Street
New York, NY 10038
Guideposts.org

Acknowledgments

Every attempt has been made to credit the sources of copyrighted material used in this book. If any such acknowledgment has been inadvertently omitted or miscredited, receipt of such information would be appreciated.

"From the Guideposts Archive" originally appeared in *Guideposts* magazine. Copyright © 2008 by Guideposts. All rights reserved.

Cover and interior design and cover photography by Müllerhaus
© Stefan Koschminder (1952 Jaguar XK120)
Stock photography from iStock
Typeset by Aptara, Inc.

Printed and bound in the United States of America
10 9 8 7 6 5

Chapter One

"Whoops!" Beverly Wheeland stumbled as she made the short trip down Newport Avenue from her home to her friend Diane Spencer's cottage. She hadn't been watching where she was going because much of her attention had been directed across the street, studying the former Simpson house that occupied the lot next to Dan and Shelley Bauer's home at the end of the street.

Happiness coursed through Beverly. Tomorrow, she and her fiancé, Jeff Mackenzie, were scheduled to walk through their new home again. One month from today, on the first of June, they would marry and move into that home very soon afterward to begin their life together. It all just seemed too wonderful to be true!

The coastal Maine May evening was equally wonderful. As the days lengthened, the weather warmed. Tonight was mild enough that Beverly wore only a shawl-necked merino cardigan sweater over her lacy top and slim denims. It was so pleasant not to be swaddled in layers of down and fleece.

Shelley Bauer, another dear friend, stepped out of her front door a moment before Beverly turned into Diane's front walk. "Hey, neighbor!"

"Hi, Shelley." Beverly smiled as the pretty young blonde crossed the street to join her.

"Is that something new to taste-test?" Beverly indicated the covered basket Shelley carried. The Newport Avenue friends all enjoyed Shelley's budding career as a baker, although their waistlines certainly didn't.

"Raspberry white-chocolate mousse."

"Oh no. I have to fit into a wedding dress in a month!"

"I know." Shelley snickered. "I'm just making sure you fill it out properly."

Grinning together, they walked up to Diane's door and knocked.

It took only a moment for their friend to pull open the door. "Come in, come in," Diane said, her eyes sparkling as she stepped back to usher them inside. "Margaret's already here. It's the bride-to-be and her baker sidekick," she said over her shoulder to Margaret Hoskins.

"Hi, ladies," Margaret said. She was seated on Diane's couch sipping coffee. She looked comfortable in blue jogging pants with a matching zip hoodie over a T-shirt. Eyeing her sturdy sneakers, Beverly suspected Margaret had been out for a stroll.

Diane might have gone with her, although she wore jeans and a navy cable-knit cardigan with rubber clogs. It was wonderful to see Diane looking so healthy. Her cheeks were pink and she looked rested. She still sometimes wore one of the two wigs she'd purchased when chemo had caused her hair to fall out during her breast cancer treatment regimen, but Beverly knew that now that she was finished with chemo, it was beginning to grow back.

"So what's the latest wedding scoop?" Diane took Shelley's basket, peeking inside and saying, "*Yummm*."

"I'm not sure much is new," Beverly said, "except that I keep worrying about what might happen if it rains the night of the rehearsal. Men never think about things like that, do they?"

"Oh, right." Shelley snapped her fingers. "Clambake on the beach. Diane and I are catering."

"I can't wait!" Diane sounded as excited as Shelley as she brought coffee to each of the new arrivals. "I'm putting in an order for good weather right now."

"I'm tempted to rent an alternative venue just in case," Beverly said. "Then it's sure to be nice, right?"

Diane laughed. "Murphy's Law. If you rent it, you won't need it."

Margaret tapped a finger against her lips. "What if we used the gallery as your backup?"

All three of the others stared at her.

"That's a great idea!" Diane said. At the same moment, Beverly began, "Oh, I couldn't let you go to—"

"That would be perfect," Shelley chimed in. "Most of the food could work in both places, and even if we can't bake the clams on the beach, I could do them at my house and bring them to the gallery."

"The only hitch is that we wouldn't be able to wait until the last minute to decide," Diane said. "You'd need to check the weather and decide in the morning, because it takes a couple of hours to get that fire hot enough to cook on the beach."

"That's doable." Beverly nodded slowly. "Thank you, Margaret. I really appreciate the offer."

"I almost hope it *does* rain," Shelley said. "I think the gallery would be a wonderful place for the rehearsal dinner!"

Beverly chuckled. "I *almost* agree." She blew out a breath in relief as the idea sank in. "Wow, do I ever appreciate your offer." She smiled warmly at Margaret. "I didn't realize how much that's been on my mind."

It was true. A clambake on the beach would not have been her choice for the rehearsal after-party, simply because of the complications the weather could throw at them. It had been Jeff's idea, and she hadn't wanted to point out the potential problem the weather could create. Otherwise, she'd liked the casual nature of the plan. It was everything her first wedding hadn't been, and this time she was determined to keep it simple and straightforward. No overly elegant formality for this wedding.

"What else is on your mind?" Diane asked. "You've got most of the details nailed down now, right?"

Beverly nodded. She couldn't control her smile as she said, "Even my dress! This month can't go fast enough for me. I can't wait to wear my dress."

"Reverend Locke is doing the ceremony at Old First, and the reception will be at the Landmark Inn." Shelley, almost as much of a planner as Beverly herself, ticked off items on her fingers as she spoke. "You've got your bridesmaids and ring bearer. How about the groomsmen?"

"Friends of Jeff's," Beverly said. "Standish Florist is doing the bouquets and church flowers, and Jeff's grandfather and Celia Patterson have offered flowers from their gardens for the reception. Mrs. Peabody is making the punch. What else? I have my mother's bracelet for something old. My dress, I guess, is the something new."

"You could wear the garter I wore when I was married," Diane offered. "That would cover borrowed and blue."

"Thank you." Beverly leaned over to hug Diane. "That's perfect."

"And I'm baking the cake." Shelley grinned, still ticking off items on her fingers. "Which reminds me, I have some pictures to show you when we get a minute."

Margaret glanced up. "Who's your photographer?"

Beverly smiled. "A colleague of Jeff's. Jeff knew exactly who he wanted, and the guy's prices were reasonable. I think he cut us a break because Jeff is his buddy."

"Is there anything important left to do?" Diane asked.

"I haven't gotten a limo yet." Beverly grimaced. "It's been on my to-do list but I put it off, and when I started calling around, every company was already booked. I don't suppose any of you know of a limo service in the area?"

All three of the others looked blank.

"I honestly can't say that I do." Margaret's forehead creased. "I imagine if you check around Augusta or Portland you'd find something."

"But that might cost a small fortune to get them to come all the way over here," Shelley pointed out.

"I already called three businesses," Beverly said. "That was all I could find within a reasonable distance." She sighed. "I'm not quite sure what to do next."

"I can handle it," Diane informed her. "Why don't you let me worry about finding transportation? If there's no limo service available, I promise I will conjure up something fun."

Beverly smiled, ridiculously relieved. "That would be terrific. Thank you!" She knew she could trust Diane to come through, and it would be lovely not to have to worry about it.

"This is all so exciting!" Shelley said. "I'm getting impatient. I can't wait to start on your cake."

"I'm excited for the wedding," Beverly said, "but now I'm equally excited about our new house. I nearly tripped over my own feet coming down the street because I was so busy looking at my house. Well, almost my house."

"When do you close?" Margaret's gaze strayed to the window through which she could see Beverly's new home-to-be.

"Early next month. I'd like to have our plans all in place for the remodel by then. The sooner I can get a contractor in there, the sooner we can move in."

"How much work do you anticipate having done?" Diane asked. Beverly imagined she was thinking back to the changes she had made to her cottage when she'd moved to Marble Cove.

"We're not sure yet. We'll be walking through tomorrow making a list." She looked around, suddenly a bit self-conscious. "Doesn't anyone else have anything exciting to share? I feel like I've been talking about me, me, me since I came through the door."

"You're the bride; that's what you're supposed to do," Diane said with a fond smile. Then the smile grew. "But, as a matter of fact, I did ask you all here tonight for a reason." She reached behind the couch and came up with three copies of a book. "My advance copies of my second book are here, and I have one for each of you."

Margaret squealed, sounding more like Shelley, and snatched the book Diane held out. "Oh, this is great!" She smoothed a hand over the cover. *"Peril on the Point,"* she read out loud, studying the seascape of ocean waves smashing against a sturdy outcropping of rock. "What a striking cover."

"I'm going to start reading as soon as I get home." Shelley hugged her copy to her breast. Then she grinned sheepishly. "Well, maybe as soon as the kids are in bed."

Everyone chuckled.

"What's next?" Beverly asked Diane.

"My book of devotionals is coming together," her friend said, "and the third book has been turned in and is scheduled for next spring."

"So what are you going to write about next?" Shelley asked. "Any research we can help with?"

"If there is, you'll be the first to know." She spread her hands. "I'm not sure what I'm going to do next. Right now

I'm kicking around ideas and researching." She smiled, looking around at each of her friends. "But I have some other news too." She hesitated, building the anticipation. "I saw my oncologist today and...I am officially in remission!"

"Diane, that's wonderful!" Shelley erupted from her seat to give Diane an enthusiastic hug. "I can't believe you waited this long to tell us that."

Diane grinned. "I didn't want to steal Beverly's thunder. The wedding plans are important—and a lot more fun to discuss than my health."

Beverly shook her head, rising to give her friend a warm hug as well. "Oh, I think not. Your health is the most important thing I can think of. This is fabulous news." She held Diane by the shoulders and looked at her intently. "Completely clean bill of health?"

"Completely clean bill of health," Diane repeated. "As boringly normal as I can get."

Margaret wiped away tears as she also stepped forward to hug Diane, but she snickered. "'Boringly normal' is the last description anyone is ever likely to use for you, lady. Congratulations."

"In remission." Beverly repeated the welcome phrase. "Best two words in the English language."

"Top of the list," Diane agreed. "Right up there with 'I do,' and 'I love you.'"

"Also important," Margaret agreed. "So now what? No more chemo, no more doctors' visits?"

"A few more doctors' visits," Diane admitted. "They want to keep an eye on me, given that this cancer was a repeat performance. But I feel certain I am done with cancer. I intend to recommit to living my life to the fullest every single day in every aspect. That includes my writing, spending time with my family, my friends, and Leo—"

"And Leo." Margaret winked knowingly at the others.

"And supporting other cancer patients," Diane finished, playfully ignoring her grinning girlfriends. "Surviving a second time gives me a—a moral imperative, if you will—to be a beacon of light for others who are engaged in their own battles with breast cancer."

Beverly's grin morphed into a warm smile. "I like that," she said. "I can't think of anyone I'd rather meet if I were dealing with that diagnosis."

"Has anyone seen Noah Henry recently?" Margaret asked, changing the subject as Diane rose to bring the coffeepot in for refills all around. "Has he come back to town?"

The others all shook their heads, their faces registering varying degrees of concern.

"I asked Brenna if she'd seen or heard from him," Shelley said, "but she hasn't."

"That's too bad," Diane said. "They seemed to be getting along so well." She winced. "I hope he didn't leave without saying good-bye."

"Brenna didn't say," Shelley admitted. "She looked a bit sad, so I didn't have the heart to pursue it."

"His grandfather pulled off a king-size disappearing act," Beverly pointed out. "Noah could be following in his footsteps. He seemed so personable, but it's a possibility, I suppose, given his background."

"Oh, goodness, I hope not," Margaret said.

Beverly could hear the doubt in her friend's voice. "It would be an awfully big coincidence," she admitted. "Just because the grandfather was a bad apple doesn't mean his descendants are."

"If he planned it, it wouldn't be coincidental at all," Diane pointed out. "But there's no motive, no reason. Noah didn't need to disappear as far as we know."

"No motive that we know of," Beverly reminded them all. "Doesn't mean there isn't one."

"What we don't know about Noah Henry would fill a book," Shelley said, frowning. "I was really hoping a meeting with him would help us find out more about how and why Elias Thorpe left town all those years ago."

Margaret sighed. "Me too. It's going to drive me crazy if we never get any resolution."

"He gets a week," Diane said. "And if there's no word from or of him in that time, I'm going to see what I can do to track him down. Either he's just plain rude or he's up to something unsavory, and I want to know which it is."

CHAPTER TWO

Margaret cleared her throat. "I cannot *wait* for my trip to Paris in July." It was a determined conversational shift, but the others accepted it with good grace.

"You're so lucky," Shelley said, longing evident in her tone. "I would love to go to Europe someday."

"Have you heard back about that art class you're hoping to take?" Diane asked.

Margaret's pleasure morphed into mild anxiety as she thought of the mailing she had just received. "Yes. My paperwork is all in order, but before I can be registered for a particular class, I have to submit a piece of art they'll use to decide which class I enroll in." She wrapped her hands around her own throat and mimed choking. "I'm terrified. What if I choose the wrong thing? What if, despite the fact that I have other wonderful work, they don't like that one piece and dump me in some basic technique class?"

Diane patted her friend's back. "Margaret, your talent is evident in every brushstroke on your canvases. Even if they—who is 'they' anyway?—don't like your work on a personal level, your skill is undeniable, and I imagine that's what they are looking for—students with the talent to absorb the information a certain class will present, to learn and to grow, whether or not the chosen piece is something they like."

Margaret regarded Diane wryly, not sure her words were helpful. "So I should choose a piece I don't like?"

Beverly chuckled. "That's not what she meant, silly. Would you like some opinions?"

Margaret grinned, relaxing a little. "Yes, actually. I've already picked out several pieces, and I'd like each of you to choose a favorite from among them. Stop by the gallery before the end of the week if you get a chance and let me know what you think."

"I can already tell you which is my favorite," Shelley began.

"Wait!" Margaret held up a hand in the universal gesture for *stop*. "I only want you to tell me which is your favorite from the ones I've selected." She inspected the raspberry mousse, selected a cup, and picked up a spoon. "With my luck, each of you would have a favorite that wasn't even on my list, and then I'd have twice as much trouble deciding."

"Okay." Shelley smiled. "But someday—maybe even after you get back from Paris—I'm going to tell you which is my all-time favorite Margaret Hoskins work." Then her face brightened. "Oh! I almost forgot! I have big news too."

"What?" Diane demanded. She too took a mousse cup, gesturing at Shelley and Beverly. "Eat!"

Shelley looked around at her three friends before she obeyed Diane's command. "I have decided to take Rusty up on his offer to sell me the Cove when he retires in October."

"Oh my gracious! That *is* news," Beverly said. She set down her dessert to pull the young woman into a hug. "How can you forget that?"

Shelley laughed. "Weddings and novels and Paris—oh my!"

Margaret laughed, appreciating the takeoff on the famous movie phrase. "This is wonderful news, Shelley."

"The timing is great," Shelley told her, "because it will give me the whole slow season to get my feet under me, to get used to managing the place before tourist season hits."

"And how's Dan feel about this?" Diane asked.

Shelley giggled. "He's almost more excited than I am! And let me tell you, I'm excited. I can't believe that my dream of owning a storefront bakery is going to come true."

"I wonder," Margaret said, thinking of the café staff, "if Brenna will want to keep working for you. She didn't have aspirations to own it, did she?"

"Oh, you mean might she be angry that Rusty didn't offer it to her?" Shelley shook her head. "I don't believe so. I found out that Brenna is really an elementary school teacher. She wants to go back to it, but right now she's working at the Cove and taking classes toward her Masters. That way, she can take care of her grandmother, whose health is failing. I think the poor little lady will soon have to go into a facility where there's more supervision and care than Brenna can give her at home."

"I didn't know that," Beverly said. Margaret imagined she was silently thanking God for her own father's relatively good health. "That's too bad."

Shelley nodded. "It's unfortunate, but she says getting to spend this time with her grandmother has been a true gift from heaven."

Diane smiled. "Brenna's a wonderful young woman. I hope Noah hasn't broken her heart."

"I guess we'll just have to wait and see." Beverly didn't look optimistic.

Noah had seemed like such a nice young man. Margaret wanted to believe there was a good explanation for his absence, but given what they knew of his family tree, it was all too plausible for the apple to have fallen right at the base of that tree.

★ ★ ★

The following morning, Shelley opened at the Cove. She had finished most of the early pastries when Brenna arrived.

"Good morning," the young woman sang out. "How are you on this fine Thursday morning?"

"Good morning. I'm fine, thank you. And what's got you in such a marvelous mood?"

Brenna shrugged. "Sun's shining." Then she looked up from the flatware she was already pulling from the drawer, and her eyes were bright. "Oh, and I got a call from Noah this morning."

"You did?" Last night's conversation immediately leaped into Shelley's mind. "Where's he been? When is he coming back? If it hadn't been a good conversation, you wouldn't have that silly grin on your face."

Brenna laughed. "Am I that transparent?"

Shelley nodded. "Clear as glass. Now spill."

Brenna sighed dreamily. "I barely know the man. I shouldn't be so thrilled. But, oh, Shelley, I like him a lot." She nudged the flatware drawer closed with a hip. "He owns a couple of technology businesses, he said, and he recently bought a new one. He got an unexpected call from his lawyer, who was handling the deal. I guess some type of complication with the sellers made him fear the deal might fall through, and he had to be on the West Coast the next day for an 8:00 AM meeting. He dropped everything and ran."

"And called you the first chance he got," Shelley said. "That's sweet."

"Oh, and he asked me to give you and your friends a message," Brenna told her.

"Really?" Shelley was surprised that the young man would even have thought twice about them. "What did he say?"

"He wanted to apologize for standing you up. He says his sudden absence was unavoidable, but he feels bad he didn't let you know. When he gets back to town, he'd like to reschedule a meeting."

"So he's definitely coming back." Shelley grinned, seeing a smile blossom on Brenna's face again.

"I don't know when yet, though. He said he'd call me when he had a flight planned." The younger woman's cheeks were rosy.

As Brenna turned and headed for the dining room, Shelley allowed herself a small private grin. Unless she was very much mistaken, there was romance in the air.

★ ★ ★

As Jeff and Beverly approached the front door of the home they soon would own, they looked around at the yard. It was the worse for wear after the winter, and there were dead branches, brown leaves, and muddy patches everywhere.

Beverly thought of Diane's and Margaret's colorful gardens. With a little help from her friends, there was no reason she couldn't turn this yard into a pretty cottage garden. Both women already had offered to give her divisions of a number of their plants, and she had started a spreadsheet of which things grew during which seasons, and what colors and sizes they were. Shelley had chuckled when she'd heard that, but to Beverly, it made perfect sense. How else would she keep track of all the different things she intended to put in her beds?

"Yikes," Jeff said as they stepped onto the porch. "I forgot how shabby this was."

"It definitely needs a new coat of paint and some new boards, at the very least," Beverly said.

"Yes, but do you like the basic structure of the porch?" Jeff asked. "I was thinking that maybe we could expand it so it stretches the length of the house. Maybe put a swing at one end, and a trellis for roses or something that would grow up it...?" He trailed off, his voice uncertain.

"Oh, I like that idea. Margaret has climbing roses. I forgot what she called them, but they're some hardy kind that does well in the seaside climate up here." She smiled. "And a swing would be lovely. We could sit out here on summer nights and wave at the neighbors."

Jeff laughed as he tested a squeaky board. "We could." He gestured to the notebook she carried. "You taking notes? We need to have this porch floor checked for rot, whether or not we redesign it."

Beverly walked over and flicked a chip of flaking paint from the exterior wall with the end of her pen. "And do we want to paint it again, or would you rather have siding or a rustic exterior?"

Jeff looked thoughtful. "Rustic? Hmm, I never thought of that. Why don't we research exterior looks and see what we think we might like?" He grinned. "If we're going to live here for the rest of our lives, we ought to like looking at it from the outside as well as the inside."

After making a few more notes, they moved inside. As they did so, Jeff's cell phone rang.

Pulling it from his pocket, he glanced at the display and said, "It's my mother." Clicking the face of his phone, he lifted it to his ear. "Hi, Mom. How are you?"

Beverly walked around the living room, trying not to eavesdrop. She hadn't spent much time around Jeff's mother, but they were very different personalities, and sometimes she wondered how well they were going to rub along as the years passed. Carolyn seemed to have tunnel vision when it came to the many different ways a person could do good in the world. If it wasn't her way and her cause, she didn't appear to respect it.

"You what?" It was impossible not to hear Jeff's voice. He sounded incredulous and angry. "Mom, there will always be people to help and relief work to do, but I am only getting married once in my life. Yes, I expect you to be here!"

There was a long silence as he listened. Glancing at him, Beverly saw his lips form into an uncompromising line. Carolyn, she imagined, was talking a mile a minute, rushing to explain why her work was more important than anything else.

Finally, Jeff said abruptly, "Your choice, Mom. But no, it's not okay with me. You skipped out on the engagement party that you planned, and now you're talking about missing the wedding."

He listened. Then he said, "Let me know what you decide. And please don't wait until the day before the wedding to decide either." He tapped the End button with perhaps more force than necessary.

"Oh, honey," Beverly said. "I'm so sorry."

Jeff stood tensely in the middle of the room. He lifted a hand to the back of his neck and rubbed, relaxing a little as Beverly came over and embraced him.

"Maybe she was just testing the waters, and she'll come now that she's gotten your reaction."

"I hope so," Jeff said grimly, "because if she doesn't, it might just affect our relationship on a permanent basis. I don't often ask things of her. Just once, would it be so hard for her to be there for me?"

Beverly massaged his shoulder. The plaintive tone in his voice broke her heart. Most of the time, she believed it had been a very good thing for Carolyn to let her parents raise her son. As flighty as his mother was, his childhood could have been far less stable than it had been with his beloved grandparents. But now she realized that his mother's choice had marked Jeff more than she'd imagined. Perhaps some part of that little boy had viewed it as abandonment. She didn't know what to say.

Jeff pulled in a great breath and slowly let it out. "Well," he said, "there's nothing I can do about it. She'll make her choice."

Beverly looked around the room. "You're right. Now. Back to business. What are your thoughts on this space?"

"I like the fireplace," Jeff said, clearly trying to set aside the moment and be positive.

Beverly smiled. "Me too. Now that I see the space again, I think our idea of knocking down the walls on the main floor and turning this into a great room is a good one. We could have an island to help define the kitchen space. Instead of a formal dining room, we'd create a table space off one side of the kitchen, maybe put in a bay window."

Jeff's eyebrows rose, and he nodded. "I agree. I wonder how difficult it would be to move the staircase. Otherwise, it's going to come down right through the middle of the space. We'll have to double-check which are the supporting walls."

"You have a good point. Maybe the stairs could be placed along the wall there by the master bedroom."

Jeff nodded. "I was thinking if we added that little room with the card table to the bedroom space, we'd have a nice suite with a good-size bathroom and walk-in closet. Then we could update that bathroom upstairs and turn those bedrooms into our home offices."

Beverly was surprised and pleased. "You really have given this a lot of thought."

"I've been playing with options in my mind," Jeff admitted. "But it all depends on what you want as well."

"I can't say I've disliked a single one of your ideas." She smiled at him. "Keep the brilliance coming."

Encouraged by her receptive response, Jeff took a deep breath. "All right. I'd also like to change the fireplace from wood to gas and maybe replace that hearth and mantel with local stone."

"Oh, I'd like that!" She looked down at the yellowed flooring with distaste. "I think this is good maple. I wonder how it would look if we had it sanded and refinished. We could do a tile floor in the kitchen area, or even extend the wood the whole way through the main floor."

Jeff agreed. "We're going to want to pretty much gut the kitchen. What if we had maple cupboards installed?"

Beverly hesitated. "I generally tend to prefer painted cabinetry...but I'm open to new ideas. How do you feel about stainless steel appliances?"

"Good," Jeff said decisively, grinning. "I feel very good about stainless steel. And a dishwasher is a must. How about granite countertops?"

"I'd like that," Beverly said.

"And new window treatments." Jeff looked doubtfully at the dusty Venetian blinds. "I'm not much of a miniblinds fan, but otherwise I'll leave the window treatments to you."

"All right." Beverly made herself a note. "There are plenty of other options."

"What do you want to do about heat?" Jeff made a face. "I'm not thrilled about that oil furnace, to be honest."

"Nor am I." Beverly spread her hands helplessly. "I don't know enough about it to have an answer. Can we research it? I'd like to find an option that's cleaner and greener, if it's not too terribly expensive."

Jeff looked thoughtful. "We need to find out how old it is. And we might want to install some solar panels as well. Solar is expensive to install, but eventually it pays for itself."

Beverly chuckled. "Ooo-kay. I'll handle the window treatments; you deal with the heating."

"It's a deal."

Beverly opened the back door and stepped out onto the deck. "This needs work, but it isn't a bad size."

"And the yard is a great size for Scamp. We'll need to inspect the fence and make sure there's no way the little squirt can sneak through it anywhere."

She looked around. "There's enough work out here to keep us busy for years."

"True. But most of the inside is going to be finished by professionals who know what they're doing, so we'll have time for this. And it'll be fun to work on it together." He crossed to her side and put his arms around her, tilting her chin up for a kiss.

He seemed to have recovered from his annoyance with his mother, but Beverly knew Jeff was as good as she at compartmentalizing his life. She hoped Carolyn understood that if she decided not to attend the wedding, Jeff was liable to put her in a compartment with a Do Not Open sign on the door!

CHAPTER THREE

Beverly left her office in the municipal building just before three on Friday afternoon. Margaret had asked her friends to come to the gallery to look at the paintings she had selected as candidates for her program submission, and she had made Beverly promise to stop by at three. After a trip to the post office, Beverly headed down the street to the Shearwater Gallery.

But as she approached the windows, she could see that the lights were off inside. Was Margaret closed? Perhaps she'd forgotten she'd asked Beverly to come. But no, the sign on the door said Open, and Margaret nearly always flipped it over to say Closed even if she just ran down the street to the post office.

It was difficult to see in the windows, because Margaret had just created a new window display that obscured the interior of the gallery. It wasn't a good move, Beverly thought. Margaret had some lovely things inside, and cluttering up the windows like that made it impossible to showcase the items inside. She debated whether or not she should say something as she tugged open the door and entered—

"Surprise!"

Shelley, Margaret, Adelaide, Diane, and a group of other women popped out from behind pillars and easels as Margaret flipped on the lights. "Welcome to your shower!" Margaret said.

"My shower…?" Beverly put a hand to her heart, completely stunned. This was her second marriage, and it had never even occurred to her that anyone would do anything like this for her. Tears stung her eyes as her cousin Charlotte moved forward to hug her and lead her forward. "Your bridal shower," Charlotte clarified.

To her astonishment, Jeff's mother, Carolyn, was the next to come forward, giving Beverly a kiss on the cheek. "You really were surprised," Carolyn said, grinning. "Your friends were sure you knew."

Beverly shook her head. "Not a clue." She was pleased to see Carolyn there; it would make Jeff happy that his mother had made the effort. Perhaps this meant that she would also consider changing her travel plans so she could attend the wedding.

Charlotte guided Beverly to a chair swagged with a large white bow near a folding table, which had been covered with white lace and held a beribboned white parasol tilted at a rakish angle. In front of it a sheet cake proclaimed with piped icing: "Congratulations, Beverly and Jeff" and displayed a beautiful design of pink roses and two intertwined silver rings. A punch bowl beside it was filled with pale pink punch in which floated some type of blossoms. A pile of gifts sat to the left of the bride's chair.

Beverly could hardly take it in. Her aunt Helen, Maddie Bancroft, and a few members of the church choir whom she'd gotten to know, Mrs. Peabody and her sister Celia, her office assistant, Angela, and others...it was hard to imagine that all these people had altered their day to come to the gallery for *her*.

"Thank you all for coming," she said, her voice quavering. Diane pushed a tissue into her hand with a smile and kissed her cheek affectionately. "Sit down and take a moment," she said.

"I'm—a little overwhelmed," Beverly said truthfully. "You've managed to completely surprise me."

"That was our intention," Aunt Helen said with a loving smile. "How soon can we open the gifts?"

Everyone laughed.

"We can start right now," Shelley said. "We decided to dispense with those silly shower games people insist on, and instead we're just going to bombard Beverly with questions about the wedding."

Margaret picked up the first box and handed it to her. "Here you go."

Charlotte sat to one side with a pen and notebook to jot down the gifts and givers, as Beverly carefully peeled away the tape and folded back the wrapping paper. The card was sweet and thoughtful, and signed "Celia and Coral."

"This is going to take forever!" Adelaide said.

"Adelaide!" Margaret said. "That's rude."

Shelley laughed. "You're right," she told the young woman. "Just tear it," she encouraged Beverly.

"No, I'm with Beverly," Maddie said as the bride-to-be folded the piece of paper and handed it to Charlotte. "That's a nice-size piece. It can be used again."

"Think green," Diane quipped.

"Oh my goodness," Beverly said. "This is *beautiful.*"

In the box lay an antique lace tablecloth. It was clearly a family treasure.

Mrs. Peabody said, "This belonged to our mother, and neither of us has a use for it anymore."

"We'd like you to have it, dear," Coral said before Beverly could voice the objection forming in her mind.

"Are you sure? This is an heirloom piece. Isn't there someone in your family who should have this?"

Celia smiled. "You've become family to us. We can't think of anyone we'd rather see this go to."

Beverly couldn't prevent a few tears as she rose from her chair to hug the elderly sisters. "Thank you," she said. "Thank you so much."

The rest of the gifts were equally thoughtful. White bath sheets and hand towels monogrammed with the initials B and J from Maddie; a set of wine glasses from Charlotte; a handmade Icelandic eiderdown duvet from Jeff's mother. Dan and Shelley gave them a stunning hammered brass lamp, while Diane presented them with an engraved photo album for their pictures from the big day ahead. Beverly's final gift was from Margaret.

"It's a painting," Beverly said, hardly daring to breathe as she carefully peeled away the paper. As she removed the sheet of protective paper, there was a collective gasp of awe from the guests.

"Oh, Margaret," Beverly said in a hushed voice. "This is...incredible." The painting was of one of their favorite places, the lighthouse. Dawn appeared to be breaking, and rays of pink and gold spilled over the horizon behind the solitary spear of the building. Marsh grasses and sand in the foreground gave the impression that the viewer was peeking over a dune at the rising sun.

The others gathered around her. No one spoke, reinforcing the sense of reverence the painting instilled.

Finally Margaret gave a nervous trill of laughter. "Goodness, I sure know how to stop a party in its tracks. Beverly, come and cut your cake."

The moment slipped away, and the sound of chattering female voices returned to the gallery. Several people lingered near the painting to tell Margaret how lovely it was, while Shelley snapped photos as Beverly ceremoniously cut the first slice of cake. Then Diane took over so that Beverly could visit with her assembled friends.

Carolyn Mackenzie pulled Beverly aside the moment Beverly stepped away from the cake table. "I have to ask," the older woman said. "How upset was my son after my phone call yesterday?"

Beverly took a moment to frame her words. She didn't want to be at odds with her mother-in-law, but her first allegiance was to Jeff. "I think he was saddened more than anything," she told Carolyn. "You're one of the most important people in his life, along with his grandfather and me, and your presence at our wedding would mean a lot to him."

Carolyn bit her lip, blinking her wide blue eyes. "He's important to me. Of course he is; he's my son. But he knows, probably better than anyone else, how important my work is on a global scale."

Beverly was silent, not knowing how to respond to that. Finally, she said carefully, "I agree that your work is very important. But so are family ties. I guess you'll have to be the one to decide which of those means more to you, and whether you're willing to risk permanently changing your relationship with your son for your work."

Carolyn opened her mouth... then closed it again without speaking. Her eyebrows rose clear up to her hairline, and she looked more taken aback than Beverly had ever seen her. Maybe she shouldn't have been quite so severe. But really, what was there to lose? Carolyn needed to know how hurt her absence would make Jeff feel.

As she escaped and joined her cousin Charlotte, who'd set aside her recordkeeping in favor of Shelley's delicious cake, she congratulated herself on her restraint. She hadn't told Jeff's mother exactly what she thought of a woman who would skip her own son's wedding, but she had let her know that an absence might have serious consequences.

Determined not to let the worry spoil the party, she took her first bite of cake, savoring the flavor. "Oh my goodness," she said to Charlotte, "this is heavenly." The cake was delicious, made not by Shelley but by Liza Cramble, a friend of Shelley's who owned the Cakery.

Finally, after a flurry of congratulatory wishes and farewells, everyone was gone except for the four friends. Coral and Celia had offered Adelaide a ride home, and Adelaide had been happy to accompany the two little ladies.

Beverly turned to her friends. "Well, you pulled this off. I was totally clueless!"

Shelley giggled. "We worked hard to keep it a secret."

"No kidding! I thought I was coming to select my favorite painting. And instead, Margaret *gives* me an astonishing painting that I believe may be the best thing she's ever done!"

Margaret smiled. "Thank you. I'm so glad you like it. But in truth, I do still need your opinion. All of your opinions." She beckoned them behind the counter at the rear of the shop. "Here are the four paintings I am considering sending to Paris. I'd like you to rank them from most favorite to least favorite."

Beverly perused the four paintings. They were very different. One was of the lighthouse. It depicted part of the boardwalk with a dog that looked suspiciously like Rocky chasing a ball thrown by a young boy who resembled Aiden.

The second painting had a rocky bluff in the foreground that looked out over the ocean where a humpback whale with her calf plowed through the waves. Beverly could remember when Margaret painted that one more than a year ago, and she had always loved it.

A third was a painting entitled simply *Peace*, featuring a seascape in which angels could be seen gathered in the clouds. The fourth, unlike the others, was an abstract titled *Sea Breeze* that Margaret had done as sort of an experiment.

"Oh my goodness," Shelley said. "How are we supposed to choose just one?" The sentiment echoed Beverly's thoughts. "These are all stunning in their own way."

"I believe I like the abstract," Diane said. "I can't even express why, but for some reason my attention keeps being drawn back to it."

Margaret nodded. "I almost didn't include it, but recently I've caught myself dabbling with more abstract themes again, so I figured why not?"

"Is there any reason you didn't consider sending this painting to Paris?" Diane stood in front of the haunting painting Margaret had done of the train station not long ago. Although it depicted the train station in its current condition of genteel decay, Margaret had superimposed a ghostly image of the stationmaster of yesteryear overseeing the train schedule, with a train and townspeople from more than a half century earlier waving farewell as the train left the station.

Margaret shrugged. "I have mixed feelings about that painting. A lot of people have called it 'interesting' and 'unforgettable.' But those aren't necessarily words of praise."

Shelley walked over to stand in front of *The Farewell*. Margaret had given it the name not just for its obvious departing passengers, but with Elias Thorpe in mind. "I think those words were meant as compliments. This painting is so compelling it's hard to look away from. Whether or not it's actually a favorite of mine is debatable, but I know I'll never forget it."

"This is the kind of painting that should hang in a public space," Shelley said. "A space where a lot of people can see it and study it."

"Like the Cove, after you buy it," Diane said.

Shelley grinned. "Now there's an idea." She glanced at the discreet price affixed to a lower corner. "Although it's way out of my price range, unless I start serving seriously high-end gourmet!"

"I thought Noah Henry might buy it," Margaret confessed. "But now he's gone again, and it's still here. Regardless, I'm not sure I'd sell it to him. I have a feeling that this painting is meant to stay in Marble Cove."

"You know," Diane said, tapping her lips with a finger, "I may change my vote to *Peace*. I think it has a very special quality to it."

"I think I like the dog and child on the beach," Shelley said. "But that's probably because it reflects my life, so it might not be a valid choice."

"It's a valid choice if it's your favorite," Beverly told her. "I like the whales for the same reason." The others laughed.

"Which one's your favorite?" Diane asked Margaret.

"I like the angels, I think. I do feel that my style is evolving, and *Peace* would be the best representative of that."

"You're the artist," Diane said. "If you like the angels, send that one."

"I agree," Shelley said. "If that little boy didn't look so much like Aiden, I'd probably like the angel painting best too."

Margaret grinned. "All right." She took the angel painting and laid it on the counter. "I'm crating this up and taking it down to the post office before I go home today. The angels are going to Paris." She gave a little shiver as she spoke. "Wow, I still can't believe this is really happening!"

"It's going to be terrific," Diane predicted.

But Margaret's thoughts apparently had moved on. "I just hope I can make myself leave when the time comes."

"What?" Shelley looked confused. "You and Allan already have your flight reservations and hotel plans in place. Why wouldn't you leave?"

Margaret sighed. "I was going to see if Adelaide could stay with her friends over at the group home while I'm gone. But when I mentioned that to her yesterday, she said the kitties would be lonely, and she was going to stay with them. I tried to explain that we wouldn't be there, and that she might have trouble, but she's having none of it."

"Well," Shelley said, "that's not an insurmountable problem. Between the three of us and our families, we can make up a little schedule and check on her daily. And I bet there are people from your church who would do the same. Adelaide's likely to have more company than she would if you were home!"

"Elsa Kling from the group home said she'd check on her," Margaret reported, "but I hate to make more work for her."

"Maybe Elsa could just check in once a week," Diane said. "We could have Adelaide over for meals too, if you're worried about her cooking when you're not home."

Beverly saw the tense set of Margaret's shoulders relax. "Oh, that would make me feel so much better. She can do a lot for herself, you know, but we've never gone away for such a long time."

★ ★ ★

Shelley heard her mother-in-law's car pull into the driveway. She walked to the front window and looked out. Her heart sank when she saw Frances pull a crumpled tissue from her pocket and blot her eyes after she closed the car door.

"Aiden, Emma, Hailey? Meemaw is here." She knew better than to try to give Frances a big hug and a shoulder to cry on when the other woman walked through the door. Being able to focus on the kids would give Frances an opportunity to compose herself.

The plan worked perfectly. Both younger children came thundering through the house, and Hailey strolled in behind them, a half-finished bracelet made of strands of intricately knotted embroidery floss in her hand.

"Hello, my babies!" Frances knelt to hug the little ones.

"I not baby," Emma informed her.

Frances chuckled. "No, indeed you're not. You're quite the big girl these days."

"We made a kite at school." Aiden made a bid for her attention.

"Oh, we used to do that too, but they never flew. I never saw a kite made out of construction paper fly in my life."

"It's not made of construction paper," Aiden said indignantly. "It's a diamond kite made of plastic bag material and electrical tape. It has a frame made out of oak dowels and heavy nylon string because cheaper string snaps."

Frances stared at him a moment. "My lands! Art projects sure have changed since my day." She smiled. "Did it fly?"

"Sure. And the man who taught us to make them said if we like, he'd come back and show us how to make a delta kite. It's a triangle shape."

"My lands," Frances said again. "You'll grow up to be a kite-maker!"

Aiden giggled. "Nah. I wanna be an electrician like my dad."

"That's an excellent goal," she said approvingly. She glanced over the little ones' heads at Hailey. "And how you are today, sweetie?"

Hailey held up her bracelet-in-progress. "I'm making you a special friendship bracelet, Grandma Bauer," she said, "but it's not quite finished. Can I measure your wrist?"

Frances held out her wrist. "Of course. Hailey, that's really beautiful. Did Shelley help you?"

Hailey shook her head. "Only when I first got started making bracelets."

"She's a pro now," Shelley said, smiling fondly.

"I know your favorite color is green," Hailey said. "And I thought it looked nice with these other shades added in."

Frances looked as if she was on the verge of tears again as she examined the bracelet the young girl held. "Hailey, this is extraordinary. Thank you for thinking of me."

Hailey smiled as she wrapped a tape measure around the wrist of her grandmother-by-proxy. "Sure thing," she said matter-of-factly and gave Frances a quick hug. "Okay," Hailey announced. "Got it!" She looked at her young cousins. "C'mon, guys. The grown-ups are going to talk about boring stuff. Let's go play."

"Thank you," Shelley said to her quietly as the two little ones thundered out of the room with the same verve with which they'd entered.

"Would you like a cup of coffee or tea?" Shelley asked Frances. "Dinner will be in about twenty minutes, so we have time to relax for a bit."

"I'd love some tea," Frances said. She shucked off her coat and hung it up, then settled at the table. "What a day."

"Were you at the rehab center?" Shelley asked as she took a mug from the cupboard, though she was fairly certain she knew the answer.

Frances nodded. "I had a committee meeting at church this morning, but that worked out well because that's when Ralph had his therapy. So I spent the afternoon there. We played Scrabble."

Shelley was surprised. "I bet that picking up those little tiles was a challenge for him." She filled the mug with water and put it in the microwave, then took a seat across from her mother-in-law.

Frances nodded, her expression glum. "He got furious with himself—and with me for bringing the game—about halfway through and quit. Refused to talk to me."

"Oh, Frances." Shelley reached across the table and put her hand over her mother-in-law's. "I'm sorry."

Frances turned her hand palm-up and squeezed Shelley's briefly, then released her hand and sat back in her chair. Shelley recognized a distancing maneuver when she saw one, but she was still pleased that Frances hadn't rejected her offer of comfort. "Thanks. The good news is that he was beating me. Cognitively, he's in great shape. But he's having a really tough time right now. He's feeling well enough that he wants to come home, but his body's not cooperating fast enough to suit him." She sniffed, and there was more of her familiar impatience in it than sorrow. "Everyone says he's progressing as fast as anyone they've ever seen. Even the staff is surprised. But, of course, it's not fast enough for him."

Shelley nodded in understanding. "I'm sure he wants nothing more than to be back in his familiar environment. Have they given you any kind of estimate of when he might come home?"

Frances shrugged. "No guarantees, but possibly in about two weeks. They have certain goals he has to meet for feeding and grooming and getting around. And I need to talk to the family about getting a safety handrail put on the stairs and in the shower." She sighed. "The biggest stumbling block is that I have to be able to understand him, or he has to be able to write well enough to tell me what he needs. He gets frustrated when I can't figure out what he's saying."

"That will change," Shelley reassured her, rising to get the promised tea. "It's still very, very early in his recovery process. And once he's living at home again, you'll get much better at translating."

"You're right." Frances rested her chin on her hand. When Shelley set the mug before her, she picked up the tea bag tab and idly dipped the bag in the mug over and over. "I just want things to be the way they were before . . . before he had the heart attack and the stroke."

Shelley nodded, sympathy swelling a knot in her own throat, making her swallow. "I know," she managed to say. "We all do. But he's doing really well, and things are going to get better again. And until then, you've got all of us"—meaning the family—"to support you."

CHAPTER FOUR

On Sunday, Dan and Shelley's family attended church with Beverly, Beverly's father, and Jeff. After going to their respective homes for lunch, Beverly's father retired to his library while the younger people strolled along the boardwalk, enjoying a mild day along the oceanfront. The skies were a bold blue, the breakers foamed white, and a breeze fluttered the women's skirts around their legs. There were a few tourists about, but it was very early yet. Families with children didn't begin to arrive until mid-June, when most schools were out.

Dan pushed Emma in the stroller after her little legs tired of walking. Ahead of them, Aiden and Prize ran, seemingly inexhaustible, while Hailey had gone down to the water's edge to see what treasures the tide had washed in.

"He'll sleep well tonight," Dan commented.

Jeff laughed. "So will he." He gestured to Scamp, the puppy he'd given Beverly. Scamp was almost six months old now. He was either playing frantically or totally sacked out, and the change could happen between one moment and the next, to their amusement.

"He goes for his first real grooming session this week," Beverly put in. "We've taken him a few times to be bathed and brushed after Leo suggested that we might want to get him used to being handled since he's going to need regular grooming."

"Unlike Miss Hound there." Dan gestured at Prize. Although the dog was a beagle-cocker spaniel mix, her adult coat was fairly short and easy to manage without the clipping that a true cocker would require. "She gets a bath once in a while and her nails clipped a couple times a year, and that's it."

As they continued their walk, keeping one eye on Aiden and Hailey down by the water, Shelley said, "Beverly, would you mind giving me some advice about loans?"

Beverly leaned forward so she could see Shelley around Dan, who walked between them. "I'll help you as much as I can, but a bank might be a better bet."

Shelley smiled. "A bank is the next step, but I wanted to talk things through with you before I went to a bank. It's about the Cove."

Beverly had assumed that was probably the case. "Okay. Want to come over when we get back?"

"Now? That would be great."

When they got back to the end of Newport Avenue, Dan, the kids, and Prize continued down the street to the Bauers' home while Shelley went with Jeff and Beverly to enter the Wheeland home.

Jeff took the puppy toward the kitchen while the two women headed for Beverly's office on the second floor.

"I'm sorry," Shelley said, appearing chagrined as she draped her jacket over the back of a chair. "I never thought about how limited your time is with Jeff. We don't have to do this now."

Beverly smiled. "It won't take long. And soon our time together won't be nearly so limited." A warm glow kindled as she thought of being married to Jeff and having a lifetime to spend together. "I can't wait."

Shelley smiled. "You two seem so right together. I'm glad you found each other."

"I'm glad Jeff found me and was persistent enough not to let me brush him off," Beverly said in a serious tone. "I was a very different person when I came back to Marble Cove, and I certainly wasn't looking for an attachment, much less a permanent relationship."

Shelley smiled. "Sometimes the best things come along when you aren't looking for them."

"Like you, Diane, and Margaret." Beverly beamed. "And like your new business." She took a seat behind her desk and grabbed a notepad. "So what questions do you have for me?"

Shelley pulled a crumpled sheet of paper from her pocket. "I've been running numbers to see how much of a loan I need and what I can afford to pay, but I need someone smarter than I am to double-check it. And I also wondered if you have a recommendation for what kind of small business loan I should look for."

"I'm no smarter than you," Beverly chided. "My skill set is just different. Heaven forbid I should have to try to produce some of the goodies you can make!" They laughed together. "Have you checked the Small Business Administration Web site?"

"I have." Shelley sighed. "Frankly, it's a little overwhelming."

"Okay." Beverly pulled up her calculator. "Let's run some numbers first and see how much we think you need, and what you'd like your payments to be. Then we can glance at some loan possibilities."

Thirty minutes later, Shelley was beaming. "Thank you so much," she said as she slid into her coat. "I thought I could make it work, but I just needed a second opinion."

"You're welcome." Beverly gestured for Shelley to precede her down the stairs. "Check your e-mail for those loan links I sent, and then you can start gathering data on who would offer you what terms, how long, and how much your payment would be."

Shelley nodded. "I'm going right home and make myself a spreadsheet to keep track of all the possibilities."

Beverly laughed. "That's what I like to hear. I'll make you as OCD as I am!"

Shelley giggled too. "A little more OCD in my life would probably not be a bad thing."

★ ★ ★

On Monday morning, Jeff went to Portland to meet with an architecture firm for which he was doing the photographs for a new brochure. Beverly had seen some of the buildings he had photographed, and she thought he had done an outstanding job of using lighting, sunrise, and sunset, to capture some really stunning photos.

After he left, Beverly shared a cup of coffee with her father before heading to her office in the municipal building annex. As she walked along Main Street, she passed the Cove, and she smiled to herself as she thought of Shelley's excitement about her impending business venture.

A movement in the restaurant attracted her attention, and she realized Martha Goodwin, one of the newer members of the town council, was waving at her. No, not just waving, she realized, even as she threw up a hand. The councilwoman was beckoning to her. Martha wanted her to come inside.

Obligingly, she entered the little eatery.

"Good morning, Beverly." Martha was seated at a booth with several other people, and she slid over so that Beverly could perch beside her. "Do you know everyone?"

Beverly glanced around and nodded, smiling at everyone as she saw familiar faces. Inside, though, she found herself tensing. Everyone at this table was in favor of unrestrained development, she knew, having read some fairly strident opinions in the "Letters to the Editor" section of the *Courier*. "Good morning," she said.

"I was just telling these folks about a conversation I had with Dennis Calder," Martha enthused. "I thought you'd like to hear it too."

Beverly only nodded. "I'm sure I would." *Oh, would I ever.*

"Dennis wants to build a little shopping center on the site of that old dilapidated train depot." Martha looked as if the train station's appearance was distasteful to her. "He's been working on the plans for a while now and showed them to me last night."

"He has the option to submit them to the council at any time," Beverly said calmly.

"Well, I'm all for it," Martha boomed. "We have to do something with that property. It can't just sit there being an eyesore."

"I think there are a number of possibilities under discussion for the train station," Beverly said.

Jules Benton, the town council president, was seated one table over with Lionel Riley, the council treasurer, and Terry Dwiggins, another of the newer council members. Beverly noticed that Jules's eyebrows had risen at Martha's statement, but she couldn't tell from his expression whether he agreed with her or not. Lionel Riley's eyes flickered as well, although she thought Terry was too busy flirting with Brenna to notice. Interestingly, Brenna didn't seem to be making much effort to flirt back, even though Terry was Marble Cove's version of a male model with his flashing dimples and warm smile.

"I think another shopping area would be a good thing for the town," said Les Johnson, Hank Roux's brother-in-law, who sported a bushy gray mustache. "I mean, the more shopping, the more tourists, right?"

"Which means more jobs," said another older fellow. "Heaven knows Marble Cove needs to add all the jobs it can. Too many people commute out of town as it is."

Beverly sighed inwardly, although she was careful not to react visibly. The world was a much smaller place than it had been, thanks to technology, and simply creating a few more jobs in town was not going to stop people from commuting.

"I think," she said carefully, "one of the most important things we need to consider is the character of Marble Cove. What makes people want to vacation here? According to a survey done three years ago by one of the vacation rental companies, our repeat tourists come here, in part, because they like the feeling of having stepped back in time a bit. They like the slower pace. They like that Main Street still feels like the heart of the community. They like the older buildings that have been preserved, even if they have modern conveniences inside. Your town council was elected to look at all the issues surrounding new development, particularly when that development would destroy one of the older buildings that contributes to the town's character. I promise you we'll continue to review all serious proposals thoroughly."

"That old train station is an eyesore," Les said. "That's about the only 'character' it has as far as I'm concerned."

"Maybe, but do we have to tear it down?" The unexpected support came from Brenna, who had moved to their table to refill coffee cups. "It would be great if there was a way to preserve the building, but still make something of it that contributes to the local economy."

"Too expensive." Les looked disgruntled at having his sentiments challenged. "It would be a lot cheaper to just tear it down and start new."

"Is that what Dennis Calder told you?" countered Brenna. "Did he back it up with numbers?"

Les's face flushed. "I haven't looked into it," he admitted. "It's just my opinion."

Brenna snorted as she picked up several empty plates in her free hand and headed for the kitchen, but she refrained from further comment.

Beverly wanted to stand and applaud her. She settled for simply standing. "Thank you for sharing your opinions," she said to the table at large. "The council welcomes all proposals for improving our local economy while preserving the character of our community." She smiled, making eye contact with every single person in the group around the table. "Have a good day, folks. I must get over to my office."

"Thanks for stopping in." Martha gave her a friendly smile, although Beverly thought there was a hint of a challenge in it. It was pretty clear that Martha was determined to see the train station demolished. It wouldn't matter a whit what Dennis's proposal entailed: Martha's vote, clearly, would be a yes.

★ ★ ★

Diane stretched and rolled her chair away from her desk, where she had what felt like a gazillion index cards spread out. Different paper colors represented different plot threads, and different ink colors represented different characters' points of view. One of the other writers in her critique group had recommended the method, but so far, all it had done was make her discombobulated and confused. Colored index cards were one thing, but colored ink…? Her thoughts were whirling a mile a minute, but nothing seemed to be sorting itself out.

She had been working on the book outline all morning, and she needed a break.

Shrugging into a fleece vest, she donned her sneakers and attached Rocky's lead. "Come on, buddy. Let's take a little walk, shake out the cobwebs." She needed to check her mailbox, anyway.

Leaving her little cottage, Diane turned toward the beach rather than toward Main Street.

Coral Peabody was standing on the front porch of her charming violet Victorian. On the front porch tubs of pansies had been artfully arranged to display the flowers' smiling faces, and more ringed the base of the black walnut tree in the yard.

"Good morning, Mrs. Peabody!" Diane called. "Your flowers are lovely."

"Thank you, Diane." The older woman beamed and put up a hand to shade her eyes. "Are you and Rocky headed for a walk along the shore?"

Diane nodded. "And a post office run on the way home. We both needed some fresh air." She realized Mrs. Peabody looked awfully well-dressed for just hanging around the house, in a powder blue wool suit that Diane suspected was a Pendleton from half a century or more ago. Then again, if her clothing was still in such excellent condition in fifty years, she'd still be wearing it too. "Are you going somewhere, or did you just feel like dressing up today?"

"I'm going shopping for a dress for Beverly's wedding today!" Mrs. Peabody almost bounced on the tips of her toes, she was so excited. "My granddaughter Belinda is picking up Celia and then coming to get me, and we're going to that secondhand shop up in Belfast that everyone's talking about."

Diane nodded. "I know the place you're talking about. I've been there. They only accept fairly new items, and I've gotten some wonderful bargains. Why pay 'new' prices when you can get 'practically new' for so much less?" She made her comments sound enthusiastic. Mrs. Peabody's budget, she imagined, would not stretch to expensive new clothing.

"You've already got your dress, right?"

Diane nodded. "I'm all set."

"I'm sorry your children won't be able to make it," Mrs. Peabody said. "They are the most delightful young people."

"Thank you." Diane felt a pang of regret. "I'm sorry neither of them will be here too. Justin doesn't have enough leave, and Jessica has to save hers for her own wedding and honeymoon."

"My goodness, it's just a few months away, isn't it?" Mrs. Peabody asked.

Diane nodded. "Yes, I'm barely going to be finished with one wedding before I'll be hip-deep in plans for another!" She chuckled.

Belinda pulled up to the curb then, and with a wave and farewell, Diane went on her way. As she headed across the boardwalk and down onto the sand, she thought about Beverly's wedding. Her dress was ready to go, but what was she going to do about that limo? In a moment of insanity, she'd opened her mouth and blithely told Beverly she'd find transportation for the ride from the church to the reception. Now she was very much afraid she might wind up hiring a horse-drawn carriage, because she hadn't been able to find a limo anywhere.

Brunswick, Belfast, all the way to Augusta she'd searched. But every single company she had come across was booked solid. She'd even offered them a bonus, but each and every one had told her they just were too busy. They all had promised to let her know if they had a cancellation, but most of their bookings were for wedding parties at this time of year and really, how many weddings were going to be canceled?

Maybe she really had better start thinking outside the box. The horse-drawn carriage idea probably wasn't such a good one unless the carriage was enclosed. The weather was just too unpredictable this time of year.

But still...maybe there was someone around with a closed carriage. It was worth a try. Energized by the idea, she increased her pace along the sand so she could hurry home and start searching for horse-drawn carriages.

Chapter Five

Shelley had a meeting with Rusty at the Cove on Monday afternoon.

When she arrived, Brenna was sliding her arms into the sleeves of a lightweight windbreaker as she finished her shift for the day. "Hi, Brenna," Shelley said. "How are you?"

Brenna smiled. "Good. Tired. Lunch crowd was crazy today."

"Crazy-busy or just crazy customers?"

Brenna laughed. "A little of both. But it was really crowded. Tourist season is picking up, a day at a time."

"Have you heard from Noah again?"

"I have." Brenna's smile bloomed, larger than before. "He's coming back to Marble Cove on Wednesday, and he wants to see me again."

"Oh, Brenna, that's wonderful. He seems really nice."

Brenna nodded. "He is. He even made time to sit and visit with my grandmother when he came to pick me up for our first date. Oh! I almost forgot. He asked me to give you and your other friends a message."

"What's that?"

"He wanted to remind you that he'd still like to meet with you all after he gets back." Brenna paused. "Say, do you know anyone who actually *knew* his grandfather?"

Shelley thought for a moment. "Augie Jackson knew him a little bit. I don't know that anyone knew Elias well, but Augie probably knew him as well as anyone, and I'm sure he'd be delighted to talk to Noah. And maybe the Inglewoods, those folks who bought his house. I imagine they'd speak with Noah too, now that we've broken the ice with them."

Brenna nodded. "That would be great. If I can find anyone who knew him, even slightly, I think it would make Noah really happy to have a chance to speak with them."

Shelley cleared her throat. "Um, you do recall some folks didn't have the greatest opinion of Elias, and I'd hate for Noah's feelings to get hurt..."

"I hadn't thought of that," Brenna said slowly. "Maybe that old saying about letting sleeping dogs lie isn't as much of a cliché as I thought."

Shelley smiled. "Guess not. You could always screen people first. You know, ask them what they recall, so then you could decide whether to introduce Noah at a later date."

"Good idea. Thanks!"

"You're welcome." She patted Brenna's shoulder as the younger woman moved past her to the door. "See you tomorrow."

The meeting with Rusty was extremely helpful. He shared additional financial information with her, including an idea that offered owner financing so the purchase would be more affordable for Shelley and would skip the middleman. They discussed other practical concerns, such as how old the appliances were and what he had been considering doing to upgrade the décor. Employee schedules, seasonal attendance, income statistics, and other nuggets of information would help her as well.

When their meeting concluded, Shelley walked home. As she walked, she used her cell phone to call Dan's sisters, Vera, Annie, Samantha, and Livvy. Dan's brothers' wives usually offered to do other things such as cook meals that could be frozen or take a basket of laundry home to wash and return.

On the final call, to Livvy, Shelley had barely identified herself when Dan's sister said, "Oh, hi, glad you called. I was going to call you tonight to ask what my assignment was this week." She laughed.

Shelley chuckled, but she was a little taken aback. "I hope you guys don't feel as if I'm taking over—"

"Oh, we do, and we love it!" Livvy exclaimed. "I didn't mean that in a nasty way, Shelley. You deal so well with Mom."

She did?

"I mean," Livvy went on, "she and Annie can't spend ten minutes together without getting into an argument, and neither of them is ever about to admit she's wrong."

Both women laughed again at the truth in that statement before Livvy went on. "Vera's willing, but working full-time makes her life insane. And Sam and I also are willing, but with elementary and middle-school activities for all our kids, we're so scattered we're lucky if we can remember our names. Please don't take offense. We're thrilled to have you pitching in like you have."

"I believe you," Shelley said, convinced. Dan's sisters had been nothing but helpful since she'd begun trying to organize the Bauer clan to help Frances after Ralph's stroke.

"Any news on when Dad might get home?"

"Your mom mentioned that it could be as soon as two weeks," Shelley said, "although I don't think anything is definite yet. I need to talk to Dan, because they need a handrail installed on the stairs and one for the shower."

"Tell Dan to call Barry. He did something like that for his grandmother last year. He'll be glad to help."

"Thanks. I will."

The final phone call had taken her nearly to Diane's front door. Glancing at her watch, Shelley smiled. Adelaide had been on babysitting duty with help from Hailey and she'd agreed to stay a bit longer so that Shelley would have just enough time to help her friends make little bags of birdseed for the wedding guests.

★ ★ ★

"I'm telling you, I felt like an unarmed soldier standing in enemy territory," said Beverly to Diane, Shelley, and Margaret. Three of them were busily cutting squares of fine pink netting, adding a small scoop of birdseed, giving the delicate fabric a twist, knotting sparkly lavender ribbon at the top, and using scissors to curl the ribbon into tight spirals.

On the coffee table, Margaret was busy making small pink and lavender bows, which she then affixed to the little food placards Beverly had printed. Although it would not be a sit-down meal, Beverly wanted to identify all the food items on the buffet so there would be no guesswork for those who might have food allergies or simply dislike a certain item.

Diane chuckled at Beverly's words. "I bet. I've met Martha Goodman. She came to one of my book signings." She pursed her lips. "She seemed nice enough, but she stayed and stayed and talked and talked, and finally the clerk who was helping me with the signing escorted her politely to the far end of the store so I could hear myself think!"

"That's Martha," Beverly said in a glum tone. "And I expect loud and opinionated from her. But it worries me that she sits in the Cove and talks at the top of her lungs about Dennis's great plans for the train station. Even Jules Benton looked as if he was listening seriously, and I thought he was a proponent of trying to save the property."

"Oh, guess what? Noah is coming back on Wednesday," Shelley volunteered. "And Brenna says he would like to talk with us."

"Really? That's great!" Diane gave a little bounce in her seat.

"She asked who I knew that might have known Elias Thorpe back in the day. I mentioned Augie Jackson and the Inglewoods." Shelley cleared her throat. "I did warn her that opinions might not be all sweetness and light, and that perhaps having Noah ask questions about him might not be such a good idea."

Margaret snorted. "I bet there are a few people left in town who would give her an unvarnished picture of Elias. Augie's probably a good choice. He'll be fair and objective."

"I think there are a lot of people who knew who he was," Shelley said, "but very few, possibly none, that really knew him well. Frances remembers him, but she was just a starstruck child who admired her dashing older cousin."

"So does Evelyn Waters," Beverly said, stripping the edge of her scissors along a length of ribbon and watching it spring into a perfect curl. "Her parents ran in the same social circles, but her memories are pretty limited. Like Shelley said, she didn't know him personally."

There was a brief silence as each woman contemplated the enigma that had been Elias Thorpe. They'd uncovered much of his history, certainly enough to understand how his life had affected their little town, but some things would be forever a mystery.

Diane snuck off to the kitchen and came out with a small cake to celebrate Margaret's birthday. With so much going on in preparing for her trip she had asked the friends not to make a big deal of her special day, but they couldn't resist acknowledging it in some way.

They all sang 'Happy Birthday' as Diane set the cake in front of Margaret.

She smiled, "Thank you so much, but you know you didn't have to do anything."

"Of course we did," Shelley chimed in.

"That's right," Beverly agreed. "We need to celebrate you, even if it's only in a small way."

"I do have the very best friends in town," Margaret said as she cut pieces of cake for everyone.

As they enjoyed the treat, Beverly cleared her throat. "So, remember how Jeff said he'd take care of the honeymoon plans, and I should just arrange to have two weeks free soon after the wedding?"

They all nodded, coming to attention, and Shelley slid to the edge of her seat. "So where are you going?"

Beverly paused dramatically.

"Oh, come on!" Shelley burst out. "The suspense is killing me!"

Everyone laughed.

Beverly said, "Jeff is taking me to Italy for our honeymoon."

"Italy." Shelley breathed the word as if it were priceless.

"That's exciting," Diane said. "Roman ruins, fantastic food, romantic gondola rides in Venice—you are going to Venice, aren't you?"

Beverly nodded. "Rome, Venice, Tuscany, Milan . . . I can't remember all the places we're going."

"Will you be taking a tour?" Margaret asked.

Beverly shook her head. "Jeff's arranged much of it himself, although we'll be taking some day tours and trips in each of the places we stay."

"Oh, it sounds so romantic," Shelley said.

Diane chuckled. "It's a honeymoon. It will be."

"I've always wanted to go to Italy," Margaret said. "Maybe in a few years, after the inspiration from this Paris trip wears off, I'll get there."

"I'd settle for either of them!" Shelley exclaimed, her eyes shining. "I hope that once the kids are grown, Dan and I are able to travel to some exotic locations." Then she hurriedly added, "Warm, though. I want to go where it's warm!"

★ ★ ★

When Dan got home that evening, Shelley had a huge pan of lasagna bubbling in the oven, along with a loaf of Italian bread she'd made that morning.

Dan's eyes sparkled as he removed his coat. "I love lasagna," he said fervently. "No, I take that back. I *like* lasagna. I *love* your lasagna!"

Shelley laughed as he kissed her and then bent to swing Aiden into his arms for a hug. Hailey and Emma weren't far behind, and Dan spent the next few minutes listening to the kids chatter about the big events in their day as Prize danced around his feet, demanding her share of the attention.

Finally, when Shelley sent the children to wash their hands before dinner, Dan said, "I talked to Mom on my way home." His tone was casual, but something in it alerted Shelley.

"Oh? Did she have news?"

Dan grinned. "Dad has a tentative release date of May twenty-first if he continues to make progress like he has been."

"Yay!" Shelley did a little dance around the kitchen, ending up in her husband's arms. "That's great news. Only two more weeks in rehab." She cleared her throat as she looked up at him. "I, uh, may have volunteered you to install a stair rail and some kind of rail in the shower before he comes home." Quickly, she said, "Livvy said Barry can help, at least with the shower thing."

"No problem." Dan grinned. "I'll call Hal and Darrell too, see if they can give me some weekend help. It shouldn't take that long."

"So will your father just be released into your mom's care?" That thought worried Shelley a little. She could imagine Frances running her own health into the ground trying to care for Ralph.

"He'll still be having therapy at Sailors Memorial every day initially, and then it'll slack off to every other day and so on. And the doctor talked to Mom about getting a home health care assistant in to help her get him bathed and dressed for the first few weeks until he can manage more things for himself."

"If she doesn't want a stranger in the home, we might be able to work out a rotating schedule so that the family can help," Shelley said.

Dan shook his head. "Shell, I think having a stranger around might be better, as long as they can afford it. I believe the first couple weeks are covered by insurance, so it shouldn't be a strain." He grinned. "Mom won't be as . . . as overbearing with a professional as she would be with us trying to help."

Shelley had to smile. "As usual, you're absolutely right."

Dan glanced at the calendar. "What's the date? Did you just tell me I was right?"

★ ★ ★

On Wednesday, Beverly met her three friends for coffee at the Cove. Shelley hadn't been sure she would be able to get away but apparently she'd found a sitter after all, because she breezed in alone at the last minute.

"Hi, ladies. What I can do for ya?" Brenna smiled as the foursome entered. Her ebony hair was confined in a French braid, and she wore casual khaki slacks and a light blue oxford cloth shirt with the sleeves rolled up.

"How ya doing, Brenna?" Margaret asked by way of greeting. "Coffee and a poppy-seed muffin for me."

"Sounds good to me too," Beverly said.

Diane grinned. "I want a cheese Danish with my coffee. I've been thinking about it all day."

"I'll have a banana nut muffin," Shelley said. "And coffee, of course."

After paying for their orders, they carried them to one of the small wooden tables and settled in, shrugging off jackets and hanging handbags over the backs of the chairs. The Cove was virtually deserted at this time of day unless it was tourist season, and today they had the place to themselves.

"Well, I sent off the painting," Margaret said. "And now I'm sure it was a mistake. I should have sent something more...conventional."

"Don't second-guess yourself," Diane said. "We all agreed that you were making the right choice."

Margaret smiled."Okay, okay. I'll let it go." Then she turned to Shelley. "When I went into the post office a little while ago, Bernie told me Ralph is coming home soon."

Shelley's eyebrows rose. "How did he find that out?"

"The postmaster in a small town knows everything," Diane intoned.

"Especially when he's as dedicated a gossip as Bernie Lanninger," Margaret said ruefully. "Is it true?"

"Sort of," Shelley admitted. "I guess it depends on your definition of 'soon.' Ralph is being released from the hospital in two weeks." Shelley shared with them Dan's news about the outpatient therapy program.

"I'm glad he's coming home, but I hope it won't make your mother-in-law's life too difficult," Beverly said. "I've heard handling a stroke patient can be pretty stressful sometimes."

"I'll organize help for her if we need to," Shelley told her, "but they're thinking of hiring a professional for a few weeks."

"That might actually be better than having a family member around," Diane said.

Shelley nodded her agreement as the door of the coffee shop opened.

Automatically, the women turned to see who was coming in at this time of day. Beverly saw Margaret's eyes widen as Noah Henry walked through the door, and she imagined her own face held the same surprised expression that her friend's did.

Behind the counter, Brenna's face lit up as if someone had flipped a switch inside her. "Noah!"

The young man didn't stop at the counter. Instead, he steadily walked right around it, a tender smile on his face as he gave Brenna a warm hug. "I missed you," he said.

"I missed you too," Brenna replied.

Noah lifted one of her hands and held it. "We need to talk."

They had spoken quietly, but even a pin drop could have been heard in the Cove just then. Beverly swallowed the lump that rose in her throat. Out of the corner of her eye, she saw Shelley dab at her eyes with her napkin.

A clattering spoon broke the moment, and Beverly turned to see Margaret stirring her coffee. "We were staring," Margaret whispered with a grin.

"That was special," Diane decided. "Very special. I'm glad we witnessed it, even if it was rude."

"Hello, ladies." Noah had noticed them. He squeezed Brenna's hands and released her. "What time do you get off?" he asked her.

"One."

"I'll be here." As she turned and picked up some things to take back to the kitchen, Noah strode across the little restaurant to the table where the friends sat. "I owe you an apology," he said, addressing Margaret.

Yes, you do. But Beverly didn't say it, because after all, he had made an effort to let them know what had happened. "We were told you had a business emergency. Thanks for letting us know. I hope everything worked out for you."

"It did indeed." His eyes flashed with a satisfied gleam, and Beverly realized he must be a very successful young man. "I was on the verge of purchasing a new business, and I thought we had worked out all the details. My lawyer called and said the sellers were trying to back out, and he felt I needed to get back to Seattle and talk with them. Fortunately, I was able to address the concerns they had, and the deal went through."

"That is fortunate." Margaret sounded a little cool, and Beverly realized her friends felt as she did. They really didn't know Noah well, nor did they know what his motives were for coming to Marble Cove.

"I'm eager to talk with all of you." Noah appeared to recognize that the women had some reservations about him.

As an awkward silence fell, Beverly quietly studied the young man. Although he was dressed casually in jeans and a flannel shirt over a knit henley, the clothes were good quality, and unless she was mistaken, that was a Rolex on his left wrist. His dark hair was wavy and could have been difficult to manage without the skillful cut that kept it looking neat. And she was willing to bet that his casual lace-up boots were Fryes or another very expensive brand. Clearly, this was a man of means.

"Again," he said, "I apologize for missing our meeting. Could we reschedule? I'd like very much to hear what you know about my grandfather's life here in Marble Cove." He grimaced. "And I'm prepared. I know he had secrets that may have been less than savory."

Beverly tried to hide her surprise. She wasn't aware that Noah knew anything about Elias's activities in Marble Cove. "I understand you would like to meet some people who knew your grandfather."

Noah nodded. "I thought there might be a few still around."

Beverly hesitated. But there was no pleasant way to say it. "We gave Brenna a few names. There may be more, but you should brace yourself for the possibility that people aren't going to have much good to say about Elias."

"It's really more of a *probability* than a *possibility*," Shelley interjected.

Noah nodded. "I am not completely surprised, although it saddens me. I guess I'll start with the names you gave Brenna and go from there. Now—is there a time that we could meet to share the information we have about him?"

Diane nodded, her expression sober, although she didn't confirm or deny Noah's statement. "I'd be happy to host all of us at my home tomorrow evening. Say, seven o'clock." She gave her address. "Would that work for you?"

Noah nodded. "Seven tomorrow night sounds fine to me. Thank you. I'll see you ladies then."

CHAPTER SIX

On Thursday evening, Beverly and Jeff's newly hired contractor met them at 6:00 PM at the Simpson cottage.

At our new home, Beverly corrected herself, while Jeff and Bernie, the contractor, discussed the best way to renovate the run-down porch.

Once inside, Beverly said, "Bernie, we'd like to open up this space into the kitchen to form a great room. What do you think?"

Bernie's eyes narrowed. He was a tall, lean man in coveralls emblazoned with his name on the pocket. "You planning to move the stairs?"

"How hard would that be?" Jeff asked. "We thought it would really open up the space if we put them over there." He gestured to a side wall.

Bernie shrugged. "It's doable, but it'll run you into a boatload more money. If you leave the stairs where they are, we can open up underneath them and box in the support beams so they look like columns. And if we put open railings with banisters on both sides of the stairs, you'd still get an open look and feel."

"That might work," Beverly said, trying to visualize it.

"I can quote you the price for each, and let you decide before we start," Bernie offered, earning a warm smile from Beverly.

"We'd like to add gas logs in here"—Jeff indicated the existing fireplace—"with a hearth made of local stone, perhaps?"

Bernie, scribbling notes, followed Beverly into the kitchen, where she explained what they wanted to do.

"What if I put in an island with two levels?" Bernie sketched on his pad and turned it to show Beverly the results. "Then you wouldn't need barstools, just your regular dining chairs at either your table or at this side of the island. And I could put in some skylights," he said, squinting at the ceiling. "They'd be angled, but you'd get some nice light. Then I'd put track lighting here and recessed lights in the living area."

"Oh, I like that!" Beverly was beginning to be able to imagine the home once it was renovated. "When will we choose appliances and countertops? Should I be looking?"

Bernie chuckled. "Sure. You see something you like, write it down, and then I'll see how it'll work in the space." He walked over to the back wall. "And if we bump out this area and put in bay windows, you could have a dining area right over here. It'd be separate enough to seem like a dining space, but it still would be part of the main living area."

Upstairs, Bernie talked about a floor plan that would allow them both to have home offices with a shared sitting area space and a second bath. They could put a sofabed in one of the offices and have it double as a guest room.

As they went on, Beverly got more and more excited. Bernie had some ideas for turning the main-floor bedroom into a master suite, using what had been the dining room.

"We could even include underfloor radiant heat in the bathroom, if you like."

"Oh," Beverly moaned. "I can see the dollar signs piling up, but everything sounds so *wonderful.*"

Jeff laughed. "We've got a pretty decent budget, and we can discuss the best way to use our dollars after Bernie gets us his proposal."

The man nodded. "I can price things out so you can pick and choose what works for you."

"That would be great," Jeff told him. "So I guess we need to head outside and talk about what needs to be done to the exterior."

Bernie nodded. "I checked the roof, and it looks okay. And since the whole place is going to need to be sided or painted or whatever, you should go ahead and do the garage as well so it will all match."

Beverly glanced at her watch. "Jeff, I need to get going. I have a meeting at Diane's at seven." She extended her hand to Bernie. "Thank you for taking the time to meet with us. I can't wait to see your proposal."

★ ★ ★

Beverly was the last one to Diane's house, although she had been just across the street.

"Hi! Come in," Diane called from the doorway as Beverly came up the sidewalk. "I saw you through the window."

"We met with a contractor who's going to do the cottage renovations," Beverly said, catching her breath as she entered the house.

"What cottage?" Beverly was surprised to see Brenna seated beside Noah, who rose and extended his hand. "Hi, Beverly," she said in belated greeting.

"Hello to you both." Beverly shook Noah's hand and explained to Noah about her impending wedding and their purchase and renovation of the Simpson cottage. "After all," she said, laughing, "I couldn't move away from Newport Avenue when my three best friends all live here!"

"And now you're at the 'right' end of the street," Shelley teased.

Everyone chuckled. Diane had made sweet tea and also had bottled water available, and Beverly was certain the clever little selection of cookies on the coffee table had come from Shelley's house. A vase of pastel-colored tulips matched those blooming in Margaret's garden.

"Oh," Beverly sighed, fingering a delicate petal. "I wish those were going to be in bloom for the wedding."

Margaret smiled. "Sorry. They'll be nothing but petals on the ground in three weeks. But we'll have lilacs and a number of other flowers in pink, white, and lavender shades that will work beautifully. I'll be happy to donate some to add to your reception flowers."

At that moment Diane handed around napkins and made everyone take a drink. "So Noah," Margaret said when she was done, "we know what brought you to Marble Cove. You were looking for information about your grandfather, whom you believed to be Elias Henry. But when he was getting old, he told you stories about Marble Cove and said that he had been, for lack of a better term, a bigwig associated with the railroad here in town?"

Noah nodded.

"And when you got here, you learned that his name was actually Elias Thorpe."

Noah nodded. "I knew—or suspected—that his last name had been changed before I came to town. You see, I found several of my grandfather's bankbooks among his personal effects about a year ago. One from Marble Cove in the name of 'Elias Thorpe' shows an average balance, but it has several huge deposits, which he appears to have spent almost immediately. Then the first account he set up in Oregon a short while later shows a large amount of money, much of which he subsequently parlayed into a successful business endeavor." He sighed, and Brenna put a hand over his. "I might not have thought much about it, except for the name." He smiled, but there was little humor in it. "I mean, how many people named Elias do *you* know?"

Margaret nodded. "I would have wondered too."

"I thought about it for months. I feared my grandfather may have come by his money unethically, and frankly, part of me didn't want to know. To say I was ambivalent about pursuing the mystery would be putting it mildly. But I couldn't stand not knowing, so I did an online search for 'Elias Thorpe.' And, of course, I immediately found a stationmaster in Marble Cove by that name in the railroad records. The age roughly matched the age my Elias would have been then. But that was all I could find.

"Then I remembered the old trunk we had found after he died with the railroad hat and the pieces seemed to fall together."

"Maine Central Rail Road," Shelley murmured, and Noah nodded.

"Is your mother still in Seattle?"

Noah shook his head. "My father died seven years ago. She remarried last year and lives in Florida now. That's how I came across the bankbooks. She gave me all my father's things when she moved. Well, almost all. Recently, she e-mailed me to say she found another small box of letters that were my grandfather's. She's going to send them to me. I doubt there'll be anything exciting in them but you never know."

"So back to the bankbooks . . . " Diane smiled. "Sorry. I'm dying to hear the rest!"

Noah smiled at her unvarnished eagerness. "After finding the Thorpe name, I decided to visit Marble Cove and see if I could learn anything."

"And did you?"

"Very little. I didn't want to go around asking about Elias Thorpe after seeing those bankbooks, you know? But then

I saw the name of the library, and I knew I had to be on the right track."

He glanced at Margaret. "When we talked in the gallery that day, I'm sorry I didn't tell you about the bankbooks. They seemed...too incriminating."

"I can see that," Margaret said.

He leaned forward, elbows on his knees, hands loosely clasped between them. "When I left here at the end of April, I hired an investigator to research public records in Oregon and here in Maine."

Diane clapped a hand to her mouth. "Seriously? Good for you! Has he found anything helpful?"

Noah nodded. "It was laughably easy...just a matter of looking in the right place, I guess. My grandfather, Elias Thorpe, who was the stationmaster here, showed up in Oregon in 1952. He called himself Elias Henry, but the long and short of it is that Henry was his middle name, and he was actually Elias Henry Thorpe. He legally changed his name in October of 1952 to Elias Henry. He didn't marry until a few years later, and there is no evidence that his wife or his son, my father, ever had any inkling that 'Henry' wasn't their real family name. I've gone through everything of his I could find."

There was a moment of silence in the room.

Beverly realized with a sense of shock that Noah didn't know about the embezzlement. Her heart sank. It was going to take some finesse to share everything they knew about Elias without painting him as a completely unsavory character.

"Did the investigator find out anything else?" Diane asked. Beverly realized her friend was thinking along the same lines.

Noah shook his head. "I had only asked him to confirm the relationship. I figured if there's anything more to learn, I can probably find it myself while I'm here."

"So do you remember your grandfather at all?" Margaret asked. "What was he like?" It was a gentle subject change, but Beverly could see all of her friends relax.

Noah nodded. "I do. I didn't see him often during my childhood, but the memories I have are good ones. He and my grandma lived in Oregon, but we moved up to Seattle when I was a child. It was more than a three-hour drive, not impossible, but my mother didn't drive, so we could only go when my father was off. And my grandparents wouldn't drive to the city, ever. I'd say we probably had a few visits a year, and he began to develop dementia when I was a young teenager, so I saw even less of him.

"In the railroad trunk, I found registration papers for a 1952 silver Jaguar 'fixed head' coupe."

"The Jaguar he owned when he lived here!" Diane clapped her hands. "How fascinating."

"My grandfather used to show me photos of that car. He must have purchased it very shortly before he left Marble Cove. He once told me he wished he'd never sold it. Anyway, those photos hooked me on antique autos as a kid, and I've never lost the fascination. He took me to a few car shows when I was young, and it was always a bond between us."

"That's nice," Beverly said softly, although she had a hard time imagining a man so focused on deceiving others spending quality time with a child.

"When I found the papers, there was a bill of sale with them. I realized I might be able to track down the car, if it even still exists." He grinned. "It was a sort of catalyst for me to come east. Or maybe just an excuse."

"That would be neat," Shelley said, "if it is still around."

"It is," Noah assured her. "I've already found out that it belongs to a man in Vermont. He's agreed to show it to me, and he'll even consider selling it for the right price."

"Oh my goodness," Shelley said. "That's exciting!"

"And the 'right price' will undoubtedly be more than it's worth, now that he knows how interested you are," Brenna said.

Noah laid his hand over hers and squeezed. "Or maybe he'll be moved by my story and let me have it at a reasonable price, since it's a family heirloom of sorts. It still has the original divided windshield!" His face reflected amazement. "And the man assures me it's been kept in pristine condition."

"You must feel as if it's a sign," Diane said.

Noah nodded. "Yes. I think I was meant to return to Marble Cove and learn about my grandfather's early life. No matter how bad it might be," he added, making Beverly realize that the young man grasped the significance of those bankbook discrepancies and his grandfather's precipitous flight from Maine. "I don't know why, but once I found

Marble Cove, I felt as if I was coming home. I've been very drawn to the community."

"Did your grandfather work for a railroad once he settled in Oregon?" Beverly asked.

Noah shook his head. "Not at all. I never heard him mention anything about railroads until those years before he died when he was losing his grip on reality and living more in his past."

"Was your father his only child?"

Noah nodded. "Yes. And I am my parents' only child." He took a deep breath. "My mother was an orphan, so I have very little close family."

There was a lull in the question-and-answer session. Noah was going to be stunned, Beverly decided, to learn that he had family members scattered all over this portion of the Maine coast.

"What did he do?" Diane asked. "I mean, how was he employed?"

"He owned a Cadillac dealership," Noah said. "He became the biggest and most respected Caddy dealer in the state. He also had a reputation for local philanthropy, although he kept it quiet. He gave money for improvements to the emergency room of the local hospital, enough that they built a whole new wing and put in a helipad."

"That's serious money," Beverly commented.

"The dealership did really well, and he also had made a number of wise investments. When my grandfather retired, my father took over the business, but he was an English professor at a local college and never really enjoyed selling cars, so he sold it."

"How nice that your grandfather did some really good things with his money." Diane smiled. "That must have comforted you when he passed away."

Noah nodded. "He donated to the fire companies, to the scholarship fund for deceased policemen's children, to the high school marching band's uniform drive—I mean, he outfitted the whole band! And that's just a tiny fraction." Noah's eyes looked into the distance. "Ever since I found those bankbooks, I've wondered if he was trying to redeem himself for some kind of wrongdoing."

His gaze sharpened, and he met each of the four friends' eyes as he spoke again. "I need to know everything there is to know about him. Will you tell me?"

CHAPTER SEVEN

Diane nodded. "Of course we will." Her heart ached for the young man, so close in age to her own children. Did he feel that he didn't really fit anywhere? His comment about being drawn to Marble Cove was telling. "First," she said, "we need to share a little historical information with you."

Although Noah's expression didn't change, she felt his sense of letdown. "All right," he murmured. "About the town, you mean?"

Diane smiled. "The town that was founded by your I'm-not-sure-how-many-times-great-grandfather, Jeremiah Thorpe."

Noah sat straight up. "You're kidding."

Shelley grinned. "No, she's not. The lighthouse, the library, Old First Church, and the train station are all linked directly to Thorpe ancestors. And speaking of ancestors . . . there are descendants of the Thorpe family living all over town. In fact, my own husband and children are your distant cousins!"

Noah blinked. Swallowed. "Wow. I—I don't know what to say," he murmured. "I came back hoping to find a few links to my personal history, and instead I've found an entire library!"

Everyone laughed.

In the next several minutes, the friends recapped Jeremiah Thorpe's storm-wracked voyage to the Maine coast, the treasure passed to him by Booth Adair, his determination that built both the lighthouse and Old First, the tragic death of his first wife, Evangeline, his second family that yielded the Mauers of Marble Cove, and his sister's penning of the hymn "Carried on the Waves." They told him about the mysterious bell that summoned them to a portrait stashed deep in the old bell tower that had saved Old First and was helping restore the venerable structure to its original glory. Then they moved on to the fact that Elias's ancestor, Henry J. Thorpe, gave the endowment that resulted in the library.

"Henry?" he asked incredulously. "I'd guess that's how my grandfather got his middle name." He paused, as if to process this new information. "But what's the deal with the train station? Someone told me it was going to be torn down. I've just discovered it! I don't want it torn down."

"There is a movement afoot to demolish the depot," Diane confirmed. "As you might expect, people are very concerned about the economy now, and they fear that the building will be a drain on the town's coffers. One group is particularly persistent about getting rid of the building and putting a shopping center on the site, trying to entice people with the promise of jobs."

"A tiny little shopping mall on that site isn't going to generate very many jobs," Noah said, a combative light in his eye. Diane experienced a small thrill as she realized that this young man was a formidable entrepreneur in his own right. Having him on their side could mean the difference between losing and saving the train station!

"Uh-oh," Margaret said. "We've lost Diane. She's thinking this might make an interesting story."

Diane chuckled. "Everything is fodder for story lines when you're a writer," she informed her friends. But she couldn't help but think that this was a story that deserved to be told…provided, of course, that they got their happy ending by saving the train station. If that building was torn down, Diane doubted she'd have the heart to try to write a fictional account with a different ending.

"All right," Noah said quietly, interrupting her introspection. "You've given me a plethora of information, and some wonderful news with it, but I'd like to hear more about my grandfather's life here in Marble Cove. In my worst nightmares, I fear he ran off and left a family behind, which would make *my* family illegitimate descendants!"

"It's not that bad," Beverly said instantly. And indeed, Noah was right. Elias could have left a far worse mess behind. "Your grandfather never married, at least not that we know of, during his life here, and I think, given that this was his hometown, we'd have heard of the scandal if he'd left a wife and children behind."

"The worst thing that we know," Margaret told Noah, taking a deep breath, "is what you already suspect. It seems very likely that he came by the money that he brought to Oregon illegally."

"He probably embezzled it," Diane said. "I'm sorry to have to tell you that."

"He was one of several investors in a local quarry, owned by the Gentry brothers." Margaret picked up the story. She explained that all the signs pointed to embezzling money from the other investors, and that the quarry shut down in 1951. "We assume that the reason he vanished from Marble Cove in 1952 was because the other investors had figured out a way to prove he'd stolen their money."

"That fits with those bankbooks I found," Noah commented.

"He liked the high life," Shelley said. "People whose parents knew him mention that he liked to spend money, throw and attend lavish parties, wear good clothes…generally, he liked a very comfortable lifestyle. But I guess you knew that already."

Noah frowned. "No. The grandfather I knew lived in the same three-bedroom modest rancher his whole life. He mowed his own grass, took care of a garden, and was a deacon in a local church. He and my grandmother canned a lot of their own vegetables, helped out the elderly folks in their congregation. It's like we're talking about two people who are opposites of each other," he said, shaking his head.

"Sounds like we are." Diane cleared her throat. "Clearly, his actions here in Marble Cove had an impact at some point. He was a changed man before you came along. It almost seems as if he made the decision to be a better man on the trip west, doesn't it?"

Noah nodded. "Maybe. I've never heard anything about him to contradict that. Still, if he truly had changed, why wouldn't he have made amends to those he wronged?"

"Even the best people are flawed," Margaret said. "He'd made so many changes for the better already...maybe he thought the scales were even."

"Or maybe he just couldn't face it," Shelley speculated. "Coming back here, admitting embezzlement, would surely have meant jail time. He'd become a new man, found a wife and a church, had a family to think of. What would have happened to your grandmother and father if he'd gone to jail?"

"What a mess," Noah said wearily. "This is a lot to process."

"I imagine so," Diane said. "We've had several months to unravel this. You're learning it all in one huge information dump. It's going to take some time to sink in."

"What was the evidence?" Noah asked them.

"You mean of the embezzling?" Beverly asked.

Noah nodded.

"Well," Diane said, "we never found any actual evidence. We heard that there were rumors back then, around the time the quarry closed. And then Elias left town, so I suppose the assumption was made that he had taken off with the money. And no one was ever able to find him."

"So we don't know for certain that Elias actually stole the money?"

Margaret shook her head. "But we know that he was accused of it at a town council meeting just a few weeks before he left town. He and two other investors, from the account I read, were accused of skimming profits. Which would have been a really terrible thing, because not only were they getting wealthy at the expense of fellow investors and those who worked there, they hurt the whole town by making the quarry less profitable. Ultimately, that's why the quarry closed, and when there wasn't enough freight to justify running the trains, the rail line closed too."

Noah looked grim. "Wow. Way to devastate the entire local economy, Pops."

"Pops?"

Noah nodded. "That's what I called my grandfather." He put his head in his hands. "It's hard to imagine he was a criminal of this magnitude."

* * *

On Friday morning, Margaret was painting when Diane walked into the gallery, setting the little bell above the door jingling.

"What a night!" Diane said without even a greeting.

Margaret laughed. "I know. This is going to sound kind of silly, but I feel a tiny sense of letdown. I mean, the mystery's solved and we know most of the details now."

"Except for concrete proof that he really did embezzle money."

"I think that the bankbooks are proof enough," Margaret said. "We may not know the 'how,' but we certainly know that Elias suddenly had a huge amount of money fall into his lap. And let's face it, if he'd earned it legally, there would be some record."

"True, but in some ways, that makes his transformation even more mysterious," Diane said. "What on earth could have caused a man to change so drastically?"

Margaret shrugged. "Don't forget he came from a long line of do-gooders and people of strong faith. As he grew older, maybe the errors of his ways began to wear on him."

"And a deathly fear of being caught."

"That too," Margaret said with a grin. "Both powerful motivators, I'd think."

"I'd feel better if we were *sure* he'd done it," Diane said.

"I agree, but Diane, we've searched for information all over this town. There's no more to be found."

"We haven't really delved into the actual embezzlement portion of the problem as much."

"And how do you propose we do that?" Margaret asked. "The bank can't show us records even if they wanted to. Elias is gone. So is just about everyone else from that era. I'm not sure what our next move would be."

"I'm not either," Diane said. "But I sure wish we had some way to know."

Beverly entered the gallery just then and greeted them both. "Did I miss something?"

Diane sighed. "We're just rehashing the embezzling thing. I wish there was a way to confirm that Elias was—or better yet, *wasn't*—a dirty rotten swindler."

"I've been thinking about it too," Beverly admitted. "Jeremiah and Henry both did so much for this town, Noah seems to be such a straight arrow, and other family members generally appear to have been pretty good guys."

"And gals," Margaret said, thinking of the young girl's journal she'd found.

"And gals." Beverly smiled. "It's almost too cliché for Elias to be such a rotter. Wasn't there *anything* redeemable about him back then?"

"It's going to be hard to find out after more than sixty years have passed." Diane grimaced. "And the guy moved clear across the country and changed his name, to boot."

"Noah said he was very involved in his church," Margaret recalled. "I wonder if it would be worth speaking with anyone there who might have known him well."

"That's a thought," Diane agreed. "If he had close relationships within the church, there could be someone still living in whom he confided."

"It's a serious long shot," Beverly said skeptically.

Diane grinned. "Couldn't hurt to try. I'll talk to Noah about it."

"While I have both of you here," Margaret interjected, "bear with me a moment while I review our care network for Adelaide during our trip to Paris."

"Didn't we just talk about this last night?" Diane's eyebrows rose.

"So sue me," Margaret suggested with a grin. "Call me Nervous Nellie. I just need to be able to have it all straight in my head before I go."

"Give up," Beverly said to Diane. "You know we're going to hear this every single day until she steps onto that plane." She chuckled. "I'm responsible for driving Adelaide to and from her activities and appointments while you're gone, for having her over for dinner once or twice a week, and for making sure she's doing all right watering your garden."

"I'm responsible for the same thing she's responsible for," Diane said, "except the flowers. I'll make sure she's caring for the cats, and if Adelaide doesn't feel well, she's to tell me immediately. I'll assess, triage, and seek professional care if necessary."

"Shelley will feed her too," Beverly said, "and stop in daily to see that the cleaning is getting done, that she has the groceries she needs, and that the milk isn't spoiling."

"Elsa Kling is also planning on having her in for occasional meals, and a few friends from church said they'd do the same and check on her from time to time." Margaret busied herself wiping off a paintbrush on a rag. "She's just not used to living alone, you know? What will she do if the power goes off, or there's a water leak?"

"Come get one of us," Diane assured her friend. "You know Adelaide won't hesitate to call on us if something unexpected pops up and concerns her."

"I know." Margaret tried to smile. "She's very sensible. I'm worrying for nothing, I'm sure." But she couldn't shake the feeling that going to Paris and leaving her intellectually challenged daughter behind, alone, had the makings of a disaster.

"I'm worrying too, but for an entirely different reason," Beverly confessed. "I think Adelaide is going to surprise you and be spectacularly independent. But I've been counting votes, and I am extremely concerned that Dennis Calder may yet pull off his demolition derby at the train station."

"Why do you say that?" Diane asked. "I thought you weren't worried."

"I wasn't. But suddenly I'm feeling that more council members are actively entertaining the idea of the strip mall. It just makes me nervous," she said dryly, "when I walk into a room and people avoid my gaze."

"Eek." Diane looked concerned now. "No wonder you're worried. Who's waffling, do you think?"

Beverly lifted her hands. "I don't know for sure, and it's driving me crazy. I thought Jules Benton was against development, but lately I've seen him sitting with Lionel Riley and Martha Goodman. Lionel isn't a voting council member, but he's very solidly in the development corner."

"Martha's your only 'for-sure' vote for development, right? Surely enough of the other council members can be persuaded to vote against it."

"I certainly do hope so," Beverly said, "but I'm feeling very antsy about the whole thing right now."

"What can we do?" Margaret asked. "Other than just talking to people?"

All three women were silent.

"I don't have any brilliant ideas," Diane finally admitted. "Why don't we think about it for a day or so? If nobody comes up with anything, we'll get together and brainstorm."

★ ★ ★

Two weeks ago, Diane had accepted an invitation from Leo to dine with him at the Landmark Inn on Saturday. He had gone out of town to a conference the past Monday, and she had hardly seen him since the beginning of the month. Although that had only been eleven days ago, she was a little surprised at the surge of happiness that rushed through her when she saw him coming up her front walk that evening.

Throwing open the front door, she called, "Hello, stranger!"

"Hello." Leo grinned, drawing her close to kiss her cheek before pulling a bouquet of white irises from behind his back.

"Oh!" Diane took them from him, studying the graceful blooms. "Thank you so much. I love irises."

"I know," he said.

Diane's eyes met his over the flowers. "I missed you," she said simply.

Leo's eyes warmed. "I'm glad. I missed you too."

But as they made small talk driving to the restaurant, Diane thought he seemed a little quiet, perhaps a bit depressed.

He perked up momentarily as they walked through the parking lot outside the restaurant. "Awesome," he murmured as they approached a sleek-looking antique car. "An XK120."

Diane laughed. "I didn't know you were an antique car buff. I recently met someone else who loves old cars."

"This one's a beauty," Leo said, circling the vehicle. "This is from the early '50s, I'm sure, and just look at the condition. It's like new."

It *was* nice, Diane had to admit. Clearly, it had been a costly car in its day.

As soon as they were seated, she said, "Are you okay? You don't seem quite yourself this evening."

Leo's face took on an expression of sadness. "You're beginning to know me well." He sighed. "I lost a dog during what should have been a simple surgery this afternoon. It happens sometimes. The animal may not tolerate anesthesia well, or could have a hidden medical condition that complicates things...but it always saddens me. The dog was only five, and of course the family was devastated."

"Oh, Leo, I'm so sorry." Diane reached across the table and laid her hand over his, and Leo turned his palm up and squeezed her fingers.

"Thanks. I did a necropsy, so I hope we get an answer as to what happened, but I can't stop myself from mentally reviewing my performance, you know? There was just no obvious reason that dog should have arrested like that." He sighed.

"What was the surgery for?"

As Leo talked through his afternoon, Diane watched his face and saw that having someone to listen really seemed to help him. He clearly appreciated her interest and forbearance. It was, she realized, the first time Leo had ever seemed to really need her, and she decided she liked it. He had been a rock for her during her recent treatments, and she knew she had leaned heavily on him at times. It was wonderful to know that he felt he could lean on her too.

They enjoyed a relaxing meal, catching up on the small details of their lives during the time they had been apart. Diane caught him up on the latest news regarding Elias Thorpe and Noah's reappearance.

The conference, Leo said, had been revitalizing. It was good for him to see new approaches, to hear other medical opinions, and to be able to discuss things with others face to face. The Internet was enormously helpful, but there was nothing better than talking with other vets firsthand.

On the way out of the restaurant, Diane spotted two familiar faces across the room. "Oh!" she said. "I don't believe it. Leo, that's Noah Henry! Let me introduce you." She waved as the couple noticed them, receiving a wave in return.

As they started to thread their way through the tables, Diane could feel Leo's hand lightly touching the small of her back, as he so often did. It was a sweet, courtly gesture.

"Hello, Diane," Brenna called as they neared the table. "How are you?"

"I'm fine." Diane smiled. "Brenna, I know you know Dr. Leo Spangler, but I'd like to introduce him to Noah. Leo, this is Noah Henry. Noah's from Seattle, although his family has deep roots in Marble Cove." And that, she figured, was the easiest way to mention Noah's background without making Noah uncomfortable. Besides, Leo already knew. "Noah's an antique car aficionado too."

Noah had risen at their approach, and the two men shook hands. "Pleased to meet you. Did you see the Jaguar coupe when you came in?" Leo asked Noah. "I may have drooled on it a bit."

Noah laughed, looking a little sheepish. "Actually, the Jag is mine. I just got back from Vermont, where I picked it up today, and I couldn't resist driving it tonight since the weather is so fine. It's going into a garage first thing tomorrow."

"Wait," Diane said. "Do you mean—is that—was that the car you were telling me about? The car Elias owned?"

Noah nodded. "The very one."

"That was Elias Thorpe's car?" Leo's gaze sharpened.

Noah nodded, his face growing solemn. Clearly, he was aware that the news might be less than welcome. But Leo merely said, "Welcome back to Marble Cove. You'd better hide that car, or Diane and her pals are entirely likely to crawl all over it with magnifying glasses, looking for clues to one of the mysteries they are always trying to solve."

Noah laughed, clearly appreciating Leo's reaction. "Well, in this case, I might help them. It appears my grandfather was quite the mysterious character."

"So do you own any other cars?" Leo asked. "I have a Model A Ford that was given to me by my grandfather, and a '61 Lincoln Continental that I restored some time ago, but for the most part, I just go to car shows and dream."

Noah's eyebrows rose. "Those early sixties Lincolns will never go out of style. That's the ultimate classy, upscale shape, isn't it?"

Leo grinned. "Thanks. I think so too."

"I have a small collection," Noah said. "My most prized possession is probably my '66 Corvette."

"Oh man," Leo said. "It was still four-twenty-five horsepower then, right?"

Noah nodded. "A blast to drive, let me tell you."

Leo almost whimpered. "I bet."

"Unfortunately, my cars are on the West Coast, except for this one," Noah said. "I'll take you for a ride someday if you like."

"That would be terrific," Leo said.

Diane looked at Brenna. "New best buds," she said, and they both laughed.

Then something occurred to Diane. "That's it!" She snapped her fingers.

All three of the others stopped talking and looked at her. "What's 'it'?" Leo asked.

Diane waved dismissively. "I just thought of something I'd like to talk to Noah about. I'll give you a call," she said to him.

He nodded. "Sounds good."

Leo took Diane's hand, and she enjoyed the feeling of his fingers enfolding hers. "It's been good to meet you," he said to Noah. "I'm sure we'll get a chance to talk again."

As they said their farewells and began to walk away, Noah said, "Oh, Diane, I almost forgot something."

She turned back to the table.

"I'd like to get together with you and your friends again. I got a package from my mother that I need to tell you about."

Diane's curiosity was immediately aroused, but there was no way they could get into that tonight. "All right. How's Monday night, my house again? I'll ask my friends if that works for them."

"That would be fine. See you then."

CHAPTER EIGHT

Adelaide had signed up to help with the nursery care for infants on Sunday, so she did not sit with Margaret and Allan as usual. During the exchange of peace, Margaret felt a tap on her shoulder and turned to see art critic Harriet Malcolm standing there with her hand outstretched. "Peace be with you, Margaret," Harriet said, sincerity in her tone.

"And with you." Margaret smiled at the woman, pleased that she was forging the beginnings of a friendship with the other woman, who had once been so sharply critical of Margaret's work.

As the service concluded, Allan turned to Margaret, beaming. "I can't wait. In just a few weeks, we'll be in Paris. We can visit Notre Dame Cathedral and all the other famous churches—"

"Oh, hi, Margaret, Allan." The speaker was Pamela Morgan, a petite blonde who was in Margaret's Bible study. The Morgans had been seated right in front of them. "Couldn't help but overhear," Pamela said cheerfully. "I'm so jealous it's a wonder I'm not turning green. I'd love to go to Paris!"

"Maybe we will someday." Pamela's husband Lon grinned. "When the kids are grown and gone, and we're retired."

"Speaking of kids, what are you going to do with Adelaide when you're gone? I work full-time, or I'd invite her to stay with us. But maybe we could have her over to dinner."

"That would be nice," Margaret said. "You could call her directly and see if there's a date that suits. Adelaide is going to be staying home alone, taking care of our cats."

She hurried on, her concerns surfacing again as she saw the surprise on Pamela's face. "I have several neighbors who are very close friends who will be looking in on her, taking her to school and other places, and keeping an eye on the cats."

"It's a great opportunity for Adelaide to test her independent living skills in a familiar environment," Allan told Pamela and Lon.

But Margaret's worry must have communicated itself to Pamela, who patted her shoulder comfortingly. "I'm sure she'll be just fine," Pamela said. "If your friends are checking on her frequently, she'll have plenty of help. And I promise I'll call her this week and get a date lined up for her to come over and have dinner with us."

"I'll pick her up and drop her off," Lon promised. "And check the house for bogeymen before I let her go in alone."

There was a moment of uncomfortable silence.

"Land's sake, Lon." Pamela elbowed him sharply. "That's *not* the thing to say to an anxious mother!"

"Sorry," Lon said. "It was a joke. I'm sure Adelaide will be fine."

"I'm sure she will," Allan said before the other couple took their leave.

When they were alone, Margaret turned to Allan. "Well."

"Well," he said in a dry tone. "Good ol' Lon. Always knows what to say."

Margaret chuckled. It was true; Lon had a reputation for putting his foot in his mouth. But still, he had a point. "Do you think I need to ask folks to check the house anytime she returns in the evening? I mean, he had a point. Someone could sneak in and be waiting for her, and Adelaide would be completely at their mercy—"

"Margaret." Allan took her shoulders and gently caressed her with his thumbs. "Adelaide is going to be fine. We can ask our friends to go into the house with her in the evenings if it would make you feel better. It might make Adelaide feel better too. Entering a darkened house in the evening can make even the strongest person nervous."

"Thank heavens it's summer and the light lasts a long time," Margaret said. "It won't get dark most evenings until after Adelaide is safely tucked into the house for good."

"See?" Allan smiled as he released her. "Nothing to worry about. Our girl has a good head on her shoulders, and you've lined up a terrific team to help her navigate her first time being on her own. She's going to be fine."

"I hope so," Margaret said, unable to shake the niggle of worry that haunted her.

"Hi, honey," Allan said.

Startled, Margaret turned to see Adelaide right behind her. "Hi, sweetie. You got out of the nursery faster than I expected."

"Only two babies," Adelaide said. "We weren't busy today."

"Ready to head home for lunch?" Allan asked.

Adelaide nodded, smiling, and Margaret relaxed. Her daughter was not good at dissembling. If she'd overheard Margaret's comments, she would be asking questions and voicing concerns. Since she wasn't, it was pretty clear she had not overheard her mother worrying about her ability to care for herself.

★ ★ ★

"I'm so excited now!" Beverly turned to Jeff and threw her arms around his neck on Monday morning. She was scheduled to work in the mayor's office that afternoon, but this morning she had set aside to deal with her own projects.

Grinning, he kissed her. "I know. Now that we can envision it, it seems more real."

Bernie, their contractor, had delivered his concept of the plans for the exterior and interior finished look of the renovations they planned. To their delight, it was within their budget. True, the two-level deck Bernie had designed at the back of the house put them near the top end of their budget, but it was a great idea, with a large, antique bronze chiminea so that they could have toasty fires on the lower-level flagstone portion of the deck.

"I was so worried that everything we wanted would put it too far out of our price range," Beverly confessed.

Jeff just smiled. "I researched a couple of different contractors before settling on Bernie. Part of the reason I ultimately chose him was because he has a reputation for delivering elegant finishing touches at a reasonable price."

Beverly turned back to the drawings that had been delivered that day, tracing the inviting front porch with its swing and rose trellis. "This will be so pretty."

"He did a great job with this master bedroom suite too," Jeff said, shuffling the large sheets of paper to bring up another one. "I like these dual showerheads and, oh man, this tile work will be gorgeous."

"And the counter with double sinks is really nice too."

"I like how the French doors open to both the closet and the bathroom," Jeff said. "Very efficient."

Jeff grabbed the plans for the kitchen. "What would you think of having glass-fronted cabinets in one or two of these? I've always liked that look, and you have that gorgeous Depression glass of your mother's that we should showcase."

Pleased that he cared about those kinds of details, Beverly smiled. "That's a wonderful idea. I'll add it to the list."

"I need to run down to the post office." Jeff held up a flat mailing envelope. "I have some finished prints I need to get in today's mail."

"I'll go with you."

Grabbing light jackets, the pair strolled downtown, holding hands.

As they turned the corner from Newport Avenue onto Main Street, Beverly saw Noah Henry striding out of the bank. She waved as he turned toward them, and the young man returned the gesture as he approached.

"Hello, Beverly," he called.

"Hi, Noah. Have you met my fiancé, Jeff Mackenzie?"

Noah and Jeff shook hands as Noah shook his head. "No. I feel as if I'm getting a crash course in 'Who's Who in Marble Cove' though, with all the people I've met since I got back. Every time I turn around, Brenna is introducing me to someone else!"

They all laughed, but then Noah's face sobered. "Beverly, it's fortuitous that we ran into each other. I was going to stop by your office this afternoon."

"Oh? What's up?"

"I've been thinking about everything I've learned about my grandfather, and I had an idea I'd like to run by you. Has anyone considered creating a museum in the old train station?"

Beverly felt her pulse pick up as she considered the question. "Yes, we had." Then she felt her initial surge of excitement wane a bit. "But that would be a costly proposition, and I can't see how I could pitch it to the town council—or the citizens of Marble Cove, for that matter. We are really struggling with our budget."

"Well, I have a solution to that, at least in part." Noah smiled. "I'd like to donate a sum of money to be used to start a museum fund, as well as additional funds to create a nature preserve at the old quarry."

Beverly was stunned. Jeff's eyebrows rose, and she imagined she looked much the same. "Noah, that would be—well, it's a wonderful idea," she managed. But did he really have any concept of how much money that would take?

"I feel an obligation to right the wrongs that my grandfather did to this town," he said. "If everything I've learned is true—and from what I can tell, at least some of it almost has to be—his actions depressed the local economy and put a lot of people out of work. Who knows how many families suffered when that quarry closed? And when the trains quit running?"

"I agree," Beverly said, "but Noah, have you any idea what such a proposal could cost? Did you have a specific figure in mind?" As her mind raced ahead, she began to feel enthusiastic. "Perhaps your seed money could help us create a campaign to designate the train station as a historic property! And we could use it as a kickoff event to get the campaign rolling, encourage other people to donate." She grinned at him. "Can you get me a proposal in writing that I could share with the town council and perhaps the historical society's board of directors?"

"Sure," Noah said easily. "I'll work it up this week." He paused. "Has Diane spoken to you about a meeting tonight?"

Beverly nodded. "She already texted me this morning, so I will see you this evening."

"Good," Noah said. "I've found something important that I want to share with all of you."

As they took their leave and continued on toward the post office, Beverly said, "Now what do you suppose could be so important he wants to meet tonight?"

"I don't know," Jeff said, "but now he's got me curious. You'd better call me the minute that meeting's over!"

* * *

"Hi, honey." Shelley was just checking a white cheddar macaroni and cheese casserole when Dan came through the door that evening.

"Hey." He barely got out a smile before the usual mad cacophony of kids and dog descended to occupy him for the next few minutes. When the eruption had fallen to a dull roar, Shelley asked, "How was your day?"

Dan smiled. "The usual. Wayne keeps me hopping, but I enjoy the work and am learning a lot." He hesitated.

Dan sat down on one of the kitchen chairs, pulling her into his lap. "I have something I need to discuss with you."

His somber tone alarmed Shelley. "What's wrong?" she asked, putting her hands on his shoulders and turning to look into his eyes.

"Nothing's wrong, exactly." Dan tried to smile. "I got a big compliment today."

"If that's true," Shelley said, "then why do you look like you're about to tell me someone died?"

Dan heaved a genuine laugh. "No one died. Today, Wayne made me an offer that could be too good to pass up. Actually,

Wayne made me aware of the offer," he amended. "It's from another company."

"Another electrical company?" Shelley's eyes grew round.

Dan nodded. "You know my work with Wayne was in an apprentice capacity. He always finds other situations for his apprentices, depending on what their interests and training are. Today he told me that he has found a position for me with a larger company on the other side of Portland."

"Portland!" Shelley slid off Dan's lap and walked to the sink. Leaning against the counter, she crossed her arms, wrapping them tightly around her middle. "Dan, that's a couple hours of driving one way. How can you do that?"

"It's a big shopping mall project," Dan said. "It would last more than a year, and it would be a lot more money. It would be a chance for me to work on a big commercial project and practice a broader range of skills."

"But . . ." The meaning of what her husband was saying sank in. "We'd have to move."

Dan spread his hands. "I think so. Commuting would add four hours, probably, to my days and cost a fortune in gas. It wouldn't be practical to stay here, honey."

"What if you commuted by the week?" Shelley asked, thinking of possibilities. "What if you found a cheap place to live and came home on the weekends?"

"Shell," Dan said softly, "what would be the point? I'd eat up any extra money I made in living expenses, and even if I did manage to save some, you and the kids would be here all week, and I'd be there. I'd be no help when someone got sick. And we've talked about having another baby...how could we live separate and you manage by yourself pregnant or with a brand-new baby?"

"What about my bakery?"

He shook his head. "You couldn't buy the Cove if we do this. But hopefully we could find some way to make your dream come true in our new home. I know it would be tough; you've already got some name recognition here, and down there you'd be starting over, in some ways."

Shelley had already begun to cry. "You're right," she said as Dan rose and went to her, drawing her against his shoulder. "The only way we can do this is if we do it together. I guess I just need to get used to the idea."

"Well, I haven't told Wayne or the other guy 'yes' yet," Dan said, propping his chin on her head.

★ ★ ★

Noah arrived at Diane's home that evening, just as she was taking Shelley's coat.

"Hi, Noah. No Brenna tonight?" Diane liked the young woman and was tremendously pleased that the two seemed to be hitting it off.

"Her grandmother isn't doing well, so she decided to stay home with her," Noah said. "Although I have strict instructions to call and tell her anything we discuss immediately after this meeting."

Diane smiled. That sounded like Brenna. "I'm sorry about her grandmother," she said. "She's not terribly old, is she?"

Noah shook his head. "I believe she is only in her early seventies. But apparently she started developing dementia at an early age."

"Is this her mother's or father's mother?" Margaret asked. "I don't believe I know Brenna's family."

"Her parents are divorced, and her father never lived in Marble Cove," Noah said. "Her mother grew up here, and Brenna moved here and lived with her mom's mother. That's the grandma who's ill."

"I wondered," Margaret said. "I didn't think there were any other McTavishes around here. What's her grandmother's name?"

Noah appeared unfazed by the Marble Cove citizen quiz. "Mrs. Harnish, that's all I know."

"Hmm. A few Harnishes around," Margaret commented. "I wonder what her maiden name was."

"You'll have to ask Brenna that one," Noah said, smiling. "She's probably related to one of you somehow."

"Nothing would surprise me less," Diane said with a dry laugh. "Everyone in this town is related if they've lived here long enough." Everyone chuckled except for Shelley, who gave a wan smile.

Diane eyed Shelley with concern. The younger woman had barely spoken yet, and she looked unusually pale. Looking closer, Diane wondered if Shelley had been crying.

Noah spoke then, drawing her attention away from Shelley. "You might remember," he said, "that my mother intended to send me a packet of letters and papers she found that belonged to my grandfather."

They all nodded. It wasn't likely, Diane thought, that any of them would forget that! "Did you find something?"

"I did," Noah said. "But I'm not exactly sure what." He took a folded piece of copy paper from his pocket. "It was a letter," he said, "so I made a copy of it. It's too fragile to be handled very much."

"A letter from whom?" Beverly sat forward.

"A woman," Noah said.

"A love interest?" Margaret asked.

"I'm not sure. There's nothing in here to suggest that. In fact, it doesn't sound as if she knew my grandfather well. Here, let me read it to you." He unfolded the paper and proceeded to read:

January 22, 1952

Dear Mr. Thorpe,

There is no adequate way to thank you for the extraordinary generosity of your financial assistance with my daughter's medical treatment. Without your intervention, Marie would be just another TB statistic, I fear. Thank you from the bottom of my heart for giving my child a second chance at life.

Gratefully yours,
Mrs. Louise Mauer

"Whoa." Diane sat back, completely stunned by the simple missive. "Elias helped a family whose daughter had tuberculosis? Why?"

"I don't know." Noah sounded as mystified as Diane. "But I sure would like to find out."

"We all would," Margaret added. "This doesn't sound much like the Elias Thorpe we have learned about so far."

"But it does sound like my grandfather," Noah said. He didn't sound angry or defensive; he was simply stating a fact.

"That letter must have meant something to him," Beverly speculated. "Why else would he have taken it with him and kept it all his life? I mean, if he really was worried about someone finding him, this would be a link to his past. So why would he have hung onto it unless it was important to him?"

"Validation, perhaps?" Margaret murmured. "A reminder that he had done something good, regardless of what else he might have done?"

"I could do some research to see if I can find out who Louise Mauer was," Diane offered. "They were probably related, right?"

"We established the connection between the Thorpe and Mauer names some time ago," Margaret told Noah. "A Thorpe girl married a Mauer a long while back, and virtually all the Mauers living in Marble Cove today are descended from that family and, of course, also from the Thorpes."

"Maybe Reverend Locke would know who Louise Mauer was," Beverly suggested. "I can ask him."

"His sister Priscilla might be a better choice," Diane opined. "She's the true genealogist in that family."

"Reverend Locke is out of town until next week," Beverly recalled. "He left after church yesterday to attend a conference in Boston, and without him, I'm not sure how to reach Priscilla."

"I hope he'll be back for the wedding," Diane said, only half-kidding.

"Oh yes. He promised." Beverly smiled. "I told him I'd come get him if necessary. Anyway, I can't ask him right away, but I will when he returns."

Noah shook his head, grinning. "I knew if I shared this note with you ladies I'd find some answers."

"Well, we haven't got many of them yet," Diane said, "but just you wait."

Everyone laughed.

Everyone but Shelley, Diane noticed. *What could be wrong?*

"Diane," Margaret said, reclaiming her attention, "did you mention our idea about the church to Noah?"

"Not yet." Diane smiled at Margaret. "Thanks for reminding me." Turning her gaze on Noah, she asked, "Do you remember anything about the church your grandfather attended in Oregon?"

Noah shrugged. "A little. They usually took me along when I visited, but as I've said before, that was infrequent, especially as I grew older. Why?"

"We were thinking that perhaps your grandfather had a few close friends in whom he might have confided something from his past. Given the role his church apparently played in his later life, we thought church friends might be the most likely to have been his confidants."

"I can ask," Noah said. "I'll call the pastor. I suppose anything's possible, although many of them are either gone or would be so old it's a real long shot, I think."

"I know. We thought so too," Diane said. "But sometimes information comes from the least likely source, so if you don't mind checking, that would be one more stone turned over."

"I don't mind at all." The young man grinned. "If anyone can help me learn anything more about my grandfather's life, I have the feeling all of you can."

CHAPTER NINE

The town council held a meeting on Tuesday evening. Much to Beverly's relief, Dennis Calder had not provided a proposal for the little shopping area he had intended to develop after demolishing the old train station.

But when she asked for a motion to table that business until new information was provided, Martha Goodman said, "I've seen the new plans, and I think they'll work."

"I have too. It would be a good step to help us pick up the economy around here." Harry Vogel, one of the new members whom Beverly had been hoping would resist Dennis's extravagant claims, said.

As Beverly's heart sank, Jules Benton, the council president, said, "You may be right, but we can't vote on it without seeing a proposal from Mr. Calder, so let's move on, shall we?"

As they moved along with the meeting, Beverly cleared her throat. "I have an item of new business."

Everyone turned to look at her. "Noah Henry, a visitor to the town whom many of you have met, I believe, has indicated an interest in providing initial funding to turn the train station into a museum and also to create a nature preserve on the old quarry's lands."

There was a moment of what she could only call stunned silence.

Terry Dwiggins whistled, a smile creasing his handsome features. "That would take a pretty significant amount of money."

Beverly nodded. "Yes, it would. I thought perhaps we could use a donation from Noah as the start of a campaign to make both events a reality."

"Did he tell you how much money he wants to donate?" Jules asked.

Beverly shook her head. "He intends to have a proposal to me later this week, and of course, I will share that with all of you at that time."

"Maybe you should tell him to hold off on that." Martha looked around the room at the rest of the council. "I mean, if we're going to approve Dennis's proposal, it would save this Mr. Henry the time and trouble—"

"Now just hold yer horses a minute, missy." Bert Atwood rose abruptly. He was the council's eldest member, a grizzled old Mainer who'd been on the council for more decades than Beverly even knew offhand. "This council does things by the book 'n' always has. Guess there's a few things you need to learn. One of 'em's not to count yer chickens afore they hatch." Bert wasn't given to long speeches. In fact, Beverly rarely heard him speak more than a sentence at a time, but he was truly irate at the moment, and he thumped a fist on the table as he spoke. "If some fella has another idea for that train station property and submits a proposal, then it's this council's duty to consider it—not to decide what we should consider or discourage and discard!"

There was silence around the council table.

Martha's face was crimson, and she looked steadfastly down at the table.

Bert slowly lowered himself into his chair with a muttered, "Hmph."

"Bert's right," Jules Benton said. "Since we don't have any proposals in hand regarding the train station at present, let's move on. Is there any other new business?"

★ ★ ★

Shelley answered a knock on the door on Wednesday to find Adelaide standing on her stoop.

"Hello, Adelaide," she said. She had a moment of panic. Was Adelaide here to babysit Emma? No, Emma had a playdate this morning. Had Shelley forgotten to tell Adelaide? "How are you?"

"I'm fine." But Adelaide made no move to enter the house.

Shelley stood aside and indicated the open door. "Want to come in?"

Adelaide nodded. "I have a question."

"All right." As the young woman came in and peeled off the sweatshirt she wore, a wave of relief swept through Shelley. Adelaide just needed to talk; Shelley hadn't forgotten anything. "What's up?" she asked. "Come on back to the kitchen. I was looking at some recipes for mousse, trying to decide what I want to make for a baby shower I've been asked to cater."

As Adelaide followed Shelley through the house, she said, "I need help, Shelley."

"With what?" Shelley indicated the table. "Have a seat. Would you like some tea?"

"No, thank you." Adelaide took a seat, wriggling her squat body until she was comfortable on the chair. "My mom is worried about me."

"Oh? How do you know that?"

"I heard her at church. She told Mrs. Morgan she was. What if she won't go to Paris?"

"Oh, honey." Immediately, Shelley had an inkling of what had happened. "It's natural for moms to worry when they leave their kids for such a long time like your mom is going to do. But she knows how capable you are, and she knows you have plenty of friends to help if you need us."

"I had an idea," Adelaide said.

"Oh?"

"So my mom will worry less."

"Ah," said Shelley. "That's thoughtful. What's your idea?"

"Will you help me make a recipe file? I want easy dishes that I could make myself. And don't forget Dad watches what he eats. I can't have food with high fat and cholesterol. I don't want him to have another heart attack."

Shelley was struck dumb for a moment. She could only stare at Adelaide as tears rose in her eyes. Mumbling,

"Excuse me for a sec," she bolted for the counter where she kept a box of tissues in a drawer.

As she blotted her eyes and blew her nose, she said, "Adelaide, that might be the most thoughtful thing I have ever heard in my whole life. What a great idea! You'll be helping both your mom and your dad with this."

"I know." Adelaide nodded once, then sat, beaming at Shelley.

Oh, what a wonderful child, Shelley thought. Adelaide's world was so simple and yet so exceptional. She had a problem, so she had found a wonderful way to address that problem. "Does your mom know you're doing this?" Shelley asked, already sure of the answer.

Adelaide shook her head. "It has to be a surprise."

"Okay!" Shelley clapped her hands. "We can make it a great surprise. Here's what I think you should do. I will help you find some Web sites that have good dishes that are low-fat and low-cholesterol. You can come over here, look through the recipes, and choose some you like. I'll look over them too, and then you and I will write each one out and go over the steps for making it."

"That would be great. Thanks, Shelley."

"You're welcome. Now. How many dishes do you want?"

Casseroles, she thought. *Casseroles would be good.*

"Five, maybe?" Adelaide thought for a moment. "I could make dinner for my parents every night for a week."

"Wow. That's pretty ambitious. You sure?"

Adelaide nodded. "I'm sure. I'll have to cook when they go away. Mom should see me cook. Then she won't worry."

Shelley smiled. If only it was that easy. Rising, she got her laptop and set it up in front of Adelaide. Going to a popular site on which she often found recipes for family meals, she opened to the search function and helped Adelaide input the information she needed.

When a list of suitable recipes for a heart-healthy diet came up, Shelley said, "Here we go. Why don't you read through these and find some you think sound good? Try to find a variety so they aren't all chicken."

"Okay." Adelaide nodded, already beginning to concentrate on the recipes.

★ ★ ★

"Hello." Beverly slid out of her coat as she arrived home Wednesday after her workday ended. "Wow, something smells great," she said as she walked into the kitchen.

"Chicken potpie," Mrs. Peabody told her. "I know it's not exactly on the mister's diet, but my mother passed on the best recipe for potpie I've ever tasted, and it's just a crime not to make it now and again."

Beverly smiled. "My mouth is watering already." She kissed her father on the cheek. "How was your day, Father?"

Her father shrugged and smiled. "Same as always. Catch the news, read a book, take a nap. Read the paper, take a walk, take a nap." He laughed, but it wasn't a sound of resignation or discontent. "Pretty simple these days. How about yours?"

"Not nearly as interesting as that meeting yesterday," she told both of her elders. "I suspect that old Bert doesn't get that mad very often. The other council members looked as stunned as I felt."

"Good for him," Mrs. Peabody said with satisfaction. "That Martha Goodman is always stirring one pot or another, looking for controversy. She's a real piece of work," Mrs. Peabody continued, shaking her head. "I couldn't believe it when she got elected to the town council."

Not wanting to encourage gossip, Beverly changed the topic. "So, do you think everything we've planned on for flowers for the wedding will be in bloom in two weeks?" Celia had already given her a pretty good rundown, but until the flowers actually arrived on her wedding day, Beverly was going to be a little bit nervous. Mother Nature could be capricious.

"Oh yes, I think we're going to have a bounty of lovely blooms." Mrs. Peabody clasped her hands together. "And I forgot to tell you that Celia found our mother's collection of handblown crackle glass vases to use on the tables. Do you think that will be okay?" she added anxiously.

"Oh my goodness, that sounds lovely." Beverly smiled. "I've always thought crackle glass was so pretty."

"Celia has some pink and lavender ribbon to tie around the necks of the vases." Mrs. Peabody began to scoop potpie out of the large copper-bottomed pot onto their plates. "I think that will be a perfect touch."

Beverly thought so too.

★ ★ ★

After the children were in bed that evening, Shelley told Dan about Adelaide's idea.

Dan tapped his temple. "Smart cookie. And very thoughtful. I hope our kids are that sweet when they grow up."

Shelley smiled. "Me too." Her smile faded a bit as she thought of the topic she and Dan had resolutely ignored since the night he'd come home to tell her about Wayne's job offer.

"Dan? Have you told Wayne you'd take the job in Portland yet?"

Dan shifted in his chair and recrossed his long legs. "No." He sighed. "I know it makes sense for us, financially. It's what we've worked for, in terms of my career. But it's not what you want, and we'd be leaving our family and our community..."

"I know." Shelley slumped on the couch. "It's a hard decision. But your deadline's coming up. Soon Wayne's going to need an answer."

"Yeah." Dan shoved a hand through his hair. "I keep hoping I'll have one soon." He cleared his throat. "Shell, I haven't really told you how much I appreciate all you've been doing for my parents. Mom especially."

She smiled. "They're family. Why wouldn't I?"

Dan grinned. "Well, I haven't noticed anyone else, even my own sisters, helping out quite like you have."

"That's not really fair, Dan," she protested automatically. "They're really busy people."

"What's going to happen if we move away?" Dan brooded.

"One of your sisters will step up when I'm not here to manage the everyday things," Shelley assured him. "Besides, things are going to get easier instead of harder as your father improves."

"I hope you're right." But Dan didn't look convinced.

Shelley wasn't quite as convinced as she had tried to sound either. It wasn't hard to see that she was the one with the best organizational skills; the family was quickly falling into a "check with Shelley" mentality when it came to who should do what when for the elder Bauers.

Chapter Ten

Diane walked to the library on Friday morning. She was itching to learn more about the woman to whom Elias Thorpe had written that letter, and since Reverend Locke and his sister wouldn't be back for several more days, she had decided to see what she could dig up on her own. She didn't feel comfortable bothering Shelley's mother-in-law with what was really a trivial question while the woman was dealing with her husband's stroke recovery, so why not check out local references?

But as she walked toward Main Street, her cell phone rang. Glancing at the screen, she saw it was her daughter Jessica.

"Hi, honey. How are you?" she asked.

"Hi, Mom! I'm fine. I guess you're getting everything set for Beverly's wedding, aren't you?"

"I'm helping," Diane agreed. "As soon as that's over, I'll have more free time to help you with whatever you need. Is there anything pressing?"

"I thought we could shop for your dress the second week of June."

"That would be fun," Diane agreed. "Any particular color you want me to wear?"

"No. Martin's mother is waiting until you decide, and then she'll find something that coordinates with it."

"All right. Then we'll definitely plan on the second week of June."

Jessica cleared her throat. "Have you talked to Justin lately?"

Alerted by something in her daughter's tone, Diane's mother-antenna rose. "Not for a week or so. Why?"

"I just wondered."

"Jess." Diane spoke slowly and patiently. "You can't ask a question in that loaded tone and then not explain what's going on. What do you know that I don't?"

Jessica giggled, and the happy sound reminded Diane of long-ago moments of sheer joy with her children. "I don't know anything, Mom, honest. But I *suspect* something, which is altogether different."

"All right, I'll bite. What do you *suspect*?" She was grinning.

"Justin asked me," Jessica began in a conspiratorial tone, "if he could bring a guest to the wedding."

Diane thought about that for a moment. "He's in the wedding party. Does he realize he may not have a ton of time for a date?"

"I pointed that out," Jessica said, "and he said, 'Well, maybe Katie could sit with Mom and Leo. It would be a good chance for them to get to know her.'"

"Wow." Diane ran her free hand through her short hair. "Just—wow."

"Exactly!" Jessica sounded triumphant. "When was the last time Justin wanted any of us to get to know his girlfriends?"

"Never," they answered in unison.

"He seemed pretty smitten when he was here at Easter," Diane pointed out, "but he wouldn't divulge any information. If he's thinking as far down the road as your wedding..."

"It could be serious," Jessica finished.

"Well, this is exciting," Diane said. "Thanks for the heads-up, honey."

"Just part of the service," Jessica said. "I'm penciling in the second weekend of June for you to come down for a shopping expedition, okay?"

"Sounds good."

"All right. Gotta run, Mom. Tell Beverly best wishes and we're sorry we can't be there. Love you. Bye!"

My goodness, Diane thought as she responded and closed her phone. *The times, they are a-changin'!*

When she arrived at the library, she greeted Gilda Harris, the librarian. Then Diane headed for the Maine Room on the second floor, where the historical society's collection of state and local history was housed. But once she was there, she had no idea where to look next. She browsed through several local history tomes, finding information about the quarry. Elias Thorpe was, as she already knew, one of several men who had invested in the project together.

"Need any help, Diane?" Gilda stood in the doorway, looking over the tops of her reading glasses. As was usual, she wore a smile, and her bright blue eyes held a warm twinkle.

Diane sighed. "Yes. I would like to look up a name, to see if the person in question ever lived here in Marble Cove. What would be the best way to go about that?"

"Census records are probably the easiest place to start," Gilda said cheerfully. "And lucky for us, that's free. The last census that was released was 1940. Hope that will help you find him."

"It's a 'her.'" Diane followed Gilda to a computer, and the two women waited while the machine booted up.

Diane watched while Gilda quickly pulled up the US Census Bureau site.

"The trick," Gilda said, "is finding the person you really want. Chances are good that there will be more than one person by that name. You can sort by state, or by several other descriptors that help you narrow the field." She pushed back on the stool and rose. "There you go, dear. You're quite capable with computers, so you can do this yourself. Just call if you need my help."

"Thanks, Gilda," Diane said. She felt a little short of breath, and she realized her pulse was racing. Oh, could it really be this easy to find Mrs. Louise Mauer who had a daughter named Marie?

It was.

Mere moments later, Diane was staring at the 1940 United States Federal Census. And there was Louise Mauer and a husband named Galen Mauer. In 1940, Galen Mauer was twenty-three years old, Louise was twenty-one, and their daughter Marie was listed as one. So Marie had been born around 1940, making her seventy-three, give or take a year, now. There was a chance she was still living!

Going back to the record, Diane saw that Galen's occupation was listed as "civil engineer" for the United States Engineers for approximately forty hours per week. Louise's occupation, at that time, had been left blank, so presumably she was a housewife who didn't work outside the home. But what happened to the family between 1940 and 1952, when Elias Thorpe had provided health care for Marie? World War II occurred during those years. Maybe Galen had enlisted in the service. Did he come back? Diane would have to search the *Courier* archives to see what she could find out about him.

After a moment's indecision, she trekked back down the stairs to the front desk, where Gilda was checking out a harried young mother with two giggling preschoolers and an infant in a carrier she wore across her front. As the young woman herded the children toward the door, Gilda asked, "Find what you need?"

Diane nodded. "Yes, but now I have another question. I want to know if a particular young local man enlisted in the armed services between 1940 and 1950. How can I find that out?"

Gilda raised an eyebrow. "That's a little trickier, but the first thing I'd do is check the records for area soldiers."

Diane felt like smacking herself in the forehead. "Ugh. You're right. How could I have missed that?"

"You could go downstairs and go back through all the obituaries in the old *Couriers*. You're talking a decade after the fire, so we should have copies of those." Gilda was speaking of a fire that destroyed the newspaper in the 1930s, one that had caused trouble for Diane on previous fact-finding missions.

"He was employed by the army before the war," Diane said. "So I need to check the obituaries between 1941 and 1945, I guess."

Gilda snapped her fingers. "Wait. There's a quick and easy way to find out if he died while serving during World War II."

The librarian started up the steps to the Maine Room again with Diane following close behind. "A couple of years ago, the historical society paid to have an archive created of all the town's war dead. So all we have to do is search that to see if his name is there. If he didn't die during the war, it won't help you, but it's a good way to start the process of elimination. If you can find out if he died and his date of death, then it won't be so tedious to look up the obituary in the microfiche."

Moments later, the two women were back at the computer. Gilda's fingers flew across the keyboard as Diane gave her the name "Galen Mauer" to input. And mere moments after that, up popped a death listing.

Diane sighed. "This is depressing. I wanted to find this, but it makes me sad."

Gilda patted her shoulder as she rose again. "Just let me know if you want to get into the microfiche."

The database was brief and succinct. It read: Mauer, Galen D. His age was given as twenty-seven at the time of his death, his rank was lieutenant, and he was killed in action in Germany on November 27, 1944. Armed with that knowledge, Diane went back downstairs, where Gilda took her down to the basement. Diane had used the microfiche collection before, so finding the *Courier* records for late November 1944 was a simple matter. In moments, she was reading Galen Mauer's obituary.

KILLED IN GERMANY. Lieut. Galen Donald Mauer, the Husband of Housewife Louise (Manchester) Mauer, Met Death There Nov. 27—Mrs. Louise Mauer, formerly of 16 Camp Street, Marble Cove, received a telegram from the War Department Friday, notifying her that her husband, 1st Lieut. Galen Donald Mauer, 27, of the Army Combat Engineers, was killed in action in Germany, 27 November.

Born, August 23, 1917, Lieut. Mauer, son of Mr. and Mrs. Lloyd Mauer of Marble Cove, was a graduate of Marble Cove High School and the University of Maine, and before enlisting in the service in May 1942 had been employed as a civil engineer with the United States Engineers. He trained at Fort Belvoir, Va., and Camp Claiborne, La., and had been stationed at Camp Gruber, Okla., and Camp Swift, Texas. He went overseas in February 1944.

May 14, 1938, he was married to Miss Louise Marie Manchester, daughter of Mr. and Mrs. Merrill Manchester of

Rockland. Mrs. Mauer and her four-year-old daughter, Marie Frances, currently reside with her parents and younger sister at 45 Stone Avenue in Rockland.

Besides his wife and daughter, and his parents, Lieut. Mauer is survived by two sisters, Miss Doris Mauer of Marble Cove; and Mrs. Lydia (Mauer) Waters of Belfast. Mrs. Waters' Husband, Sgt. Ronald Waters, has been at Camp Swift in Texas and shall shortly embark for overseas.

"Mauer. Manchester. Waters. The apples didn't roll too far from the tree, did they?" Diane muttered, thinking of local people she knew who bore those same surnames seventy years later.

But she still didn't have a connection between Louise Mauer and Elias Thorpe. Could Louise Mauer have worked at the quarry after her husband died in Germany? How could she find that out?

She went back to find Gilda for advice.

"Hi again, Gilda." Diane said as she approached. "I'm making progress. But I'm wondering if there's a listing of employees of the Burr Oak Quarry anywhere in here. It's the last piece of the puzzle I'm working on today."

Gilda looked stumped for a moment and then looked like a lightbulb went on. "Well, we do have lots of documents in the Maine Room from when some of the quarry investors were under investigation for mishandling of funds in the early 1950s. Maybe there would be some employee lists in that material," Gilda noted. "But you'd have to do a lot of sifting."

"That's what I was afraid of," Diane said. "But I've come this far, and I'd really like to get some confirmation of my hunch."

"Okay," Gilda agreed. "You know where to go then. Good luck."

Diane headed back to the Maine Room ready to pour over memos and documents for hours, but some of the first pieces of paper she found were dictations of letters from the quarry president taken by none other than Louise Mauer, whose name was on the dictation pad. Diane had hit the jackpot once again.

She made a copy of the letter and put it with a printed copy of the obituary and rose, reflecting on all she had learned that afternoon. Elias Thorpe apparently had paid for lifesaving medical treatment for Marie Mauer, the twelve-year-old daughter of quarry office employee Louise Manchester Mauer and her deceased war hero husband, Lieut. Galen Mauer.

The question was: why?

* * *

"Beyond the obvious, you mean?" Margaret asked an hour later.

"Right." Diane nodded.

When Diane had entered the gallery, Margaret took a break from her painting-in-progress and made them each a cup of tea. It was a quiet afternoon, still a bit early for a lot of tourists to be shuffling around the shop, and the two women leaned on the back counter, sipping and chatting.

"I mean, Elias was almost certainly related to Galen Mauer," Diane went on. "Did he do it to make himself look good?"

"Perhaps," Margaret said. "It could be that he was worried his embezzling would be suspected. Maybe he wanted public opinion on his side."

"Maybe they were friends as well as family," Diane suggested.

"They'd have been roughly the same age, I think," Margaret mused. "Maybe Elias looked up to his cousin. Being an army officer would have had some cachet, especially during the war, and being killed in action—that might have made an impression, even on Elias."

"We know he wasn't a complete blackguard," Diane agreed. "He couldn't have been, to have done such a complete about-face when he started his new life in Oregon."

"The only way to know is going to be to find someone who knew them all back then. And perhaps to find Marie herself. She could very easily still be living."

"I'm going to give Shelley's mother-in-law a call," Diane said. "I'll ask Shelley when might be a good time. If there's a connection to the Mauer family, Frances Mauer Bauer knows about it, I'm certain."

Margaret laughed. "You're probably right."

The two women fell silent, sipping their tea and watching passersby on Main Street.

"Do you remember when we first started seeing the lights?" Diane asked. "Right after I moved here?"

"Ayuh." Margaret smiled. "Hard to forget."

"I saw a light flash the day I first saw Rocky." Diane thought back to the sequence of events. "Of course, I didn't think anything of it at the time."

Margaret laughed. "Yes, I guess it did take awhile for us to catch on. I'll never forget the adrenaline rush I got when I saw that arm in the surf and realized someone out there was in trouble."

"We'd never have known if it hadn't been for the light." Diane wrapped both hands around her mug and fell silent.

Margaret eyed her friend. "Why the sudden journey down Memory Lane? You thinking about writing another story featuring a lighthouse?"

Diane shrugged. "I'm just toying with ideas, trying to find one that feels like a good fit right now."

Margaret smiled, knowing Diane would confide details once she had them worked out in her head.

★ ★ ★

Beverly was just about to shut down her computer and leave her office in the municipal building annex on Friday afternoon when her office assistant, Angela, appeared in her doorway.

"Noah Henry is here to see you," Angela announced. She winked one heavily made-up eye as she added, *sotto voce*, "And boy, is he handsome."

Beverly burst into laughter. "I think he may be taken," she said equally quietly.

Angela heaved a deep breath of disgust. "Figures. All the cute ones are."

"You know," Beverly said as the young woman turned to go back to her desk, "'cute' is only good for so much. Finding someone you really connect with and can build something long-term with is much more important."

Angela cast her a questioning glance. "Listen to you talk—you're marrying one of the best-looking old guys I've seen around here in ages!"

Beverly burst out laughing. She couldn't wait to tell Jeff.

She was still chuckling a moment later when Noah appeared in her doorway. He cast a quizzical look in her direction. "What's so funny?"

Beverly made a dismissive gesture. "Never mind. It was a girl thing."

Noah nodded. "I probably don't want to know then." He waved a portfolio that he'd carried tucked beneath his arm. "I've got that proposal I promised you."

Beverly was dumbfounded. "Already? We only talked on Monday!"

Noah grinned. "Why waste time? I know a contractor who specializes in historic restoration. Of course, he couldn't be too specific without seeing the building for himself, but I sent him several photos and a description of the age and the state of the building now, so he was able to ballpark some costs for me." He extended the folio. "Want to take a look?"

"I'd love to." Beverly motioned him over to a love seat she had placed beneath the window. Perching on an adjacent chair, she opened the leatherette folder and slipped aside the vellum that covered the opening page.

The first page was as professional as anything she could have imagined. It bore the name of the train station and the town, along with a surprisingly well-done image of what the station might look like once it was restored.

Successive pages held cost estimates and information about the process of restoration. The proposal was polished and comprehensive, and the conclusion about the cost did not seem inaccurate to her, based on what she knew. She had to force herself not to gasp out loud when she saw the amount of money Noah was willing to donate to the project.

"This is only for the train station," Noah told her. "Of course, it isn't sufficient for the entire project, but I hope the people of Marble Cove will be willing to pitch in when they see how much of a start we can get with my donation. I've commissioned a study of the quarry area too, so that we can see what would be needed to create a nature preserve. I envision native plants and animals, informative displays about the ecosystem, maybe an area designated for local schools to conduct studies..."

"That sounds wonderful." Beverly tapped the folio. "And you must know this is truly outstanding." She realized she wasn't dealing with a callow youth who had taken a fancy to honor his grandfather, but with a seasoned businessman with sound instincts and a solid understanding of finance.

"I'm hoping to be able to donate enough to get both projects off the ground," he said. "I think it would make me feel much better knowing I had done something, even if it's far too little, far too late, to rectify the wrongs my grandfather did. Marble Cove is a very special little community. I like it here."

Something in the way he spoke the final words got Beverly's attention. Was Noah considering staying in the area? Beverly thought of Brenna and of the romance that appeared to be flowering between them. Then she thought of Noah's business instincts. *My gracious, he could probably revitalize the entire county all by himself.*

Noah reached into his pocket and withdrew a sealed white envelope. "Oh, I almost forgot. Here's something for you and your friends to look at. You can return it to me at your leisure."

"Thank you."

"I also wanted to tell you I spoke to the pastor of my grandfather's church yesterday, and to my mother last night. I am afraid they both agreed that we would have little luck trying to learn anything about his early life from anyone on the West Coast. He had two close friends at church who are both deceased now. Neither of them could think of another soul who might know anything about the years when he lived in Marble Cove. Mom had no idea he'd ever even lived on the East Coast until I started digging."

"I guess I'm not surprised," Beverly said. "Your grandfather was a man of many secrets."

"And since he apparently decided to start over on the right foot in his new life, I guess I'm not surprised either," Noah said. "It makes me think he just wanted to forget about his past."

Chapter Eleven

So I think we're at a dead end." Beverly's shoulders sagged after she relayed Noah's information to her friends that evening. The four of them had gathered around Margaret's kitchen table for some carrot cake and a quick catch-up. "I always feared we would get to a point where some of our questions couldn't be answered."

Margaret nodded. "After so much time has passed, it becomes much more difficult to figure it all out."

"Especially when most or all of the principal players have passed away," Shelley noted.

"I made some progress finding out who Mrs. Louise Mauer was," Diane reported. "She was a secretary or office worker at the quarry in 1950, I learned, so I assume she was still working there until it closed."

She went on to relate the rest of the information she had found about Louise Mauer's soldier husband who had died in the war, and the fact that their daughter Marie would have been about ten in 1950.

"But you don't know how or if Galen Mauer is related to the Mauers that Frances is related to?" Shelley asked.

Diane shook her head. "I have his parents' names and his sisters' names. Want to ask her?"

"Sure." Shelley smiled a little. "If I can get her talking about family history, maybe she'll take a break from fussing about Ralph's progress."

Beverly laid the envelope Noah had given her in the middle of the table. "Who wants to do the honors? Noah gave me this, said he thought we'd find it interesting."

Diane gestured at Beverly. "Go for it!"

Beverly smiled, carefully lifting the flap of the square envelope. "It's heavy. I can't imagine what's in here—oh!"

She pulled out two small items. "Look! These must be the bankbooks he said he found."

She opened one, handing the other to Margaret. "This one is from a Citizen's Bank of Astoria, Oregon. So it must have been established after he left Marble Cove. Yes, right here: the first entry is in May of 1952, and it shows a balance of...oh my heavens!" She gasped at the amount shown in the opening balance. "There's almost a million dollars here. Back in the early fifties, that was, well, it was a fortune!"

"It was *several* fortunes," Margaret said. "Look, this is from Marble Cove Bank & Trust, and there's only a few thousand dollars in here." She gasped as she scanned earlier entries in the little book. "But Noah wasn't kidding. Elias made some enormous deposits in the years before 1952. And it looks like he spent most of it almost immediately."

"What happened to the money he had at the end?" Diane asked.

"It was all withdrawn and the account closed out on February 28, 1952."

"Which fits with the timeline. The last train left Marble Cove on March 1st."

"But where did he get all that money?" Shelley wondered.

"He must have had a separate account somewhere or he carried it with him in cash." Beverly shook her head. "Clearly, he planned to disappear."

Diane upended the envelope and several photographs and folded papers spilled across the table.

"Check this out," Shelley said, picking one up. She studied it, then flipped it so the others could see it as she read the back, "'Elias Henry Thorpe, 1947.' So this one was taken when things were still going well, before all the scandal broke, I guess."

"Here's a newspaper article about a party he had." Diane skimmed the print. "It's from 1948. Sounds like quite a party. Ice sculptures, a string trio, champagne fountains...wow!"

Beverly held up yet another newspaper article. "Here's a photo of his house on Sullivan Street. He's posing with a group of women at the foot of the grand staircase—it says 'grand staircase' right here in print!"

"And look at that chandelier," Shelley said. "Too bad that isn't still hanging in the foyer."

"It really is a beautiful example of Victorian architecture. I bet it was really something back in his day." Margaret grinned. "Good thing we already know where it is and who owns it, or Diane would be over there trying to convince the owners to let her scour every inch of it for clues about Elias's life."

Diane laughed. "Am I that bad?"

"Yes!" All three of her friends chimed in, looking at each other with amusement.

"Well," she said, "I would ask the Inglewoods to let me do exactly that, but I kind of doubt there are many clues to Elias's life still left there. So other than tracking down these two women, Louise and Marie Mauer, I don't know that we have many more ways to find out information about him. And anyway, at this point, we'd mostly be doing that for Noah's sake. What we need to concentrate on is how to help Noah pull off this train station museum before Dennis Calder manages to talk people into his development plans."

The women began to talk about the wedding then, asking Beverly how final details were slipping into place.

Beverly smiled, not even flustered by the questions. "Honestly, the wedding feels as if everything is totally under control. I'm not even worried about it—which is quite a miracle."

"Indeed," Margaret said, nodding sagely, and they all chuckled.

"Well, I might be worried about one thing," Beverly amended. "Diane, have you managed to find a limo yet?"

"Not yet." But Diane had a mysterious smile playing around the corners of her mouth. "But you're going to have to trust me. I had an idea that I think is going to work out."

"And we've got the renovation plans on the house arranged. The contractor will be starting just as soon as we close. He says he should be able to have everything done in a couple of months so we should be moved in this summer."

Shelley smiled. "That would be nice, being able to wave across the fence at you in the mornings." But then her smile faded.

What was wrong with Shelley? Beverly wondered. She couldn't put a finger on it, but her youngest friend seemed strangely subdued.

★ ★ ★

Adelaide was on Shelley's doorstep bright and early Saturday morning. As she came in, she took a folded piece of paper from her pocket. "My list of recipes," she said. "I didn't want Mom to see it."

Shelley smiled. "You're getting sneaky."

Adelaide laughed. "I know. Sneaky Adelaide. Ha ha!"

The young woman's merry expression both delighted Shelley and made her feel sad at the same time. She would miss Adelaide—and all the Hoskins family, and everyone else—terribly if they really did move. She knew Dan hadn't accepted Wayne's proposition yet, but it was just a matter of time. They couldn't afford to turn it down. Not just because of the money, because she figured if they stayed here, her own business would get off the ground much faster than it would if she had to start over somewhere new where no one knew her, but because they had chosen this career path for Dan, and this was essentially a promotion. They should be looking at it as a gift, not a terrible event.

"What's wrong, Shelley?"

Shelley gave a start. Adelaide was far too perceptive, and she didn't want the younger woman worrying. "Oh, nothing," she said. "Just thinking we should get started, because I have a lot to do today."

Adelaide frowned. "If you're too busy, I can come back later."

"No! That's not what I meant." Shelley took a deep breath. She was bungling this badly. "Let's check out your recipes." She held out her hand for Adelaide's list, forcing a smile. "I can't wait to see what you're going to make!"

"I numbered them," Adelaide told her as they headed to the kitchen. "Number one is the one I want to make the most. And I looked to make sure there were different things too."

"Good for you." Curious about Adelaide's choices, Shelley smoothed out the paper and began to read:

Bow-Tie Pasta with Chicken and Peas

Mushroom-Chicken Skewers

Vegetarian Lasagna

Peppered Steaks

Asian Grilled Tuna

Mushroom-Spinach Pizza

There were nine more recipes on the list, and Adelaide had a Web site URL listed after each one. "Where did you find these?" Shelley asked.

"On vegetarian heart-healthy Web sites," Adelaide answered. "There was some other stuff that sounded good. But when I read the recipes, I think I would need Dad's help." She tapped a stubby finger on the paper. "These I can do myself." She grinned. "I think."

"Awesome!" Shelley gestured to the table. "Let's look at them and see which ones would be best."

Adelaide fairly bounced to the table. "Okay! I really wanna do the pizza."

"Then we'll start with that," Shelley said.

They looked at the first seven recipes on the list, culling it down to five. "I think this is plenty for you to prove to your mom that you can cook," Shelley said.

"That I can take care of myself," Adelaide corrected. "I will clean up too."

"I'm sure you will. Shall we make a list of what you'll need to make each of these dishes?"

"Yeah. Dad can take me to the store. I will make him wait in the car while I shop."

Shelley's eyebrows rose. "He could probably help with the shopping. Just don't tell him what you plan to make."

"Maybe." Adelaide seemed entirely committed to this plan. "But he can't tell Mom. Not one word."

Shelley was unable to hide her amusement. "I'm sure he won't if you tell him how important it is to you. Your dad can keep a secret."

Adelaide chuckled. "Dad's a good secret-keeper."

★ ★ ★

Jeff and Beverly attended church together on Sunday. As they slipped into their pew with her father, Jeff nudged her. "In less than two weeks, we'll be saying 'I do,' in this room."

"I can't wait." She sent him a private smile. "I'm ready to be married now. And I *really* can't wait until our new home is finished and we can move in."

Jeff smiled. "I'm looking forward to that too. Our own place."

After the service, they were just about to exit their pew when Maddie Bancroft, Old First's choir director, came bustling up. "Beverly," she sang out. "Do you have something for me?"

Beverly regarded Maddie blankly. "Um, no . . . Should I?" Frantically, she searched her memory. She knew she hadn't promised to bake anything for one of the never-ending fundraisers Maddie was always involved in—

"Oh no!" She clapped a hand to her mouth. "Wedding music!"

Maddie smiled. "Yes. Wedding music."

"I was supposed to get you some suggestions for pieces that we would like." Beverly felt terrible. How could she have forgotten? True, she'd been immersed in her new role as mayor, learning on the job, as it were, and she'd been thinking about the new house and still worrying over the latest information on Elias Thorpe, but—"I just told my friends that everything was under control! Oh, Maddie, I am so sorry."

"It's not a big problem," Maddie said. "Two weeks is plenty of time. The organist plays weddings all the time, so she's going to be familiar with just about anything you choose. Tell you what, why don't I e-mail you a list of the pieces I most often recommend?"

"Oh, would you? That would be so helpful."

"Look over the list, and then shoot me an e-mail or call me and we can talk about them. We need about thirty minutes of prelude music to play while the guests are seated, you'll need to select something special to use as your processional, and you may also want to use a special piece during the ceremony. Are you lighting a unity candle or taking communion?"

"Lighting a candle," Beverly replied.

"Oh, good. Malotte's 'The Lord's Prayer' is a lovely choice, but there are other hymns and songs that will be equally nice."

"I adore that one," Beverly said. "Jeff, what do you think?"

He nodded. "Compelling piece of music. I think it would be very nice to include it. Do you have recommendations for a soloist?"

Maddie's eyebrows rose. "Oh. I assumed perhaps you had someone in the family or a friend you'd invited to sing. Um, let me give that some thought. Do you want a male or female?"

Beverly was taken aback. "I don't know. I—" Inspiration struck. "Would you consider singing?"

Maddie's eyes widened. "Oh, I don't—"

"Please? Maddie, you have a lovely voice. I know you don't often perform solos. I guess the choir director can't really assign solos to herself, can she? But I'd be so happy if you would. You're my friend, and I can't think of anyone I'd rather have sing at our wedding."

Maddie was silent for a moment. She looked away, clearly touched. Then she leaned forward and enfolded her in a hug. "Thank you, Beverly. I am honored, both to be asked to sing and to be considered your friend." She smiled, blinking back the tears in her eyes. "I'd love to sing on your special day," she said to them both.

"Wonderful," Beverly said. "Thank you."

As they greeted the pastor and moved outside, Beverly saw Brenna and Noah strolling hand in hand down the street just ahead of them. Clearly they'd attended Old First as well.

"Hello," she said as she and Jeff came abreast of the slower-moving pair.

"Hi, Beverly, Jeff." Brenna greeted them, her pretty features glowing. Beverly was so used to seeing her with her hair pulled back and wearing practical work clothes that she sometimes forgot how lovely Brenna really was. Today was the perfect example: her long dark hair curled around her shoulders and she wore a lightweight floral skirt that floated around her, with a short-sleeved jewel-neck sweater in a matching peach hue.

"Hello," Noah said.

"I wanted to thank you for sharing your photos and other information with us," Beverly told him. "We all looked at it Friday night. If you want to stop by my office one day this week, I'll return it to you."

"Sure thing." He smiled.

A new thought occurred to Beverly. It felt right, and she knew Jeff wouldn't mind. "You know we're getting married in two weeks," she said to the couple. "I realize it's short notice, but we'd like to invite you to the wedding. I'll get invitations in the mail tomorrow."

"Thank you," Noah said. He sounded sincerely pleased. "We'll let you know as soon as possible if we can attend."

CHAPTER TWELVE

When Beverly arrived at the mayor's office on Monday morning, Angela was already seated at her desk. The young receptionist's brow was furrowed as she stared at a sheaf of papers she'd just pulled from an envelope. Beverly had never seen Angela look angry and was concerned.

"Good morning, Angela. What's wrong?"

"Oh, I'm just so angry I could spit." Angela thrust the pack of papers at Beverly. "Dennis Calder has submitted his plans to 'develop'"—her fingers made angry quote marks in the air—"the land where the train station stands. His version of development is nothing but destroying the history of this town as far as I'm concerned!"

"Angela..." Beverly hesitated, searching for the right words. "Don't let yourself get too upset. This isn't a done deal yet, you know."

"I know." Angela sighed. "But I'm afraid if enough people start listening to him talk about all the jobs he's going to create, they're going to start believing that snake."

Beverly smiled. "I have another proposal for the train station too. Noah Henry would like to preserve it as a museum."

Angela's eyes widened, and she straightened. "He would?" Then her shoulders slumped again. "But...how can this town afford to do that? It might eventually bring in some income as a tourist attraction, but I can't imagine it would pay for itself up front."

"No, but Noah might give it a good start. He's interested in donating money for the project. Don't say anything, though. I haven't presented this to the council yet, and some of them will get their noses out of joint if the whole town hears about it before they do."

Angela laughed. "Isn't that the truth?" Then she sobered. "Beverly, if that should come to pass, I'd be really interested in serving on a committee to work on the restoration of that old building."

Delighted to see a young person displaying such civic interest, Beverly patted Angela on the shoulder. "If it does work out and we go ahead with it, I would be thrilled to invite you to join such a committee. I think it's very important for the young people of our community to have an opportunity to get involved in projects like this."

As Beverly went on into her office and pulled her planner toward her to review her calendar, the telephone rang. She heard Angela answer it, and moments later, her line buzzed. "Call for you."

"Beverly? It's Diane. Are you going to be in your office this morning?"

Beverly glanced at her schedule. "Yes. Why?"

"I want to get Noah Henry to meet us there. We have some news for you." Diane sounded excited.

"Okay. What time do you want to come by?"

"How's ten?"

"Ten it is." That, she thought, would only give her an hour to obsess about whatever secret Diane was waiting to share.

The hour passed slowly, but finally, a few minutes before ten, she heard voices. She could have sworn she heard Shelley's voice—

"Hi, Beverly." It *was* Shelley. And Margaret and Diane and Noah. And even Brenna, who would normally be working at the Cove right now. Probably had been, if her clothing was any indication, Beverly thought as Noah slipped Brenna's coat from her shoulders.

"What's going on here?" Beverly came to the door of her office and beckoned them all inside as Angela assessed the crowd. "Not, of course, that I'm not glad to see you all."

Brenna grinned. "I can't stay. I just wanted to be here for a minute or two."

"Because...?" Beverly was truly mystified.

"Two reasons," Noah said. "First, I heard you were having a little trouble finding a limo for your wedding day."

Beverly nodded. "Yes. Diane's on the job, though I'm not sure she's had much more luck than I have." She glanced past him to her friend, who was beaming. "Why?" she asked, slowly and suspiciously.

Noah reached into his pocket and came up dangling a car key beneath her nose. "I don't have a limo, but I do have a 1952 Jaguar coupe in mint condition that I would be delighted to loan you. Can't get much more stylish wheels than that."

"You'd loan us your...Elias's car?" Beverly was stunned. After all the work she and her friends had done to uncover the stories of Noah's ancestors, this seemed to fit perfectly into the circle. "Oh, Noah, thank you! How perfect!"

He grinned, restoring the key to his pocket. "Tell Jeff I'll have the car at the church for you right after the ceremony."

"All right." She still couldn't believe it. "That's why all of you came down here? So you could see my reaction?"

Margaret chuckled. "No. We were pleased when Diane told us, but there's something else..." She turned and looked at Diane, who nodded.

"I couldn't wait to share this with all of you," she said. "Shelley knows, because she talked to her mother-in-law."

"You learned something about the woman from the quarry that my grandfather helped?" Noah looked eager.

Diane nodded. "Louise Mauer's husband Galen was some kind of second cousin to Frances Bauer. That's not really important. What *is* important is that now we know Louise Mauer was indeed related by marriage to Elias, and her daughter is as well. Unfortunately, Louise passed away about ten years ago."

"Oh, too bad...," Beverly began.

"But her daughter Marie is still living!" Diane looked around the group. "Marie married a local man by the surname of Harnish."

"Harnish!" Brenna looked uncomprehending. "But that's—"

"And had one daughter," Diane went on, eyes twinkling. "Her daughter married a man by the last name of"—she paused, then she and Brenna said together—"McTavish."

"Whoa. Wait. You mean my grandmother is the girl from the letter?" Brenna appeared completely stunned, as did the others.

"Is your grandmother's name Marie?"

"Yes. Marie Harnish."

"And do you know if she had tuberculosis when she was a girl?"

Brenna shrugged helplessly. "I don't know. I never heard if she did."

"That's not unusual," Margaret said. "People with TB where shunned, avoided, sent to sanitariums. A lot of former TB patients still wouldn't mention it to anyone, even today."

"Wait." Noah sat down slowly on the little love seat beneath the window. "So Brenna and I are actually..."

"Kissing cousins, at best," Diane said, grinning. "You probably share a few common ancestral genes, but nothing to get excited about."

Noah looked dazed. Then his expression cleared, excitement filling his eyes. "We can ask your gran what she remembers!" he said to Brenna.

She smiled sadly. "We can try. She may or may not remember. You've seen how she is." To the others, she said, "She has the occasional good day, but she doesn't even know me some of the time now. Still, when she does remember things, most often then it's older stuff, like from her childhood. So who knows? Maybe she will remember Elias."

"Would it be possible for me to visit her?" Diane asked. "Or do you think she'd find that upsetting?"

Brenna shrugged. "On the right day, she'd enjoy it. On the wrong day, it would get her all bent out of whack for hours. I suppose we could always set up a tentative time to visit, and I'll let you know if it isn't going to be a good day."

"This might be our only shot at finding out why Elias helped Marie," Diane said. "Did he help because they were related to him? Or was he simply moved by a little girl's plight?"

"If my gran doesn't know," Brenna said, "you may have to accept that you'll never have an answer."

★ ★ ★

On Tuesday morning, the extended Bauer family was in a total tizzy. Shelley's phone rang at least half a dozen times before noon.

"Is he home yet?"

"Do they need anything?"

"Have you been over?"

"How does he seem?"

And Shelley's personal favorite from Annie: "Has Mom been awful?"

Shelley's father-in-law Ralph had been released from the rehab center, as they had hoped, early that morning. Dan had driven his mother over, and together they had brought Ralph home.

Shelley had gone to the house while Frances was out, placing a casserole and a fruit salad in the refrigerator for the evening's meal, and leaving Ralph's favorite chocolate cake with peanut butter icing on the counter. She'd made the beds up with fresh sheets and put clean towels in the bathroom and kitchen, then thrown a load of dirty laundry in the washer.

Then she'd taken Emma home and waited to hear from Dan how the excursion had gone.

According to him, Ralph was moving pretty well on his own with a walker. "If I can just impress upon Mom that she can't do everything for him, he'll be fine," Dan said. "Fortunately, Dad doesn't want her doing things for him. They'll probably fight like two cats in a sack, but at least he's home."

Shelley told him what she had done in preparation. "Your sisters and sisters-in-law are going to take turns stopping in daily to see if they need anything, to help with laundry, and to bring a meal. Until your mom feels like cooking, that at least is something they can do. I made them all promise not to rush right over there today, but just to call, and to wait until it's their day to visit."

Dan shook his head. "Shell, you are amazing, you know that? No one else I know could get Vera and Annie to cooperate and actually listen."

Shelley laughed. "They're not so bad."

The telephone rang, and she rose to answer it. "Hello?"

"Hi, Shelley, it's Frances."

"Hi," Shelley said with genuine pleasure. "How are you doing now that you finally have your fella home?"

Frances laughed. "It's wonderful. It really is." She sounded on the verge of tears for a moment. Then her voice firmed. "Thank you for making the beds and starting that laundry. I could've done that myself, but it was nice of you. I saw the list you left for us, the one of who's going to stop by on what day. Shelley, I really don't need that kind of help—"

"It's not all for you," Shelley said. "They're all terribly anxious about seeing Ralph, and I thought this way would be a lot less exhausting for him than having the whole clan show up on your doorstep today."

"Oh." Frances sounded uncertain. "I suppose that would be better, wouldn't it? I mean, we love the whole big bunch, but maybe you're right. That might be too tiring for Ralph. I see you left us a meal too, which I appreciate. But you can't do that every day, Shelley. You've got enough to do with your own family."

"I don't plan to. The other kids are dying to help, so they'll be bringing in some meals. They need something to do, Frances. They've been worried sick, and we all feel so helpless." Before her mother-in-law could voice another complaint, Shelley said, "Besides, it's just silly for you to run yourself ragged when the most important job of all is to oversee Ralph's therapy and recovery. You can't do that if you let yourself get exhausted by minor stuff like housekeeping. That's what family is for."

There was a deep silence on the other end of the line. Shelley felt a moment of panic. Had she been too bossy?

"You're right." Frances sounded apologetic. "I'm sorry, Shelley. I'm tired and grumpy, and very, very glad I don't have to make dinner tonight, so thank you for that and for setting me straight. I am grateful for the help, you know. I'm just not very good at showing it."

Shelley chuckled. "It's okay. We're all just happy Ralph is home. The rest will sort itself out, and things will be back to normal before you know it. In the meantime, just let the kids help you once in a while, okay?"

As she hung up the phone, she could see Dan smiling from his seat in his recliner. "What?"

"Nothing." Dan shook his head. "I was just thinking that you've become a pro at managing my mother." His smile faded. "And I'm about to take you away from her."

Shelley tried to smile. "I can still manage from a couple hours away, honey. It's not like Portland is on the other side of the country."

"I know." But Dan sounded as unhappy and conflicted as Shelley herself felt about the prospect of moving. Still, her job was to be supportive.

"It'll work out," was all she could think of to say. It felt trite, and judging from Dan's expression, it didn't do much to allay his concerns either.

★ ★ ★

"Mom?"

Margaret had barely set foot in the door on Wednesday evening when Adelaide came to greet her. "Hi, honey. How are you doing?"

Adelaide gave her a sweet smile. "Fine. Mom, I'm going to cook tonight. Dad said it would be okay."

Margaret tried to hide her amusement. "Well, then it's fine with me. You know I don't adore cooking like Shelley does, so that'll be fine. What are we having?"

"Pasta with chicken."

What? Had she misunderstood? Margaret had expected her daughter to say "grilled cheese sandwiches" or "scrambled eggs," two of Adelaide's typical choices. In fact, Margaret worried that Adelaide would be eating eggs and cheese on a daily basis while she was in Paris. "Did you say pasta with chicken?"

Adelaide nodded matter-of-factly. "Bow-tie pasta with chicken and peas."

"Do you need help?"

"No." Adelaide shook her head. "I studied the recipe." She moved to the pantry and got out a can of cat food, popped the top, grabbed a fork, and began to dish out the food while the family's three cats wound around her ankles, yowling.

Margaret studied her daughter for a moment, but Adelaide apparently had nothing more to say. "Great," Margaret finally said before she headed toward the bedroom to change out of her work clothes.

Allan was sitting in the living room as she walked through. "Hi, honey," he said.

"Hi." She walked to him for a brief kiss, then gestured toward the kitchen. "Did you hear that?"

Allan nodded. "I was informed that she was cooking pasta with chicken, and that she did not need help. In fact"—he rustled the newspaper he held—"I got a directive to go read my paper. We, my dear, are not needed in the kitchen."

Margaret shook her head. "I wonder what brought this on."

Allan shrugged. "Who cares? She's cooking, and we're not."

Margaret laughed out loud as she headed back to the bedroom.

At the dinner table a short while later, Margaret sat back with a smile. Adelaide's pasta casserole was delicious, and she'd set out salad with dressing as well.

"Honey, this is a terrific meal," Allan said.

"Thanks." Adelaide beamed.

"Did Shelley help you with this?" Margaret couldn't help but ask.

"She looked at the recipe after I found it. We read it together—to make sure I could do it. And I did!"

"You certainly did. This is very tasty."

"May I cook every night for the next four days?" Adelaide looked anxiously from one parent to the other.

"What? You really want to cook every night through Sunday? What do you want to make?"

"I'll surprise you," her daughter said firmly. "I already know what I'm making. We have all the ingredients for tomorrow night. Dad, will you take me to the store to shop for the rest?"

Allan nodded, smiling. "Sure."

"Um, honey? Why do you want to do this?" Margaret asked.

Adelaide looked at her very seriously. "I want to practice for when I'm alone," she said. "If you see me cook now, then you'll know I can do it."

The simple reasoning left Margaret speechless. She and Allan looked at each other, exchanging a glance of surprised approbation.

"You're absolutely right," Margaret said. "That is a wonderful idea." She knew Adelaide could do it, but she was pleased that her daughter was so interested in showing off her competence.

CHAPTER THIRTEEN

Beverly awoke on Thursday morning and, as she had every day for the whole month, arose and crossed off another day on her calendar. Only ten days left now until the wedding!

It was a glorious morning, chilly but sunny, and her run along the beach left her feeling invigorated and charged up for whatever life threw at her during the day. Returning home, she showered and dressed before going downstairs to start breakfast. Jeff was coming over for blueberry pancakes this morning.

"Good morning!" she greeted Jeff at the door when she heard his footsteps on the porch, before she realized he was on his cell phone. She clapped a hand over her mouth, motioning him in and helping him remove his light jacket while he talked.

As she hung up the jacket, he moved into her father's library. Her father was still sleeping at this hour, so the room was empty.

Beverly went back to the kitchen, knowing he would soon join her. She wasn't trying to listen in, but Jeff's smooth baritone carried through the downstairs, and she couldn't help but hear his side of the conversation. Some other photographer was asking him to step in as a substitute on an assignment. Jeff declined.

Moments later, he came into the kitchen. She was mixing the blueberries into the pancake batter as the skillet heated.

"Good morning." He slid his arms around her waist and kissed the side of her neck. "Sorry about that."

"No problem." She smiled as she returned his kiss and then spooned the first ladle of batter onto the skillet. "I take it that was for something out of the country?"

Jeff grimaced. "No, but across the country. Washington State. I'd have had to be gone for several days, and I just don't think that's a good idea this close to the wedding. I mean, what if you've forgotten other things like you forgot the music?"

She could hear the teasing note in his voice, and she pretended to sock him in the arm. "Ha! I haven't forgotten a single other thing. That was just—just—oh, I think my brain went on vacation. Probably because I knew Maddie would never let anything bad happen once I asked her to do the music for the ceremony."

Jeff laughed. "She certainly is capable."

That evening, Mrs. Peabody had left a pork shoulder in mushroom sauce in the Crock-Pot. Beverly added whole wheat pasta and steamed broccoli, and for dessert she served some sugar-free blond butterscotch brownies that Shelley had given her.

As she served her father a brownie, she said to Jeff, "I haven't been able to get that phone call from the man who needed your help out of my head today. Do you think he found anyone?"

Jeff sighed. "I don't know. I hope so."

"What was the assignment?"

"It's on Mt. Rainier, and it involved photographing a handicapped climber's ascent of the mountain."

"Sounds interesting," Father commented.

"I'm sure it would be," Jeff said. "But it's too close to our wedding date. The weather up there is unpredictable."

"But even more than that," Beverly said, "mountain climbing is so risky. I have this image of you clomping to the altar on crutches."

Jeff laughed. "I've never been hurt on assignment in my whole life."

"I know. You're careful, and I appreciate that care. I never imagined myself falling for a man whose job involved dangerous situations."

"But I was just so irresistible," Jeff put in.

Beverly laughed, reaching for his hand. "Not to mention determined."

"You weren't the easiest woman to charm," Jeff admitted. "So yes, I was determined." As she covered his hand with her own, he lifted it to his lips and kissed her knuckles. "And I'm not taking a chance on missing this wedding."

★ ★ ★

Beverly was in her office the following morning when there was a knock at the frame of her open door. She glanced up questioningly, expecting to see Angela, because she hadn't heard the office door open.

Instead of Angela, Jules Benton stood there. The council president had come in around the same time she had. After exchanging civilities, each of them had headed for their own office. Beverly hadn't found Jules difficult to work with, exactly, but she couldn't say they saw a lot of issues the same way. Nor had they found the easy working relationship she'd expected, which would have made sharing a secretary much easier.

"Hello," she greeted him. "Come on in. What's up?" Still, as Jules entered her office, he closed the door behind him. Beverly sat up a little straighter. Jules was a pretty relaxed man. If he felt the need to close the door, whatever was on his mind was probably going to be interesting, to say the least.

"Beverly." Jules crossed the room and sat heavily on a chair across from her desk. For a moment, he was silent.

"What's going on, Jules?" She leaned forward, concerned. The man looked upset.

"I need to speak to you in private," he said. "This has to be completely confidential until we figure out what we're going to do about it."

Heart hammering, she nodded. "You've got my word." She was only five months into her first term as mayor. Was she ready for a crisis?

Jules cleared his throat. "I had a breakfast meeting with Dennis Calder today."

Dennis! She should have known he'd be involved in this. But she only said, "And?"

"He wants me to support his new development package, which he spent considerable time explaining to me." Jules sighed and ran a hand down his face. "In fact, he offered me an outright bribe in exchange for my vote."

Beverly gasped. "Oh my word."

"Yeah." Jules looked distressed. "I was flabbergasted. And pretty upset that he thinks I'm the kind of person who would accept a bribe. I've always prided myself on my civic involvement. What makes him think I'm for sale?" The older man looked angry now as well.

"I don't know," Beverly said honestly. "I've never, ever thought of you that way."

"I'd hope not!" The anger went out of him abruptly and his shoulders sagged. "Just a few minutes ago, Dennis sent me an e-mail. In it, he reminds me that he wants to give me a 'thank-you gift' for my consideration in supporting his plans."

Beverly cringed. "Oh dear."

"We're going to have to address this," Jules said. "If Dennis is bribing me, he might be trying it with some of the other council members. Just for the record," he added, "I had decided before I spoke to him today that I was not in favor of tearing down the train station. I've given this a great deal of thought."

"As have I," Beverly said. She couldn't resist doing a mental head count. With Jules on her side, that meant there would be four council votes against Dennis's development plans. Then she went on. "I know people are anxious about jobs and would welcome anything that would create them. And I know there's also anxiety about any plan that might require a financial commitment from the town for upkeep." She sighed. "I can't say that I'm not relieved, Jules, to hear that you're opposed to Dennis's plan. But what on earth do we do now?"

Jules lifted his hands, palms up, in an equally clueless gesture. "I'm not sure either. He approached me directly with the actual bribe. Unfortunately, I wasn't wearing a wire, so it's my word against his."

Beverly smiled wryly. "How about the e-mail?"

"It could be incriminating," Jules said, "although he was very careful not to mention anything specific. His exact wording was what I said to you." He produced a crumpled piece of paper and read out loud: "'As I mentioned, I would like to offer you a thank-you gift for your consideration and support of my project.'"

Beverly shook her head. "Oh, Dennis." She felt very sad. She'd known him a long time and considered him a friend until recently.

Jules looked up from the paper. "I honestly don't know what to do. I don't think this is enough to have him arrested. Should I pretend to accept?"

"No!" Beverly was emphatic. "Absolutely not, unless for some reason the police would ask you to do so as a decoy. If you were to do that on your own, it would make you vulnerable to charges of collusion, and you could be arrested if this gets out." She sighed. "I guess we need to talk to the police about this. How about I call Fred Little? He's my neighbor and a good guy."

"Works for me," Jules said, his face gloomy. "I'm going to hate doing this, but I can't believe Dennis Calder would stoop so low."

"I feel the same way." Beverly slowly reached for the phone. Part of her wished they didn't have to make this call. How could Dennis have become this person she truly didn't know anymore?

But after a moment's hesitation, she hit the key that would connect her to the police front desk. If they were lucky, Fred might be available.

* * *

Adelaide made a tuna-noodle casserole for dinner on Friday evening. She added mushrooms, cheese, and broccoli, and produced an exceptionally tasty dish. Afterward she cleaned up the dishes and then pulled out a ring binder and opened it.

To Margaret's surprise, it was filled with clear sleeves that held recipe cards. "That's nice," she said. "Where did you get that?"

"Shelley gave it to me. She said every chef needs a recipe file."

Margaret grinned. Bless her friend. "Great idea."

Adelaide got a pencil and paper from the drawer and sat down in front of her recipes. "I need to check the 'gredients. So we can get everything I need."

Allan, standing in the doorway, said, "If you like, we could run to the store when you're done making your list."

"Okay!" Adelaide beamed.

Margaret walked into the living room and perched on the edge of Allan's recliner. "Mind if I go along to the store with you?"

Allan looked up quizzically, knowing grocery shopping was perhaps one of Margaret's least favorite chores. "Not at all. What brought this on?"

She grinned. "I want to watch Adelaide shop. I'm so proud of her, and rather in awe of how great our last two evening meals have been. She puts me to shame."

"I know one thing," Allan said. "Now that we know she can cook, she's not getting out of taking her turn every week!"

Adelaide came into the room a few minutes later, waving her grocery list. "I need sweet potatoes. And parsley."

"If it were summertime, we could grow those in our garden," Allan commented.

Adelaide nodded. "Good idea, Dad. I'll start a list of stuff to grow."

Allan grinned over his daughter's head at Margaret. "This could get interesting."

CHAPTER FOURTEEN

Jeff and Beverly snuggled on the couch. Her father had just said good night and gone to bed. She had told Jeff about her day, even about the bombshell that Jules had dropped on her that morning. She knew Jeff would never breathe a word of it to anyone.

Unfortunately, Detective Little had been tied up in a meeting when Beverly had called down that morning, but Fred had promised to call Beverly and Jules if he thought he could carve out a little time to meet with them. So there was nothing to be done until Sunday at the earliest.

Instead of worrying about something over which she had no control, Beverly thought of the plea Jeff's photographer friend had made the morning before. She had tried to put it out of her mind after their earlier conversation, and yet something within her couldn't let it go.

"So what, exactly, is this assignment you were asked to take on in Washington State?" she asked.

Jeff hesitated. "Why?"

She shrugged. "I keep thinking about it. Just curious."

"The guy who's making the climb is a double-amputee army vet." Jeff took a deep breath. "He's climbing to raise funds for wounded warriors, and he wants to increase awareness of the need for continued research to produce superior prostheses, particularly in light of the number of young, athletic amputees this country has as a result of the recent wars. The photographer was going to donate his time, but the poor guy got the flu, and there's no way he'll be well enough to climb in a few days."

"Oh, Jeff," Beverly said. Her heart was touched. "Perhaps you should reconsider. That's not just any old assignment."

Jeff shook his head. "I'd love to, but I don't think it's a good idea."

"I agree, the timing could be tight. And, of course, I don't really want you to go, but . . . I have a feeling this is something you need to do. Maybe even something you're being *called* to do." She hadn't been able to stop thinking about it—the insistence with which the idea had stuck in her mind made her suspect there was more at work here than simply her subconscious.

"I would really like to be a part of this," Jeff said. "I know what you mean—I feel as if there's a reason I got that phone call."

"You should reconsider this job." She turned and put her hands on his shoulders, looking into his eyes. "I have enough faith in you, and in our relationship, to know that our wedding will be fine even if I have forgotten some last-minute details." She grinned. "Although I'm sure I haven't."

Jeff laughed. "Hello? Music?"

"You're never going to let me forget that," she groaned.

He shook his head. "Probably not." Then his face grew serious. "I appreciate the vote of confidence. It does sound like an awesome assignment, but seriously, honey, I think it's just too close to the wedding. Forget about the last-minute details. What if something happens and I can't get back for the ceremony?"

"I think we should trust God on this one." Part of Beverly marveled that the words were coming out of her mouth. "If He really wants you to do this, He's going to get you back here for our wedding. There can't be that many good photographers who also could climb with this fellow. And it sounds to me as if he deserves the best."

Jeff hesitated. "I won't deny that I'd really love to do it. Not just because it's the type of physical challenge I enjoy, but because it's for such a good cause. I would be honored to help our wounded warriors with this work." He shook his head. "If it was any other time, I'd have said 'yes' in a heartbeat. But the timing is terrible. For us, I mean. For the climb, it's really a pretty good time. The weather's less predictable in May and June than it is later in the summer, but for my money, this is a safer time to climb. Wait until later in the summer, and you're looking at a lot of crevasses that are tough or impossible to cross."

Beverly didn't want to talk—or think—about dangerous elements of climbing like crevasses, or she'd never get her next words out of her mouth.

"Jeff, I want you to go. I think you should follow your heart." She tilted her face up against his shoulder for a kiss. "It's a wonderful effort that this soldier is making, and he needs an equally wonderful photographer. Your friend knows you're getting married. He'd have called someone else already if there was someone to call."

Jeff smiled down at her. "Got this all figured out, don't you? All right. If it's really okay with you, I'll do it."

Beverly leaned forward and picked up his cell phone from the coffee table where he'd set it. "Call him now so the poor guy can stop worrying about finding a replacement."

Jeff took the phone from her hand. "It's a one-day climb. I promise I'll only be gone for a few days, and I'll be back in plenty of time for the rehearsal and the rehearsal dinner."

As Beverly rose to take their iced tea glasses to the kitchen, she could hear Jeff on the phone, asking if he could still be of help.

Moments later, he came into the kitchen. "He was thrilled. He hadn't found anyone else; he was trying to figure out how he could get himself out of bed and up the mountain." He shook his head. "Rainier is exhausting when you're well and in good shape."

Beverly nodded. As badly as she would have liked to have had Jeff around during the final week before the wedding, he wouldn't be the man she loved if he didn't do this type of work, and if he wasn't moved to help someone in need. How could she have held him back? "When do you leave?" she asked, drawing a deep breath.

Jeff shifted. "I, uh, have to take a flight out first thing in the morning."

"Really?"

He nodded. "The climb was originally scheduled for Sunday, but since I can do it, they'll postpone until Monday. That'll give me time to get organized and get a little rest on West Coast time before we start. Then I'll fly home again on Tuesday." He pulled her close. "And a few days after that, you'll be Mrs. Jeff Mackenzie."

"I can't wait." Beverly linked her arms around his neck, smiling. "I really cannot wait."

★ ★ ★

The first thing Beverly thought of when she awoke early Saturday morning was Jeff. He'd be in Seattle today.

She sighed, missing him already. But she felt a strange certainty that she had made the right decision to encourage him to go. That young climber's story needed to be shown through the right lens, and she knew Jeff's skill made him one of the best for the job.

As her gaze fell on the light streaming through her bedroom windows, she remembered what she'd been doing yesterday afternoon when she'd taken a break from work.

Smiling, she padded to the desk in her robe and slippers and pulled up a file labeled "window treatments." Now that they had the contractor in place, they had chosen floor coverings, wood trim, and paint colors. Window coverings were next on the list. The windows would need to be measured and curtains or blinds ordered. In many old homes, the window dimensions were not the same as the standards of today, and their cottage was no different.

Grabbing her phone, she texted Diane, Shelley, and Margaret. *Want to look at window treatments over breakfast?* Diane had done some nice things when she had redone her own little home, and Shelley and Margaret both had an artistic eye. Beverly could use a second opinion.

When each of them texted back in the affirmative, Beverly dressed and hurried downstairs to let Scamp out. After putting the puppy out in the yard, she checked the contents of the fridge. Omelets and sunflower-seed bread would work with halved grapefruit.

She let Scamp in and fed him, grinning as the puppy's tail made wild whirligigs the entire time he was scarfing down his breakfast.

Diane arrived shortly afterward. Judging from her friend's clothing and the sand on the sneakers she toed off at the door, she had already been out and about, probably walking Rocky. Her cheeks were pink, she'd begun to regain some of the weight that had melted off during her chemo, and Beverly thought she looked absolutely terrific. When she told her so, Diane said, "That's what Leo said this morning too. Thanks."

"You've already seen Leo this morning?" Beverly's eyebrows shot up. "Details, please?"

Diane laughed. "We met on the boardwalk and walked our dogs on the beach together. No big deal."

"Would you have done that six months ago?" Beverly asked.

Diane looked thoughtful. "You've got me there," she finally admitted. "No. Probably not, because I wouldn't have wanted to encourage him."

"And now?"

Diane's smile was mischievous. "I want to encourage him."

Margaret and Shelley arrived next, and then they all trooped back to the kitchen. Diane greeted them and then pointed at Beverly's laptop, which she had set on the kitchen table. The window was open to a site where she had found a particular Roman shade Beverly really liked over a sheer fabric roller blind. "Is this one of the contenders?"

Beverly nodded. "We're going to have a bay window in the back where the dining table will sit. I'd like to have plenty of light there, but of course privacy is necessary too. Do you think those would work?"

Margaret perused the page, reading the specs. "These sound like an excellent choice. Energy efficiency is a must when you live here."

Beverly nodded. "I was afraid it would be too cold in that little nook if I didn't do something to help beat back the cold. That's a lot of windows."

"Then I think these window coverings will work just fine. What else are you looking at?" Diane sat back and let Beverly find a different "favorite" link.

"This is what I'm thinking of for the bathroom. It would let in plenty of light, but that rippled effect would give privacy, I think. Have any of you seen this installed?"

Beverly made omelets and the four women sat and ate, scrolling through dozens of ideas for window treatments and nixing or adding to Beverly's list of potentials.

"Jeff is out of town," Beverly told them, "so I won't really be able to make any decisions until he gets back. But at least I can narrow it down."

"Jeff's out of town?" Diane looked surprised. "When did that happen? I didn't realize he had any trips planned." She looked a little concerned. "My goodness, the wedding's in a week!"

"I know." Beverly explained the circumstances of his friend's illness and the charitable nature of the event. "I'd really appreciate it if you'd pray for a safe and uneventful trip. I mean, it's just a day hike up a mountain and back down. But it's a tricky mountain. And there's not a lot of extra time built into this if he should, say, fall and break a leg—"

"Which is *not* going to happen," Shelley said sharply. "It's just not."

"I am a little frustrated that he's not here to help me deal with the last-minute preparations," she admitted. "And I feel like a jerk even saying that when I was the one who urged him to go. I really *did* want him to, you know? This is the kind of thing that makes Jeff the man he is. I've made peace with the less-than-conventional timing of many of his projects—"

Shelley snickered, and Margaret and Diane guffawed outright.

"Given your liking for having everything just so, I think you've done a marvelous job of adjusting," Margaret told her.

"Jeff's wonderful," Beverly said. "I wouldn't change a thing about him."

Diane's expression softened as Beverly spoke. "He really is a wonderful man, isn't he?" Her eyes twinkled.

"I feel like a different person since moving here and meeting Jeff," she confessed.

The other women chuckled.

"I think maybe you just had your eyes and your heart opened," Margaret said.

"I like that." Beverly nodded. "That's a lovely way to describe how I've changed."

"We all have, I think," Diane said reflectively. "My friendships with you three are deeper and stronger than any I've ever had in my life outside my family. And that's saying something. I wasn't friendless before. Far from it. I had some dear friends who helped me through my first bout of cancer and Eric's death. They're still dear friends. But you three...you three are truly the sisters of my heart."

Touched, Beverly put a hand over Diane's and squeezed. "If I had thought of those words, I'd have said them first. You're absolutely right." She smiled. "I can't tell you how happy I am that all of you are involved in my wedding."

Everyone agreed. And then Beverly was struck by a thought that stopped her cold. "Oh no! You're not going to believe what I've forgotten! First it was the music, but Maddie rescued me from that—"

"What did you forget?" Diane asked.

"Programs. I haven't given a single thought to providing a wedding bulletin or program listing the music, the order of the service, those participating—oh, I'm such a dunce! Jeff's been teasing me, but wait until he hears this."

"Jeff didn't think of it either," Diane pointed out. "I hardly think he's going to be upset with you."

"Probably not," Beverly agreed. "It's not a guy thing. But it was important to me." She thought of all the details she needed to take care of this week, and of all the work waiting for her on the mayor's desk. "Well," she said, lifting her hands helplessly, "I'm just going to have to let it go. There is no way I am going to have time to get it all put together and get it printed." She closed her eyes, exasperated with herself. "I'll just be happy to have Jeff back in plenty of time. And I know he will be."

"I could do programs," Margaret offered. "It wouldn't really take much time at all if you send me an e-mail attachment with the info you want in it." She smiled. "I could do a pencil sketch for the cover."

"Oh, Margaret, I can't ask you to do that," Beverly said. "Not that I don't appreciate the offer, but—"

"It's not much work at all." Margaret cut her off, smiling. "And if I know you, you've already got all the information neatly typed into a file, just sitting there waiting..."

Beverly nodded sheepishly. "I do."

"Then send it to me. Let me help you."

Beverly stared at her a moment, then blew out a breath and nodded. "Thank you, Margaret. Thank you so much."

"You're welcome." As she often did, Margaret deflected the moment of gratitude by asking, "So have I told you about Adelaide cheffing it up for dinner this week?"

"No, and you haven't mentioned Paris either." Diane linked her fingers and rested her chin on them. "Have you heard anything about the seminar?"

"Not yet." Margaret cleared her throat. "I'm trying hard not to let myself get worked into an anxiety attack. What if they hate my painting?"

"They're not going to hate your painting," Beverly said. "Those angels are an incredible work of art, and anyone who sees it is going to recognize that fact. Now tell us about Adelaide's cooking."

Margaret was strangely reassured by Beverly's crisp assessment. "Thanks. I guess I need to keep telling myself that."

Shelley explained Adelaide's request to her friends.

Margaret grinned at Shelley. "Thank you for helping her."

"I didn't do much," Shelley said.

"Ha. I detect the fine hand of a master chef behind Adelaide's success."

Shelley just smiled and shook her head. "She had it all planned. She only needed a little guidance with menu selection and finding recipes that would be easy for her to manage."

"I'm so proud of how self-sufficient she's become," Margaret said.

"What's she doing?" Diane asked.

Margaret said, "Adelaide's serving us meals all week. She wants to show me that she can cook for herself. Tonight is going to be free-range chicken, stove-top stuffing with onions, and fresh beans. And Allan and I are both banned from the kitchen. She doesn't even let us help clean up!"

"That's my kind of kitchen help," Shelley said with a laugh. "Not that it's ever likely to happen at my house." Then the young blonde's ready smile faded. "Guys, I have something to tell you," she said hesitantly, her words falling into the silence as her friends registered her somber mood.

"What's wrong?" Diane asked. "Has Ralph taken a turn for the worse?"

It was easy to understand why Diane would gravitate toward such an idea, Beverly thought, but—

"No. Oh, it's nothing like that." Shelley tried to smile. "In some ways, it's good news. Dan has been offered a new job. It would be a promotion, and a really great opportunity for him."

"But?" Margaret cocked her head expectantly.

"It's on the other side of Portland," Shelley said. "Looks like we are going to be moving away."

"Moving?" Beverly was stunned.

Margaret and Diane looked equally distressed.

"Away from Marble Cove?" Margaret sounded as if she couldn't quite take in Shelley's words.

"Oh, Shelley." Diane's eyes had already filled with tears. "I want to be mad at you, but I can't," she admitted. "I know what an opportunity like this means for Dan and your family."

"I'm not mad either," Margaret said. "Diane's right—it's great that Dan's hard work has been recognized. But what about your business? Shelley, you have worked so hard to turn your love of baking into a viable source of income, and now you have the chance to buy out Rusty...You won't be doing that now, I guess."

Shelley shook her head, biting her lip so hard Beverly feared it might bleed, and she reached over and took her young friend's hand.

"No," Shelley said. "If this happens, we'll be too far away for me to own a business here. I guess I'll have to look for something closer to home."

"Oh, sweetie..." For once, Diane didn't have any words of comfort. She just pulled Shelley to her and let the younger woman sob for a moment, until finally Shelley sat back and grabbed a napkin to wipe her eyes.

"So now you know." She shrugged. "I'm happy for Dan, I really am. His education has been a vital step in making things easier for us. He's worked hard, and this is such a great opportunity. But it's so hard to give up my dream of a little bakery when it was almost right there in my grasp, you know?" She sighed. "I guess one of the hallmarks of growing up is realizing that sometimes you have to sacrifice your dreams for the betterment of your family. But it's going to be wrenching. Don't say anything to anyone else. We haven't even told his family yet."

There was a heavy silence.

"Well, perhaps this will give you something happier to think about." Diane smiled. "I have finally figured out what I want to write about next."

Beverly sat forward. "Oh, good. I can't wait to hear this."

"Me neither. Let's end this gathering on a bright note," Margaret said.

"Okay. It's actually going to be a series of books," Diane said. "The stories will feature the same core characters set in a small town, and throughout the course of the stories, the main characters will pursue and ultimately solve small mysteries."

"Oh!" Shelley clapped her hands. "Diane, are you writing about *us*?"

Diane laughed. "The books are fiction. But I won't deny that my inspiration comes from a source very close to my heart."

CHAPTER FIFTEEN

Dan and Shelley approached his parents' home on Sunday after church.

Dan carried a large open box in which Shelley had placed a decorated sheet cake. "I still don't know why she insisted on having the whole family for Sunday dinner when he's only been home for five days."

Aiden had run ahead to open the door, and Shelley and the girls stood back so Dan could carry in the cake. "Because she's desperate to get things back to something like 'normal.' Be nice."

"Shelley!" Most of Dan's siblings had arrived already, and his sisters Annie and Vera began to chatter before she had even gotten in the door.

"Thank you for organizing a visiting schedule," Annie told her. "Mom said she'd have been totally exhausted if we'd all shown up right away."

"And you know we would have if it hadn't been for your thinking ahead." Vera grinned at her, and it looked so like Dan that Shelley wanted to chuckle.

She squeezed past a knot of teenage nieces to get into the kitchen. "Here I am," she said to Frances. "How's the turkey coming along?"

Because she'd been worried about Frances trying to do too much, Shelley had arisen at 5:00 AM and gone over to Dan's parents' home early that morning. She had helped Frances make dressing and stuff the bird, and after it had gone into the oven the two had peeled a mountain of potatoes that could be boiled and mashed closer to noon. Then she had peeled and chopped large quantities of oranges, kiwi, banana, and several other fruits to make a massive fruit salad for the Bauer clan.

And then she'd gone home to get ready for church.

As she entered the kitchen, she saw Sam and Livvy, Dan's two youngest sisters, efficiently setting the table in the adjacent dining room, while Annie had gone into the parlor to supervise Darrell and her husband who were pulling out the leaves and setting up the huge table known as the "kids' table."

Darrell's wife, Patsy, was industriously mashing a vat of the steaming boiled potatoes. "Hi, Shell. I understand we have you to thank for getting these started this morning."

Frances rushed toward her, grabbing her and pulling her into a hug. "I'm so glad you're here. Whatever possessed me to have everyone here? Ralph's going to be exhausted."

Shelley put her own hands on Frances's shoulders when the older woman released her. "Breathe," she ordered. "Now let's stop and think for a minute. The gang is all helping. The meal will get done. Where's Ralph?"

"In his bedroom watching baseball. He said he wanted to stay out of the way. Hal's with him."

That sounded pretty good to Shelley. "All right. Why don't you check on them and remind all the children to stay downstairs today? He shouldn't get too tired out if he's not bombarded with company for hours."

Frances nodded. "Good idea. I'll have Dan put twine across the stairs with a sign on it."

Shelley chuckled. "That ought to do it."

Annie bustled up, stopping in front of them. "The adults' table is set, kids' table soon will be. What's next, boss?"

It took a moment before Shelley realized that Dan's sister was addressing her and not Frances.

Frances began to laugh while Shelley was still trying to process the affectionately uttered moniker. "You're soon going to be as bossy as I am, Shelley."

How to answer that? As diplomatically as possible, Shelley said, "There's only one you."

Annie and Vera both hooted with laughter. "Isn't that the truth?" Annie managed.

Vera seemed a little more sensitive to Shelley's dismay. "You know we're just teasing you, right?" she asked Shelley. "Without your stepping up and keeping us all organized while Dad and Mom were going through this nightmare, I don't know what we'd have done."

"Someone," Annie predicted darkly, "would probably have killed someone else by now." They both began to laugh again, and Shelley and Frances joined in. Shelley knew Annie and Frances rarely saw eye to eye on anything, and the jest was rooted in a grain of truth.

Frances, not the most demonstrative person, shocked Shelley by drawing her into a second hug. "I don't know what any of us would have done without you," she said. "My son Dan is officially the smartest man on the planet for having had the good sense to marry you."

★ ★ ★

Beverly had just finished painting the fingernails of her left hand in five different shades of ivory on Sunday afternoon when her cell phone rang. For a moment, she got excited, thinking that perhaps it was Jeff. But then she remembered he was probably at the base camp today, going over a thousand things in preparation for the climb and, she hoped, resting, getting acclimated to the time change. Even if he had cell service at all, she doubted he would be calling.

As she'd suspected, when she checked the screen, it wasn't Jeff, and she was glad she'd talked herself down from that anticipation. It was Fred Little, and he wondered if she and Jules could meet with him about whatever they wanted to discuss. After a quick call to confirm it worked for Jules and another back to Fred, Beverly scrubbed off all her nail polish. She'd gotten enough of a look to decide which shade she wanted to use at the end of the week.

She got ready to leave the house. "Sorry, baby," she said to Scamp, who danced around her feet, thinking there might be a walk in store. When she said, "Kennel," the little dog's ears and tail went down, and his whole little body expressed dejection, although he went meekly into his crate. "I promise we'll go for a w-a-l-k when I get back," she told him. After explaining to her father where she was going, she strode out the door and headed downtown at a brisk pace.

As she approached the police station, she saw Jules walking toward her from the opposite direction.

"Hello, Beverly." Jules looked tired and unenthusiastic. She felt equally joyless. This task wasn't going to be fun.

"Hi, Jules. I guess we may as well get this over with."

The council president nodded. "I guess. I've gone over it and over it in my head, wondering what Calder could have been thinking. But the only conclusion I can come to is that money means more to him than his reputation or the heritage of his hometown."

Beverly immediately thought of Elias Thorpe, who must have been swayed by the same single-minded desire at one time. "I fear you're right."

Together, they turned and walked into the station, where they were quickly shown into a conference room.

Fred Little joined them moments later. He was in uniform since he was on duty, and even indoors he wore his tinted glasses. The buzz cut he normally wore looked even higher and tighter than usual, as if perhaps his wife Cindy had just touched it up for him that morning.

He shook hands with each of them. "Sorry." He glanced around at the spare decor in the room. "Didn't mean to treat you like criminals. We don't have many nice accommodations around here."

Beverly smiled, although she couldn't summon up a chuckle. "It's all right."

Fred leaned back against a windowsill and crossed his arms. "So what's going on? Since you're both in here on a Sunday afternoon, I'm thinking this is something serious."

"It is. We need your advice." Beverly took a deep breath and then explained what had occurred on Friday. She turned the tale over to Jules after a moment, and Fred asked him detailed questions about the exact sequence of events and the exact vocabulary used.

"I didn't record the initial conversation," Jules said, "because we were face to face. Sitting at a table at the Cove," he added, outrage in his voice. "Brenna McTavish wouldn't have heard the conversation, but she can verify that the two of us were there together." Then he drew a copy of the follow-up e-mail from his pocket and handed it to Fred. "He sent me this a little while after I got back to the office. He's sneaky, but if you know the whole story, you can clearly figure out what he's saying here."

Fred took the piece of paper and studied the e-mail. Finally, he straightened and set down the paper on the table. "You know," he said, "unless we can prove he broke the law, there's not a lot I can do. I believe you," he said as Jules opened his mouth to object, "but without proof, this probably wouldn't ever make it to an arrest, much less a trial. Your word is good enough for me, but it would help if someone had overheard you. Calder could claim it was just an innocent breakfast and this"—he flicked the edge of the e-mail copy—"while it sounds shady, doesn't promise anything specific enough for us to go after him with." He cleared his throat. "I'll be happy to run it by the district attorney—in confidence, of course—and you're welcome to talk to him, but I suspect he's going to say the same thing I just did."

"Thanks, Fred," Beverly said. "We'd appreciate it if you could talk to the DA and that way we'll know we've covered all the bases."

"Yes," Jules agreed. "I'm sure you're right, Fred, but I wouldn't mind hearing what the DA thinks as well."

"You got it," Fred assured them. "I'll keep you posted."

Beverly and Jules left the station and Beverly headed home to work on her remarks for the Memorial Day celebration that would take place the next day. Her thoughts drifted to Jeff. Though she wished he were here with her, it seemed fitting that on Memorial Day he would be accompanying a wounded veteran in a fund-raising effort to help and support others.

CHAPTER SIXTEEN

Shortly before noon on Monday, Beverly had an appointment with Shelley to discuss the final preparations for the cake.

"Hi, come on in!" Shelley met her at the door and practically dragged her inside. "You did a wonderful job at the Memorial Day flag-raising ceremony."

"Thanks." Beverly shook her head. "I thought I was going to lose it there for a minute. It was very moving, very emotional to be a part of the town's history in that way."

"I bet." Shelley continued to pull her through the house. "I did a minimodel of your cake yesterday afternoon and took pictures, and I can't wait to show it to you!"

"I can't wait to see it," Beverly responded.

Shelley led her back to the kitchen, where she had her laptop open on the table. Beverly could hear the children, who were off school for the holiday, playing in the next room, but her attention was riveted on the monitor that displayed a stunning ivory wedding cake. Each of three layers had been decorated differently, but a two-inch wide ribbon of pale pink with a lavender stripe wrapped around the base of each, creating a theme. One layer appeared to be interwoven lattice work, one was dotted with icing pearls, and the smallest layer at the top was draped in icing scallops. Pale pink hydrangea blossoms formed a cluster on the top and at strategic points flowing down the side of the cake in a curving pattern to another cluster at the bottom.

"Oh, Shelley," Beverly said. She wanted to reach right into the picture and touch it. "You have outdone yourself."

"If there's anything you don't like or if you have suggestions for changes, I'll be glad to do it," Shelley said, sounding worried. "I got a few tips from my friend who owns the Cakery for working with the fondant. It turned out rather well, I think. But it's your wedding, and it has to be perfect, so tell me what you want done differently."

"Not one single thing. It's beautiful, Shelley. Just beautiful." Beverly wished Jeff was here so he could also see what a wonderful job Shelley had done. But today was the day of the climb. She glanced at the time displayed in the bottom corner of the monitor. She hoped they'd made the ascent and gotten to the summit hours ago and were well on their way back down to the base camp.

As Shelley pointed out features of the cake, the voices of the children became louder.

" . . . an' you be the bride, Hailey," Aiden was saying.

"F'ower girl!" That was Emma. "I f'o f'owers?"

"That's right, Em. The flower girl reaches into her basket and throws flower petals. And she goes first, before the bride." Hailey appeared to be demonstrating.

"Look at me! F'owin' f'owers!" It was a squealing giggle.

Suddenly, a huge arrow of guilt struck Beverly deep in the heart. Oh heavens, what had she been thinking! Months ago, she'd invited Aiden to be the ring bearer. She had two attendants, her cousin and Diane, and she hadn't given a single thought to junior bridesmaids or flower girls! She had completely overlooked Shelley's other children and how being excluded from the ceremony while Aiden participated might make them feel. And then what about Adelaide? Wouldn't she notice that she didn't have a job while practically all of the other children in their little clique did? Adelaide wasn't technically a child, but in many ways she thought like one, and Beverly realized she could hurt Adelaide's feelings deeply if she wasn't careful.

She almost opened her mouth and impulsively attempted to rectify her error, when she thought of Jeff. This was his wedding too. Would it be fair to him to make a change so close to the ceremony after all the plans they'd made together? Taking a deep breath, she attempted to focus on what Shelley was showing her, making appropriate noises of delight—which she didn't have to feign, because the cake really was gorgeous.

Finally, she was able to leave. She whipped out her phone as she walked toward her father's home. Punching in Jeff's number, she waited tensely. It would only be about breakfast time on the West Coast, so maybe she'd catch him before he started his day. Either way, he might not get signal.

As she'd feared, the call went straight to voice mail. "This is Jeff. Leave a message, and I'll return your call."

"Hi, honey." She tried hard to make her voice upbeat and cheerful. "I hope everything went okay. I, uh, had a thought when I was at Shelley's approving the cake just now. Would it be okay with you to ask Hailey and Emma to be flower girls and Adelaide to be a guest-book attendant? I just thought since we asked Aiden..." She trailed off, regrouped. "All right, I hope I hear from you soon. I love you, and I can't wait for you to get home and *marry me!*" She was smiling when she hit "end."

As she made the rest of the short walk home, she couldn't stop thinking about the little girls playing "wedding." And by the time she had reached the door, she had made a decision. How silly was she? She knew Jeff Mackenzie. She was marrying him for many reasons: he was flexible, he was kind and compassionate, and people would always be more important to him than having a perfectly balanced wedding party. He was going to chuckle when he heard her message, and then he'd phone her and tell her to call her friends and invite their children to be in the wedding.

Pulling her phone back out of her pocket, she tapped Shelley's number. "Hi, Shelley," she said, when her friend answered. "I have a question for you..."

And ten minutes later, she had two flower girls, and Shelley assured her they each had a dress from Easter that would work.

She entered the house, hung up her jacket and called Margaret next. Her friend was at the gallery, she knew. Unfortunately, the beginning of tourist season precluded taking the holiday off for most downtown merchants.

"Hello, Beverly."

"Hi, Margaret. What are you up to?"

"Just working on another painting. I'm glad you called. If I don't take a break, my wrists are going to give me a fit tonight."

"Glad I could help." Beverly grinned to herself. "Margaret, I know this is rather last-minute, but I was wondering if you think Adelaide would like to be our guest-book attendant? It truly didn't occur to me until a little while ago, or I'd have asked earlier."

"Oh, that's sweet," Margaret said, her voice warm. "I bet she'd be thrilled. Does she need to wear anything special?"

"Just a nice dress of her choosing. You know the wedding is mostly pink and lavender, but it really doesn't matter as long as she's comfortable and feels pretty."

"I'm sure she has something suitable," Margaret said. "Remember, you're talking about Miss I-Love-Pink herself."

Beverly laughed. "That's great. Shall I call her and ask her?"

"She would be thrilled if you did." Margaret's voice changed. "Beverly, I feel as if she has grown up so much since we decided to take this trip to Paris."

"The cooking, you mean?"

"Not just that, although last night she made this sweet potato and lentil casserole that was so good we all had seconds." She chuckled. "There was supposed to be enough left for a leftovers meal this week, but we scarfed it all down."

"Wow. I'd like that recipe."

"I'll make sure Adelaide gets a copy to you. But as I said, it isn't just the cooking. She has always helped scoop the cat litter, but now she's bleaching and scrubbing out the box herself instead of waiting for Allan to do it, and yesterday she wrote me a note telling me we were almost out of food and litter. Which I have to say was helpful, because I always forget and then poor Allan ends up making an emergency run to the store."

Beverly laughed.

"And on Saturday morning, she stripped her bed and washed all her sheets and towels before I even had to remind her. Usually she forgets until I bug her about it, and remembering to wash the towels too is unheard of!"

"Sounds like this vacation is going to be good for you in more ways than just the ones you'd expected," Beverly commented.

"I think so," Margaret mused. "It's certainly changed our family dynamic, and we haven't even left yet. We—oh. Oh my dear heavens. Beverly, I just got a special edition of the paper!"

"What? What's wrong? The paper?" She was confused. "I thought the *Courier* was closed for the holiday." She stuck her head into the study. "Father, did you get a paper?"

"What?" Mr. Wheeland frowned. "Oh yes, the special edition came early this morning. I have it right here."

"Okay, good. Father has it. I'll read it and call you back."

"Oh my," she exclaimed as she held up the paper.

"Calder Attempts Bribe" was the huge, above-the-fold headline plastered across the top of the front page right beneath the *Marble Cove Courier* banner. Reading the accompanying article, Beverly put a shaking hand to her mouth. The piece had been written by Gerald Kimball. Whomever he'd spoken to had given him quite a bit of information—information that would have been almost impossible to come by unless that person had been in a meeting with Beverly and Jules recently.

She thought of Jules, and she thought of Fred Little. Fred would never divulge privileged information like that, she was certain. But neither would Jules. They might not always see issues from the same direction, but she was as certain the council president was honest and ethical.

But then...who could have done it? She reread the article, and as she did, she realized that while the information about Dennis was specific, nothing about the council members was. Who else had Dennis tried to bribe? Was it possible some other council member had taken offense and gone to Kimball?

Quickly, she hit Margaret's number again. But after a rehash of the article, her friend had nothing helpful to add. Nor did Shelley or Diane, when she touched base with them.

Jules called just as she was ending her call with Diane, and they decided to meet again at the office.

"Who could have done this?" Jules asked. Closing the door, they moved into Beverly's office, flipping on the lights and sinking onto chairs.

Beverly opened the newspaper she'd brought along, and they reread the article again. "I have no idea," she said. "It could be any one of the council members, I suppose. Except for Martha. I can't imagine her betraying Dennis. She thinks his development plans are the greatest thing ever."

"It wouldn't be Lionel either." Jules referred to the council treasurer. "For two reasons—first, and most important, he's not a voting member. And second, he also is a proponent of development."

"So who's against it?" Beverly asked. "Who's against it enough to be highly offended that Dennis would offer a bribe? Who would go to the newspaper?"

Jules lifted his hands, palms up, and shrugged, looking frustrated. "I have a hard time imagining any of them doing this."

"It wouldn't make sense that Dennis would approach Bert anyway. He knows how he feels." Beverly got up and paced. "What about Terry Dwiggins, Everett Quinn, and Harry Vogel? I don't know them well, and I don't really have a good idea of how any of them feels about the development. Do you?"

Jules hesitated. "Harry's opposed to it, I'm pretty certain. He's quiet, but he has asked a lot of good questions, and he's expressed concern about destroying a building that is a part of Marble Cove's history. Terry?" He shrugged. "I have no idea. He's pleasant, he listens, but he doesn't give away much. Same with Everett."

Beverly sighed. "I haven't been able to get much of a read on them either. Do you think we should just call each member of the council and ask?"

Jules paused. "I don't know. What if none of them had anything to do with it? Do we want anyone to know that I'm one of the ones Dennis tried to bribe?"

Beverly tried to think through all the possible complications. "I don't know. I wish I could see the future. This thing might have legs we haven't even thought of, and speaking up could make it even worse!"

Jules smiled. "I know. I feel as if there's critical information out there that I'm not privy to. Or that I've missed, or something."

"Let's wait a little while and think this through," Beverly suggested, "before we speak to anyone else."

"That works for me," Jules agreed. "If Gerald Kimball calls, I'm just going to tell him I have no comment."

"So will I." She rolled her eyes. "I'm sure there are a few other council members who will have plenty to say to fill up his follow-up articles."

Jules laughed. "I suspect you're right."

As they concluded their meeting, Beverly's phone rang. Her heart leaped. Jeff! She hadn't talked to him since Saturday. But then she remembered he was climbing today. So she strongly doubted it was he.

Checking the readout, she was glad she had dampened her expectations. Shelley. Tapping the screen, she took the call. "Hi, Shelley. What's up?"

"Hey, I know it's short notice, but do you want to go shopping?"

Beverly shrugged, although her friend couldn't see her. She didn't have anything else exciting going on this afternoon. "Sure. What are we shopping for?"

"Flower girl dresses! I was going to have Hailey and Em just wear their Easter dresses. But I just found out about this secondhand bridal shop over in Rockland that's supposed to have great deals. Adelaide is coming too."

"But it's Memorial Day," Beverly said. "Won't they be closed?"

"I called and checked," Shelley said, "and they're open until five. Since May and June are *the* big bridal months, I guess the store doesn't want to miss out on any chance for business."

"All right," Beverly said. "I'm downtown at my office. What time do you want to leave?"

"I can drive. I'll pick you up in ten minutes."

Chapter Seventeen

After an exciting and productive afternoon shopping for dresses, the friends drove back to Marble Cove. While they were still on the road, Beverly heard her cell phone ring. Digging it out of her handbag, she checked the readout automatically—

And nearly dropped her phone in surprise. "It's Jeff! He's supposed to be climbing Mt. Rainier today. I didn't expect to hear from him."

Quickly, she accepted the call. "Hi, honey. This is a surprise."

"Hi, sweetheart." Jeff sounded...not very perky. "How are you doing?"

"I'm fine. I miss you. Is everything okay?"

"Not exactly. That's why I'm calling."

"Oh dear. What's wrong?" She felt her heart leap into her throat.

"Nothing horrible," he hastened to assure her. "No accidents, nothing like that."

"Okay." She felt the adrenaline drain out of her so suddenly it left her feeling weak. "Whew."

"We do have a little problem, though. The weather's bad."

"Are you stuck on the mountain?" There went the adrenaline again.

"Beverly..." Jeff paused, and her imagination began to make wild, frantic loops into dangerous territory before he spoke again. "I'm not even on the mountain yet."

"What? But I thought the climb was postponed until today—"

"It was. But a storm rolled in overnight. We were supposed to start the ascent at midnight, to take advantage of the firmer snow and give us plenty of time for alternate routes descending. We thought maybe we'd get off before 5:00 AM, but there's a blizzard in progress. So we're all just hanging out today, hoping tomorrow will be better."

"Tomorrow's Tuesday..." Beverly couldn't hide her concern.

"And if we make the ascent tomorrow, then Wednesday we'll come down from Muir and I'll get a flight home on Thursday. It should still be fine."

"Oh my goodness," she said faintly. "That'll be cutting it really close."

"Yeah, but I'll make it." Jeff sounded confident and positive. "I'm not missing this wedding for anything." He paused, and his voice dropped. "I love you. I'll be in touch, okay?"

"Okay. I love you too." And before she knew it, he was gone.

Slowly Beverly turned to Shelley. "I guess you heard enough of that to know Jeff's going to be delayed."

Shelley's eyes were wide and worried. "A storm kept them from making the climb?"

Beverly nodded. "So they're planning on tomorrow. But what if tomorrow's bad too?" She took a deep breath. "He's already at Camp Muir, which is the base camp for climbers ascending the summit. But it's no walk in the park to get to Muir, so even if the climb was canceled for some reason, he could still be stuck at Muir until the weather changes."

"It's going to get better," Shelley tried to reassure her. But Beverly wasn't very reassured. She'd absorbed a lot of knowledge from Jeff as he talked about some of his assignments, and she'd Googled Mt. Rainier climbs when he'd decided to go. From what she'd been able to tell, the more reliable weather was later in the summer. May could still be problematic, and blizzards could easily delay a team for several days.

She tried to remind herself of the surety she'd felt, the calm sense that Jeff was meant to make the trip...but all she could think, as her anxiety rose, was that problematic was *not* something she needed to be dealing with the week before her wedding!

After Shelley dropped her off, Beverly headed into the house. But then, obeying an impulse, she walked into her father's library and told him she wouldn't be home for dinner. "I'm sure Mrs. Peabody will feed you well," she told him with a smile.

"No doubt, after she talks my ear off," her father said wryly, but with a latent twinkle in his eye.

Less than an hour later, she pulled her car into the driveway of Jeff's grandfather's bungalow. His Chevy pickup was parked in the driveway, she noted with relief. She had decided not to call before coming, hoping to surprise him.

His terra-cotta pots were newly planted with petunias, she saw, and the huge garden on the lot next to the house looked as if he'd already put in some early vegetables. As she walked up the front walk, the door opened, and Edward Maker appeared.

"Beverly! What are you doing here?" He sounded quite surprised.

She smiled. "Coming to see you, if you have the time to visit."

"Always got time for you, young lady." His blue eyes twinkled, and she realized that in a few decades, Jeff might look very like the man standing at the top of the porch steps.

She embraced him as she reached him. "I'm glad," she said.

They went inside, and Mr. Maker puttered around making tea, urging her to take a seat at the kitchen table. He joined her in a few moments, setting a plate of tasty-looking no-bake cookies on the table before her.

"Oh no," she said. "I won't fit into my wedding dress if I eat these."

"No calories in those," he told her solemnly.

"Ha! Where did you get these, anyway? I know you didn't make them yourself."

"I might have. But there's this widow down the street who thinks her fine cooking might get her an M-R-S degree one of these days."

Beverly burst out laughing. "And will it?"

"Not a chance. But as long as she brings me cookies, I'm not telling her that."

She shook her head affectionately. "You're too much."

They sat in silence for a moment. Finally, Mr. Maker said, "Where's Jeff?"

She tried to smile. "Mt. Rainier in Washington State."

"What?"

Genuinely amused by his surprise, she told him the story of Jeff's job offer. "I felt very strongly that I should encourage him to go," she said. "There aren't very many photographers with the ability to complete an assignment like that, you know?"

Jeff's grandfather nodded. "The boy has a gift."

"But at the same time, now I'm worried it was a mistake. What if he can't get home in time? Or worse, what if he gets hurt or—or—"

Edward Maker reached over and placed a rough, gnarled old hand over hers.

Near tears, feeling as if she was being silly and a terrible worrywart, Beverly turned her palm up and took comfort from the touch.

"Jeff would not have gone if he really thought there was a chance he couldn't make it home for the wedding," his grandfather said. "The boy's only going to do this once, and I know he intends to do it right. He chose you, so he's already got most of it right."

Beverly smiled through tears that had suddenly sprung up.

"He won't take chances. He'll be careful. And there's no one out there that could do a better job. You did the right thing," he said, squeezing her hand. "You followed your instincts and let him go, and I believe there's a reason for that. This story might make a difference in a lot of lives, and Jeff will be a part of telling it."

Beverly sighed, feeling immensely comforted, although she wasn't sure why. It was as nice to simply be sitting here with someone who loved Jeff as much as she, and his words had helped to quash the nerves that had arisen as the day passed.

"Thank you," she said, rising and brushing a kiss across the old man's cheek. "I needed to hear that."

★ ★ ★

Only four days until the wedding! Beverly woke up in a happy moment of anticipation on Tuesday morning, until she remembered that her groom-to-be was thousands of miles and one high mountain away. She wondered if the storm had eased and the party had been able to start their ascent around midnight, as they had hoped. No way to know until she heard from Jeff again, although she had to admit her visit to his grandfather yesterday evening had helped to calm her nerves.

Then she recalled yesterday's crazy ups and downs with Dennis Calder's attempted bribe. She had a feeling that the day was going to be hectic. As she cared for Scamp, ate a quick breakfast, and dressed for the office, she decided that the only answer was one she often overlooked when she needed to take time for it the most.

And so she sat down on the edge of her bed before she left for the day. Reaching for the Bible that had belonged to her mother, she found a passage in Second Corinthians that reminded her that she didn't need sight to have faith. She thought about that for a while, realizing that she *did* have faith. Jeff had left at her urging to give of the gifts the Lord had given him— his skills with photography and his physical health and strength that allowed him to vigorously pursue a job on one of the highest peaks in the country. She trusted God to bring him back safely, to get him here in time for their wedding so that they could share their love for each other and their commitment to a faith-filled life together with all the friends and family whose care was such a vital part of their life together.

She trusted Him! And with that thought buoying her, she lifted her mother's Bible to her lips and kissed it. Then she gently set it back on her bedside table and walked downtown, conscious of the spring in her step and the radiance of the pretty morning around her.

Before heading into the municipal building annex, she stopped at the Cove to see if anyone was talking about yesterday's special edition of the paper.

"Beverly! What do you think—"

"Hey, there's the mayor."

"Mayor Wheeland, are you going to press charges—"

Beverly held up both hands in a universal gesture: stop! "Give me a minute to get some coffee before you come after me," she said, smiling. Looking around, she saw Jules Benton waving, and she made her way across the unusually crowded little room to the table where he pushed out a chair for her.

Mary Henderson, a former council member, was also there, and she shook her head with a sad smile. "Hello, Beverly. I wish I could say good morning, but that rotten Dennis Calder has got this whole town in an uproar."

"Actually, it was the newspaper article," Jules reminded Mary.

"Can you believe this?" Martha stopped in front of their table, her face rigid and angry. "I had such high regard for Dennis Calder. His plans for the shopping center were simply stellar. Why on earth would he have felt he had to extend *bribes*?"

Jules's gaze met Beverly's across the table. "It's unfortunate," was all he said.

"Indeed it is," Martha affirmed. "Now we're back to square one. We'll have to find another developer to work with."

"We do have other options," Beverly reminded the woman. "I expect that at our next board meeting we'll have information to share on the museum idea that Noah Henry proposed."

Martha looked scornful. "I can't imagine anyone voting for that," she said before she turned and stomped away.

"Gracious," Mary said quietly. "Apparently she is unaware that not everyone in this town thinks like she does."

Beverly had to chuckle. "And thank heaven for that."

"Dennis Calder oughta go ta jail." The speaker was Hank Roux, sitting at a nearby table. The three men with whom he was sitting all nodded vigorously.

"Nobody can prove that he did anything illegal," Beverly reminded them, the conversation with Detective Little echoing in her head.

"Are you doubting my integrity?" Gerald Kimball had come in for coffee to go. He was almost at the door, but he turned back when Beverly spoke.

"Not at all," she said honestly. "I'm merely saying that without proof, we shouldn't be jumping to conclusions. Are you willing to tell us—or the police—where you got your information?"

Gerald shook his head, looking taken aback. "Not a chance. Who would ever trust me again if I revealed a source?"

Just then, the door opened, and Detective Little appeared in the doorway. "Kimball. You want to come down to the station for a chat?"

"Am I under arrest?" Gerald asked.

Fred raised his gaze briefly to the ceiling. "Of course not. But I want to talk to you. We can do it at your office or mine. If we go to yours, I might take a notion to ask a *whole lot* of questions, come to think of it. Might take *hours.*"

"Never mind," Gerald muttered. "I'll come down to the station."

"That's thoughtful of you," Fred said. He held the door for Gerald, then winked at Beverly as he followed the reporter out.

Beverly couldn't prevent a snicker. Jules was grinning, as was Mary, but it didn't last long.

"This news is going to upset a whole bunch of apple carts," Jules told them. "Before you came in, Ed Marchette was in here." Ed Marchette owned a local construction company. "He said his company had decided to back out of that Rocky Beach Condos project Dennis was working on, and right after him, another guy who was supposed to be doing a new office building out there near the hospital said the exact same thing."

Mary cleared her throat. "I heard that Dennis is up to his ears in debt and overextended. If he can't get these projects moving, he's going to lose money faster than he can recoup it."

"Lotta construction companies aren't going to be interested in hitching their names to his now," Jules said. "Could get dicey for Calder."

"Dicey as in bankruptcy," Mary clarified. "But I guess only time will tell."

* * *

Diane had been afraid to hope that the visit she had scheduled with Brenna's grandmother on Tuesday afternoon would work out. But when she called Brenna after the young woman got home from her shift at the Cove, Brenna said cheerfully, "Yes, she's pretty good today. Why don't you come over in an hour or so? Oh, and bring your dog, Rocky. Gran loves dogs. She used to have Irish setters when she was a girl."

When she was a girl. A tingle went through Diane at the casual words. If their information was correct, Marie Mauer-now-Harnish had been a tuberculosis patient as a child. She could hardly wait to meet her.

Three o'clock finally arrived, and Diane and Rocky walked several blocks across town to the small brick rancher in which Brenna's grandmother—and currently Brenna—lived. It was a gloriously warm almost-summer day, and Mrs. Harnish was sitting in a rocker on the porch when Diane arrived. She wore a thick fisherman's sweater over slacks and a top. A scarf was wound around her neck and tied about her head in a style reminiscent of the Kennedy era.

Brenna and Noah sat on a porch swing near her, their hands clasped between them.

As Diane pushed through the gate and started up the walk, the old lady clapped her hands. "Here, pretty boy. Come up here and say hello to me."

Diane grinned. She led Rocky up the steps and stood back while Mrs. Harnish ran her hands over him, and he leaned against her knees. "Oh, you're a gorgeous fellow, you are."

As Diane mounted the porch steps behind Rocky, the old woman looked up and held out a gnarled hand. "Marie Harnish. I understand you've got some questions to ask me about when I was young."

Diane gently clasped the old woman's hand, feeling the fragility of her frame. "Yes, ma'am. I'm Diane Spencer. It's a pleasure to meet you."

"Diane Spencer. You're not from here." It wasn't a question.

Diane grinned. "No. We used to vacation here when my husband was living. I moved to the area a few years ago after he passed away. Are you going to hold it against me?"

Marie wheezed out a laugh. "Not likely." She indicated Noah. "If I let this one come around courtin' Brenna, guess I'll have to put up with you too." The words were good-natured. "Do you know him? This is ... this is ..." She trailed off, searching for the name.

"It's Noah, Gram," Brenna said quietly.

"That's it. Noah. He's not from here either, but Brenna tells me his granddaddy was Mr. Thorpe that was part-owner of the quarry when I was a girl."

"Do you remember him?" Diane leaned forward, delighted to have the topic introduced so easily.

"My daddy worked there, you know." Diane's question went unanswered, but the snippet of information provided another piece of the puzzle. "Before he went off to college, for a little bit he worked there. And after he got killed in the war, my mam got herself a job there too."

"So you don't recall Mr. Thorpe?"

"'Course I do." Mrs. Harnish frowned. "He was my daddy's cousin a couple times removed, you know. Tall, dark-haired. Good-lookin' man." She flicked a finger in

Noah's direction. "This fella puts me in mind of him some."
It appeared Brenna's gram had forgotten already that Noah
was Elias Thorpe's descendant.

"Yes, I'm not surprised that he was engaging." Not given
the charisma that so many of the Thorpe men appear to have
had, at any rate. Towns and buildings and quarries didn't
get built by fade-into-the-woodwork types of personalities.
"Mrs. Harnish, did Mr. Thorpe ever come to dinner or
anything?"

Marie shook her head. "We weren't grand enough for the
likes of him. Besides, he was sweet on my mam before she
married my daddy, you know. But she chose my daddy, and
that was that."

Diane felt another puzzle piece clink into place in her
mind with an almost audible snap. "Elias Thorpe courted
your mother before she married your father?"

Marie shook her head. "Don't think it ever got to that.
But he fancied her. Still fancied her after my daddy died,
too, that's what my grandma said, but Mam was too sick
with grief to notice."

"But you noticed."

"My old grandma noticed," Marie corrected. "Told him to
get along and leave Mam in peace. Told him he wasn't good
enough for her Louise Marie. And I reckon he believed her,
because he never did come around again." She grimaced.
"But I know he put in a good word for her when she went
to hire on at the quarry. And when I took sick with TB, he
helped, you know."

"I just learned that recently," Diane said. "Do you know why?"

"Mam said he was a nice man." Marie frowned. "But a lot of other people in town didn't much like him. He was good to us, though, me 'n' Mam. Said I was his kin and if he could help, he would. And then he went and called some special doctor from the city that made me take this medicine. Nobody else ever heard of it before, but it sure fixed me right up!" Her old face wrinkled even more and a tear tracked down her cheek. "Never did get to thank him," she mumbled. "Quarry closed and he left town. Woo-wee, people were mad about that. I always hoped he'd come back some day so I could thank him proper." She fumbled for a tissue, and Brenna slid off the swing to kneel and place her arms around her grandmother.

"Gran, he knows," she said. "Wherever he is now, Mr. Thorpe knows how grateful you are."

The old woman leaned her head against her granddaughter and sighed. "I'm a bit tired."

"I know." Brenna rose and put her hands under her grandmother's elbows. "Let's go inside now. It's getting a little chilly for you."

"Okay." But before she rose, Mrs. Harnish placed her hand on Rocky's head and stroked his short, sleek coat. "You're a handsome boy, you are."

As Brenna helped the old woman to her feet, Noah went around them and held open the door. When they had vanished inside, he turned back to Diane. "Wow. I have never seen her that animated, or heard her talk that much. And she's usually not nearly that lucid." He ran a distracted hand through his hair, shoving it back from his brow. "Then again, she was talking about her past. The present seems to be much more difficult. Recent memories don't stick."

"That's not uncommon, from what I've read." Diane recalled a visit a year or so earlier with another aging resident of the community named Odessa. "You get some of these folks talking about the past, and you just never know what you might learn."

CHAPTER EIGHTEEN

Dan texted Shelley and told her he would be late for dinner that evening. When he finally got home, she turned and smiled as he came through the door.

"Hi, honey. Long day?"

Dan walked over and kissed her. "My own fault," he told her. "At the close of the day, I drove back over to the main office to talk to Wayne before he went home for the evening."

"Oh?" Shelley stirred a pot of minestrone soup she had started earlier in the day, then set down the spoon and turned to lean against the counter.

Dan sighed. "I told Wayne I wasn't sure I wanted to move."

Shelley's eyebrows rose. "And how did that go over?" She could probably guess.

"Like the proverbial lead balloon. I didn't know this, but Wayne told me he's being pressured by the IBEW to take on two new apprentices. They want him to move me on."

"Oh, Dan." Now she was the one who sighed. Wayne had been a tough boss, but he and Dan had developed the beginnings of a real friendship, she'd felt, and she hated to hear that Dan really wasn't going to be able to stay with Stover Electrical.

"Wayne says this new offer is a great opportunity, and that I'd be a fool not to take it. He says he can't think of anyone he'd rather see have this chance." Dan sounded both elated and unhappy.

She could understand why. Moving had been the last thing on their mind since they had made the decision not to leave their home just two months ago. "When do you absolutely positively have to let him know?" she asked.

"He told me to take a few more days and think about it," Dan said. "I just don't know what to do, Shell. If I say no, then I'll have to get someone else to take me on to finish my apprenticeship, I guess. It looks like Wayne's going to be too tied up with his new kids to keep me on."

★ ★ ★

"Mom? Do you like my new dress?" Adelaide twirled in a circle in Margaret's living room. "Isn't it beautiful?"

"It is. You did a great job finding a wonderful dress in your price range," Margaret said. "And it's very pretty."

"I look grown-up." Adelaide came and leaned on Margaret's shoulder. "Can we get my hair done special for Miss Beverly's wedding? I'm gonna see a lot of people."

Margaret laughed. "I suppose we can manage that. I'll call tomorrow and make you an appointment."

"At Cut 'n' Curl? I can call them myself."

"All right. If you want to do that, that's fine."

"I'll ask for Carlie. She always makes my hair look really nice."

Carlie did do a particularly nice job with Adelaide's hair. Margaret was pleased that her daughter had realized it. It was another affirmation of Adelaide's growing independence. "Why don't you come sit down, honey?" Margaret patted the seat beside her. Allan had left for a deacon's meeting at church, and it was just the two of them. "We can look at some of my Paris information together."

"Okay." Adelaide held up one finger. "But I have to go clean the kitty litter first. Then I want you to show me things. All the things you're going to do in Paris."

Margaret smiled. "All right." She pulled a folder of information from the art school toward her. "Thank you for cooking again tonight. That quiche was delicious."

Adelaide paused on her way back down the hallway. "Mushroom, cheese, and spinach," she recited. "That was an easy meal to make."

"Tomorrow evening is the last night that you're going to be cooking, right?"

"Mm-hmm."

"What are you going to make?"

"It's a s'prise." Adelaide's predictable answer made Margaret grin. "No peeking."

"No peeking, I promise."

As Adelaide rushed from the room, Margaret sat back with a smile. She realized that a small part of her hadn't truly believed Adelaide would ever be independent.

Yesterday, she'd purchased a dress without Margaret by her side for the first time ever. Granted, Beverly and Shelley wouldn't have let her go wrong, but it still was a wonderful sign. It boded well, she supposed, for the time when Allan and Margaret would be away. For over twenty-six years now, she'd been standing beside Adelaide, helping her every step of the way. But Adelaide's recent seizing of the reins of her own schedule, her own life, had showed Margaret how capable her daughter really was.

But she'd still worry. Didn't every mother?

★ ★ ★

Mrs. Peabody had left one of Father's favorite casseroles for dinner that evening at the Wheeland home. While Beverly set the table and got the rest of the meal ready, she put the phone on speaker and listened to Diane repeat the story of her visit with Mrs. Harnish. So Elias had been sweet on Louise, and even though his regard apparently had come to naught, he'd taken some responsibility for his fallen relative's family. She wondered if he'd ever considered enlisting after Pearl Harbor thrust his country into war, or if he might have felt some guilt for not doing so. That would explain a lot as well.

There was no way to know, though, and she doubted they ever would.

Later, as Beverly dished out the steaming meal and set a plate before her father after their prayer, he said, "I wonder how Albert Calder is holding up."

"Holding up? You mean because of the article about Dennis?" She felt a little guilty that she hadn't given the old man even a passing thought.

Her father nodded. "I might walk down to his house for a few minutes tomorrow."

Beverly thought of the crusty older man who so rarely left his house on the corner of Newport and Main. "Really?"

Father snorted. "Old grouch will probably kick me off his property instead of thanking me for coming."

Beverly smiled.

"But," he continued, "I want him to know the community isn't judging him, just because his grandson may have made some missteps."

Beverly opened her mouth to speak but found that she was a little choked up. So she closed her mouth and laid a hand on her father's arm, squeezing gently. Her father and Albert Calder had lived on the same street for many years now. They'd never been close or had much in common, so it spoke volumes to her that he was concerned enough to want to reach out.

If the tables were turned, she doubted Mr. Calder would be thinking much about how her behavior might affect her father—which, sadly, probably explained more about Dennis than she'd ever thought before.

"Heard from Jeff yet?" her father asked, after a moment passed.

She smiled. "No. His ascent was delayed yesterday because there was a storm on the mountain, so they were hoping to be able to do it today. I haven't heard from him yet, so I don't know how it went."

"You didn't tell me that yesterday!"

"I didn't want to worry you." She fiddled with her fork. "I did enough worrying for us both yesterday. And earlier today."

"Still worrying?"

She looked up, about to say "of course," when she realized that wasn't strictly true. "No," she said. "I've been thinking of him off and on, but this morning, I gave the worry to God. Jeff will be home in time for the wedding."

As if on cue, her cell phone rang. Leaping to her feet, Beverly pulled it from her pocket and checked the readout. "It's Jeff! Excuse me, Father."

He smiled as his daughter raced from the room. "I'll clean up the dishes."

"Hello? Jeff?" Beverly went out the front door and perched on the steps. It was a lovely evening, and she was more than comfortable in the lightweight sweater she had donned before dinner.

"Hi, Sweetheart."

Her heart lifted and swelled. It was so good to hear his voice. "Hey. How are you?"

"Doing okay," he assured her. "We made the ascent today and the worst of the descent is behind us now."

"You're on the mountain?" She was startled. "I didn't think you'd have much cell service there."

"Me neither, but when I saw I had five bars I thought I'd better grab the chance to call you. We'll be back at base camp in less than two hours now."

She could hear his breathing, and she remembered how thin the air was at the high altitude. "Was it a tough day?"

Jeff chuckled. "It was no picnic. But when we got up there, the air was clear and the cloud cover was below us. Beverly, it is such a gift from God to be able to see and do that. And the guy I'm photographing—he is a living, breathing miracle. It humbles me that a man would lose two of his limbs in service to our country and still be inspired to reach out and help others going through the same awful journey he's taken. Thank you so much for encouraging me to take this job."

"You're welcome." She smiled. "I'm glad you were able to help."

"Yeah. Now if only I can get out of here."

"Well," she said, "tomorrow, you'll be able to leave Camp Muir, right?"

"I hope." Jeff didn't sound particularly hopeful though. "I just heard that the weather's deteriorating again. In fact, it's already starting to snow again, and I don't know how long it might last. We could be delayed leaving Muir."

"Oh." Beverly took a deep breath. The worst was over; surely Jeff would be able to get off that mountain in time for the wedding now. "I am confident you will make it back in time, and I am not going to worry about it."

"You're not?" Jeff sounded surprised. "I'm kind of worried, if you want to know the truth."

She laughed. Actually laughed. "God will work this out for us. I'm just giving my worry to Him. You might want to do the same."

"I'll try." Jeff sounded a little mystified, and she couldn't blame him. He knew he was marrying one of the biggest worrywarts on the planet, and suddenly she'd been replaced by this calm woman who told him not to worry? She couldn't really even explain it, but ever since her little devotional session this morning, she had felt better about Jeff's absence. So much so, in fact, that she intended to make time for a real devotional period tomorrow.

CHAPTER NINETEEN

On Wednesday, Beverly walked to the municipal building. She had risen early enough to walk Scamp and still have a short devotional period as she'd planned, and her mood was cheery, despite the rain clouds that threatened. With luck, Jeff would be on his way home today. She couldn't wait!

She was nearing her office on Main Street when she heard someone calling her name. "Mayor Wheeland? Beverly?"

Turning, she saw Noah Henry coming her way. "Good morning, Noah. How are you?"

"Fine, thanks." He smiled, and she thought again that he was a very handsome, compelling young man. "Have a minute to talk?"

"Of course." She gestured to the door. "I'm just getting into the office. Is this a good time?" When he nodded, she preceded him into the building.

Angela had already arrived, but her back was to the door as she stood on tiptoe peeking into a filing cabinet. "G'morning," she said over her shoulder.

"Good morning." Beverly hung up her light jacket. "Noah Henry is going to be meeting with me for a bit. Will you please hold my calls?"

"Ayuh."

Noah followed Beverly up the stairs to her office and took a seat across from her desk. "How was Mrs. Harnish after she rested yesterday? Did she continue to be as mentally capable as she appeared when Diane was there?"

Noah grinned. "Why am I not surprised that you've already heard about that?" His face sobered. "No, sadly, as good as she was then, by evening she was about the worst Brenna has ever seen her. She couldn't remember Brenna's name. Didn't remember she was her granddaughter. She thought maybe Brenna was a neighbor who'd come in to give her a hand."

Beverly winced in sympathy. She could only imagine how difficult it would be to look into the eyes of someone you loved, only to realize that they didn't know you. "I'm sorry to hear that. It must be terrible to lose someone in little pieces like that."

Noah nodded. "My grandfather had it too, but I don't recall a lot about it." His lips twisted as he said, "Teenage boys are remarkably self-absorbed. I remember him from my childhood when he was vigorous and quick-thinking, and it seems as if the next thing I knew he was just a sad little man in a wheelchair who never spoke."

They were silent for a moment. Then Noah cleared his throat. "Anyway, I didn't mean to get maudlin. I came to talk to you about something else altogether."

Beverly smiled, seeing that he wanted to change the topic. "No problem. What would you like to discuss?"

"I read the speculation about Dennis Calder's business difficulties in the paper. It got me thinking. Marble Cove needs ethical developers to ensure that its small-town atmosphere is honored. There's a lot of history here, and it would be a shame to let it be bulldozed by someone out to make a quick buck."

When Beverly nodded in agreement, Noah took a deep breath. "I'm planning to make Calder an offer on his business, if he can show me the books and prove that he doesn't have a lot of fishy stuff going on. And by 'fishy stuff' I'm not talking about trying to bribe an official. I'm more concerned about tax fraud and things like that."

"Oh, I hope he hasn't gotten himself into that kind of unsavory activity," Beverly said sincerely.

"I know." Noah paused, thinking something through. "It feels like something I need to do. Like I would be closing a circle, nullifying or maybe just mitigating some of the wrongs my grandfather did with his schemes that took advantage of local people."

"I think it's a lovely idea," Beverly said. "And heaven knows, you have a great deal more integrity than Dennis appears to. But Noah, I am not sure you should go into this thinking that you have to 'make right' the wrongs of your ancestor. Each of us has our own life story, and it doesn't need to be affected by those who came before."

"I know. I don't feel *compelled*, or responsible. I just think it would be a good thing to do." He grinned boyishly. "And I'm considering staying on this coast, so I may as well get underway with business plans here. I have scheduled a meeting with Calder tomorrow."

"Good luck," Beverly told him. "I hope it goes well. Marble Cove would be delighted to have you here on a permanent basis."

★ ★ ★

"What are you smiling at?" Shelley, who had invited Diane over so that they could sew and chat at the same time, eyed her friend with a grin.

Diane was indeed grinning as she hemmed the dress she would be wearing in the wedding. "Nothing special." But Diane chuckled. "Just thinking that maybe I won't tell Leo I decided to wear a lower pair of heels so that I won't tower over him. Not that he would mind, but I'll feel better if we're eye to eye when we're dancing."

Shelley chuckled too. "Yeah, I imagine he'll appreciate that." She reached for scissors. She was switching the bright pink ribbons on the girls' dresses they had just bought. She had found some really lovely pink-and-lavender plaid that both Emma and Hailey had liked, so she was painstakingly replacing all the pink bows with plaid ones. It was a time-intensive labor of love, one that she knew would be appreciated by Beverly, to whom little details like color mattered.

"So what are you doing to celebrate your birthday?" Diane asked.

"Not much," Shelley replied. "Dan says he and the kids have a special surprise for me when he gets home."

"That's sweet," Diane said. "I wish we all had more time so we could celebrate with you as well."

"Oh, Diane," Shelley explained. "I understand that we've all got a lot on our plates. I'm just glad to know I have you as friends. That's the best gift I could have."

When her cell phone rang, her eyebrows rose. Dan didn't usually call her in the middle of the morning. Clicking on the phone, she said, "Hi, honey. What's up?"

"Shelley!" Dan's voice on the other end of the phone was panicked.

"What's wrong?" Instantly, she was filled with dread. "Is your dad—?"

"Dad's fine," Dan said, "but this birdseed isn't!"

"What?" That morning, she had given Dan a basket piled with the small beribboned bags of birdseed they had filled. He had to go by the Landmark Inn on the way to his current job, and he had offered to drop off the basket on his way.

"I left the window down in the truck by accident, when I stopped to get some supplies," he reported, misery in his voice. "The birdseed basket was on the front seat. I forgot the forecast called for rain, and now everything's soaked."

"Oh. *Oh no!*" Shelley's mouth fell open. She looked at Diane. "The birdseed got soaked when Dan left his window down. What are we going to do?"

"Oh my gosh." Diane looked a little stunned. "I don't know, but tell Dan not to worry, we'll figure it out."

"Honey," Shelley said, "can you drop it by the house? Diane's here, and we'll see if we can salvage any of it. Don't worry, we'll fix it."

When she ended the call and looked up, Diane was smiling at her. "That was really sweet, Shelley. You could have screamed at him. A lot of people might."

"What would be the point? He feels terrible already." Shelley grimaced. "Although I have to say I'm feeling a little panicky right now. No, not a little. A lot!"

Diane blew out a breath. "We probably can't use the seed now. Even if we are able to dry it out, half of it's liable to germinate. And it's too risky anyway. I read an article about birdseed because Jessica's thinking of using it too. You have to be really cautious not to let it get moldy, because it can kill birds."

"All that net and ribbon . . ." Shelley looked mournful.

"I know. Maybe we can use it again. But wow, that was time-consuming. I don't know about you, but I'm not sure I have time between now and Saturday to tie all those little bags of birdseed up again!"

Shelley nodded. "I know."

Both women fell silent, continuing to sew as they considered the problem.

Within ten minutes, Dan's truck pulled into the driveway, and moments later, he loomed in the doorway between the kitchen and living room, where they were seated. "I'm so sorry." He looked completely shamefaced. "I can't believe

I did this." He held out the basket, its pink and lavender ribbons now limp and bedraggled.

"We'll fix it," Shelley said. "You go on and stop worrying, okay?" She stretched up on tiptoe to kiss him.

"Okay." But Dan looked crestfallen as he headed back out the door again.

"Oh dear." Diane rose from her chair with a wry smile. "Poor Dan. We'll have to fix this, or he'll never forgive himself."

Shelley tentatively fished a soaked bag of birdseed from the basket and examined it. She untied the ribbon, and opened the net, emptying the waterlogged seed into the trash. "If we open all of these and let them dry out, I could iron the ribbon and net and we could reuse it."

"I can get more birdseed," Diane said. "But when on earth are we going to do this?"

Shelley shook her head. "I don't know. Only three more days until The Big Day...this isn't good."

"Wait!" Diane held up a hand. "What if we got Hailey and some of her friends to help? It would go a lot faster. We only need about sixty, right?"

Shelley looked doubtful. "I don't know. Usually, when a group of preteen girls starts a project, they take *more* time and *more* supervision."

Both women chuckled.

"I could supervise," Diane said. "Why don't I go get the seed right now, and when Hailey gets home from school, we can ask for her help."

Shelley nodded. "I don't have a better idea. And the last thing I want to do is stress Beverly out, so I'd rather just fix this quietly if we can."

Diane nodded. "We'll tell her after the wedding."

★ ★ ★

Not long after Noah took his leave, Angela came to the door of Beverly's office.

Beverly glanced up, smiling. "Thank you for holding my— Angela, what's wrong?"

The young woman was pale and wan, wearing only a faded touch of the makeup she usually slathered on. "Oh, Beverly, I did something awful." The girl burst into tears, covering her face with her hands.

Beverly surged to her feet and was across the office in two strides. Sliding an arm around the sobbing young woman, she guided Angela to the love seat and sat down with her, rising briefly to pull the box of tissues from her desk into a more available spot. "Would you like to talk about it?"

Angela nodded. She took a deep, hitching breath. "I'm the one who talked to the paper."

Beverly understood instantly. "About Mr. Calder's bribery attempt, you mean."

Angela nodded. "I turned on the intercom to tell you something, but I guess you didn't notice, and then I heard Mr. Benton telling you about that e-mail, and I...I left the intercom on so I could listen." Her face contorted. "That train station is a piece of Marble Cove's history, and I was just so angry and upset at the thought of Mr. Calder tearing it down. I was hardly off the phone with Mr. Kimball when I was sorry, but when I called him back, he said he was already writing the article and as I hadn't said it was off the record, I couldn't stop him from printing it."

Beverly sighed.

"I really am so sorry, Beverly." Angela blotted her eyes with a tissue, then twisted it between her fingers. "I'll understand if you decide to let me go. I wish I'd thought for a few seconds before I opened my mouth. You can't imagine how much I wish I had a do-over. I'm not really a terrible person, even if I did a terrible thing."

Beverly looked at the young woman, hunched into a miserable ball on the love seat. Her head was down, her gaze trained on the floor. Her shoulders held a hopeless slump.

Beverly remembered herself at Angela's age. The world had seemed so perfect and full of hope. But it had only been a few short years before she had made an enormous mistake in judgment. No, she certainly wasn't perfect, and she didn't know anyone who was. Even aging didn't always seem to guarantee that one would get wiser, although in her own case, Beverly felt that it had helped.

"Angela," Beverly said. She put a finger beneath the young woman's chin and waited until Angela met her gaze. "Nobody is perfect, and we all make mistakes. What is important is that when we make those mistakes, we take the time to learn from them. It sounds to me as if you've already learned something from this lapse in judgment."

Angela nodded. "I have."

"Then I forgive you. Eavesdropping is a bad habit, and one I hope you'll break. From now on, I expect one hundred percent professionalism, both in the office and out. Anything you learn here stays here unless you have specific permission to share it. Is that going to be a problem?"

"Oh no, ma'am, it isn't." Fresh tears welled as Angela realized she wasn't going to lose her job. "I promise I'll never reveal office secrets again."

Beverly smiled. "Good. Then let's get to work."

As Angela rose, Beverly said, "You know, it took a great deal of courage to come in here and confess your error. I appreciate your honesty."

Angela shot her a grateful glance. "I couldn't have lived with myself if I hadn't," she said quietly. "I don't know how Dennis Calder can look himself in the eye, that's for sure."

As the young woman returned to the front office, Beverly settled into her chair and pulled her planner toward her. Her cell phone rang and she reached for it absently, intent on all the things she hoped to get done today. "Hello?"

"Hi, honey."

"Hey!" It was Jeff. "How are you? Better yet, *where* are you?"

Jeff sighed, and she could hear the dejection in his voice from clear across the country. "I'm at base camp. It's still snowing like crazy."

Beverly was silent for a moment. Panic fluttered in her chest, but she remembered her prayers that morning and the day before, and her resolution to give her concerns to God. "All right," she said. "We still have the rest of today, Thursday, and most of Friday. You'll make it in time."

After a moment of silence, Jeff said, "Who is this and what have you done with my fiancée?"

Beverly laughed. "It's really me."

"You sound a lot calmer than I thought you'd be. In fact, I think you're a lot calmer than I am right now!"

"Maybe." She hesitated, seeking the words to explain. "When you mentioned this trip, I agreed with you at first. It just was too close to the wedding. But I couldn't get it out of my head, and after you told me more about it, I felt that it was important for you to go. Not just for your career, but because it was the right thing to do, to help out a friend and support your handicapped climber. And I'll admit, when you had to delay the ascent, I was worried. But I wasn't kidding when I told you I'm handing over my worries to God. Trying to," she amended with a giggle. "I believe that you'll be back in time."

"All right." Jeff took a deep breath. "I'm going to try it your way. I believe this storm will soon end. I believe I'll get off this mountain soon. I believe there will be a flight bringing me back to the East Coast in time to rehearse my wedding with the most wonderful woman in the world."

"I believe," Beverly repeated in a near whisper. "I love you, honey. See you soon."

★ ★ ★

The rest of Beverly's day was hectic. She and Angela reviewed several grant possibilities, hoping to begin some proposals to present to the council and the community to help with the costs of the museum and nature preserve. It would be good for the community to know that the council was serious about Noah's offer. In the fall, if all went well and Noah's proposal was approved, she hoped to convince the town to hold a festival and possibly a charity auction to raise funds to supplement what they had found.

She was just finishing getting her files in order so that Angela could take care of anything she needed over the next few days when a shadow fell across the floor.

Glancing up, she saw Jeff's mother standing in the doorway. "Hello, my almost-daughter-in-law," Carolyn said gaily. "Father and I arrived about an hour ago and are all settled in our suite. I hope you can join us for dinner tonight?"

"Absolutely." Beverly smiled. When Jeff's mother was directing the full force of her charm at someone, it was almost impossible not to smile. "So I take it you've decided to attend the wedding?"

Carolyn's face fell. "Yes, and I have to apologize to you both for even considering missing it. I understand Jeff's point. Sometimes my enthusiasm carries me away, but he was right to fuss at me. There should be nothing more important than family, and he's never asked me for much. I'd have felt churlish if I'd missed your big day."

Impulsively, Beverly came around the desk and gave her mother-in-law-to-be a hug. "Thank you. I know Jeff will be thrilled that you are here."

"Father wants to take us both and your father out to dinner at Captain Calhoun's tonight. Will that be okay?"

"That would be lovely." Beverly hoped Mrs. Peabody hadn't spent a lot of time getting a supper together, but she would understand. And after all, Carolyn was *asking* rather than *telling*. "Let me call home and let him know so he can start getting ready."

"All right. And if there's anything I can do, you'll let me know, I hope? I feel bad that I haven't been around to help you at all."

"You can read over the program for me," Beverly offered. "Margaret gave me the proof today. She says as soon as I've looked it over and caught any errors, she can print and fold it. So I'd love to have another pair of eyes on it."

Carolyn clapped her hands. "Goodie! I'd be delighted." She fished in her pocket and came up with a small box gift-wrapped in lovely silver paper and ribbon. "This is for you, Beverly. I know you probably already have something old, new, borrowed, and blue, but I thought perhaps you could wear this too."

Beverly took the box from Carolyn. "I'm sure I can make it work." Quickly, she unwrapped the little package, trying not to worry. She already had earrings, a necklace, a blue garter . . . if this was jewelry, it could be problematic.

As she removed the lid from the box, a velvet jeweler's case came into view. Flipping open the lid, Beverly sucked in a breath of awe. "Oh my goodness, Carolyn. This is stunning! Are these...?"

"Yes, dear, those are sapphires. Jeff's father gave this necklace to me for our wedding day, and I'd like you to have it and wear it for yours, if you don't already have something else." A brief moment of sadness crossed her pretty face. "My marriage may not have worked out, but it gave me Jeff, the single best gift I ever received, and I believe this necklace will bring you luck."

Beverly burst into tears. "Oh, Carolyn, thank you so much. I will treasure it, and I know Jeff will be so happy to see me wearing it."

A few minutes later, Beverly smiled as she shut down her computer and got her jacket. Jeff's mother had a good heart. She was a little impulsive—okay, a lot—and sometimes a bit single-minded, but she wasn't selfish or self-serving, and Beverly knew that Carolyn was genuinely delighted to be welcoming her into the Mackenzie family. They might never see the world in exactly the same way, but they both loved Jeff and Mr. Maker, and that would be enough glue to bind them together.

Chapter Twenty

Later on Wednesday afternoon, Margaret looked over the wedding program one more time. Beverly would proof it that night, and tomorrow Margaret could get them printed and folded and ready for the wedding. The drawing had turned out beautifully, and it gave her a warm feeling to have been able to help out. With tourist season on the cusp of arrival, she hadn't been nearly as free as she was earlier in the spring when things were slow, and she felt bad that she hadn't been as available as Shelley and Diane.

Her cell phone rang, and she pulled it from her pocket. It was the house phone number. Surely it was Adelaide since she had been due to arrive home from helping out at the community center not long ago. "Hello?"

"Hi, Mom." Adelaide didn't sound as cheery as she normally did.

"Hi, my sweet girl. How was your day?"

"Good. How was yours?"

"Mine was fine too."

"I think we have a problem."

"Oh? What's wrong?" Margaret wasn't sure what she expected, but she hoped everything was okay.

"Oreo is crying. He keeps getting in the litter box and crying."

"Oh dear."

"Mom, I think he needs to go to the vet."

"All right. Let me call and see if we can get an appointment. I'll call you right back."

Margaret glanced at the time as she dialed the vet's number, hoping they could still get an appointment today.

"You can fit us in?" she asked, a little surprised.

"Yes. Can you make it?" the receptionist asked. "If he's blocked, you don't want to wait until tomorrow."

"Um, yes, we can make that work. See you then." Quickly, Margaret called home and told Adelaide about the appointment. "Do you think you can manage to get Oreo into a carrier and be ready to roll when I get there?"

"Sure, Mom, no problem."

When had her daughter become so confident?

When Margaret pulled into the driveway at five fifteen, she was surprised to see Adelaide immediately come out the door, lugging the cat carrier. From the awkward way she moved, Oreo clearly was already inside.

"Gracious!" Margaret put the car in park and hurried to help Adelaide secure the carrier on the backseat with the seat belt. "I wasn't sure you could get him in there without help." Oreo hated the cat carrier. "How did you do that?"

"I turned it on its end. Then I opened the door and stuck him in back feet first. Just like you showed me." Adelaide looked immensely pleased with herself. "Didn't I do a good job?"

"You did a *great* job," Margaret corrected, chuckling.

Oreo meowed and wailed the whole way to the vet, raising Margaret's level of concern. Usually, once he realized there was no escape from the carrier, he settled down.

A vet tech called them into an exam room almost the moment they arrived. After she weighed Oreo and took his temperature—which made him even more unhappy—Leo Spangler entered the room. "Hello, ladies," he said. "I know I'm seeing you at a wedding on Saturday, but I didn't expect to see you here today."

"I'm helping with the guest book," Adelaide informed him.

"I heard. I bet you're going to do a great job." Leo smiled at her as he began to examine Oreo. "Now who wants to tell me what's going on with this guy?"

Margaret opened her mouth to repeat what they already had shared with the technician, but Adelaide forestalled her. She explained that she'd heard Oreo crying and that as she'd observed him, she'd seen him repeatedly trying to use the litter box without success.

"You're pretty sharp," Leo commented, making Adelaide grin.

"I know."

Margaret and Leo shared an amused glance. But then he reverted to a more serious expression. "Oreo is 'blocked,'" he told them, palpating the cat's lower belly. "His bladder is very full. Something has happened to prevent urine from passing. With your permission, I'd like to admit him for a day or two, anesthetize him, and get him unblocked."

Margaret nodded. "All right."

"The receptionist will have you fill out some paperwork, and I'll call you as soon as I have more information. We'll set up a time for you to pick him up then, okay?"

Adelaide had tears in her eyes. "But he'll be lonely here without me an' Lizzy an' B'rscotch."

Leo put a hand on her shoulder and rubbed gently. "Maybe a little, but we're going to make him feel better, Adelaide. Just as soon as he does, he can come home again, I promise." He bent his knees so he was looking directly into her eyes. "You might have saved Oreo's life today. If you hadn't noticed his problems, he might have gotten very sick very quickly."

"I'm ob-thervant," Adelaide informed him, knuckling away a tear.

Leo laughed. "Indeed you are, my friend. Indeed you are."

★ ★ ★

True to her word, Diane had come over to Shelley's after Hailey got home from school. Shelley had ironed out the ribbon and net, and it looked as good as new.

With three of Hailey's friends giggling and helping, retying the birdseed bags took less time than it had the first time they did it.

While Diane and her four helpers finished the birdseed bags, Shelley assembled everything she would need to make Beverly's cake. She planned to bake the layers tomorrow. Then when they were completely cool, she would place filling between the layers and add a thin layer of buttercream icing to keep all the crumbs from getting into the icing when she began to decorate. The crumb coat would be dried and ready for decorating Friday morning. She already had the flowers she'd be placing on the cake finished, and they should be dry by Friday.

Dan came through the door just minutes after the birdseed team had disbanded. Diane and Hailey's friends had gone home, and Hailey was starting her homework while Shelley breaded haddock filets.

Dan still looked glum, she noted as she kissed him hello. "I'll help you with those tonight," he said, indicating the basket of birdseed before he'd even greeted her.

"With what?" Shelley pretended not to understand. "There's nothing for you to help with." She reached into the basket and picked up one of the bags, tossing it to him. "See?"

Dan caught the little bag, obviously realizing it was dry. "But this—how did you—you must have worked all afternoon on these, Shelley."

She shook her head, indicating Hailey. "Not at all. Your amazing niece called a couple of her friends."

"Miss Diane helped us," Hailey volunteered, "and we got it all done again really fast!" She grinned at Dan. "That was kind of a dumb thing to do though, Uncle Dan."

"I know." He nodded, slowly returning her grin. "Hailey, I guess I owe you a big favor for getting me out of this fix."

"I'll come up with something *good*," she said, rubbing her hands together gleefully.

"Oh yeah?" Dan started around the table toward her, a gleam in his eye.

With a shriek, Hailey slammed her book shut and bolted from the room.

"Dinner's ready in fifteen minutes," Shelley called after her, grinning at the pair's antics.

Dan went to the sink. As he began to wash his hands, he said, "I need to talk to you."

Alerted by the seriousness of his tone, Shelley braced herself. "Do we have a moving date already?"

Dan shook his head. "No. We don't have a moving date." He came to her and cupped her elbows, holding her before him. "Shell, we're never going to have a moving date. I've decided not to accept Wayne's offer."

Shelley gasped. "What? But, Dan—"

"Even if it means leaving Wayne and finding another electrician to help me finish my apprenticeship, I don't want to move to Portland. Wayne's terrific. I doubt I will find anyone who's as thorough and who is as good a teacher as Wayne, but I can deal with that. What I can't deal with is picking up and leaving Marble Cove. We love our life here. My family is here, all of our friends are here, we like the kids' schools. You're the core of Mom and Dad's support network."

Happiness all but suffocated her, but still, she felt concern that Dan might really be doing this just to please her. "Oh, Dan, are you sure? I mean, I agree with everything you've said, but—"

Dan put a finger to her lips. "No argument. You supported me wholeheartedly when I had a chance to make a major career change, and now it's your turn. I wouldn't feel right keeping you from the opportunity to realize your dream now. I don't think it's just luck that Rusty's decided to sell the Cove, honey. This is part of God's plan for our lives."

"That's a lovely way to think of it," Shelley said, reassured.

"I'm going to tell Wayne in the morning that I can't accept the Portland job." Dan took a deep breath. "This decision scares me to death. I mean, it could be a huge mistake. But there's something inside me that says it's the right thing for us, and I have to listen to it."

Shelley slid her arms free and took her husband's hands. "Then I'm sure it's the right thing too."

* * *

Thursday morning dawned as brilliantly sunny as the previous day had been gloomy. As she walked to the mayor's office that morning, Beverly wondered if it would be selfish to pray for a pretty day on Saturday.

Her heart felt light. The first thing she'd done that morning was check the weather forecasts on the Internet for Washington State. It looked as if Jeff's storm was clearing out, and there would be a good window of opportunity for him to leave Camp Muir and return to his rental car. They'd spoken briefly, and she'd told him he didn't need to share every detail with her, that she'd be surprised and delighted to see him whenever he arrived.

As she walked, she checked off last-minute wedding details. Shelley had the cake well under control. Shelley also had the birdseed baskets; Margaret had the programs, which Carolyn had helped to proof the night before. Margaret was overseeing the flowers for the church and she, Mrs. Peabody, and Celia were making sure there were flowers in the crackle-glass vases on each table at the reception. She knew Victoria wouldn't miss a beat with details at the Landmark, so things were definitely coming together nicely.

Her dress was ready, as were the accessories that went with it. They weren't leaving for their honeymoon immediately, but she had packed a small bag for their wedding night stay at the Landmark. Shelley was going to take Scamp overnight so Beverly's father wouldn't have to worry with the lively puppy.

"Beverly. Hey, can I talk to you for a minute?"

She was yanked from her reverie by a masculine voice. When she saw Dennis Calder striding toward her, she groaned inwardly. This was guaranteed to be unpleasant. Still, she pasted on a smile. "Of course. How are you, Dennis?"

He shot her a sardonic smile at the question. "Just peachy. Want to grab coffee? No, scratch that. If we go into the Cove, every busybody in there will be turning up his hearing aid. Do you mind just walking a bit?"

"That would be fine." Her work could wait, she reminded herself. Dennis was one of her constituents; as mayor, she represented this man as well as everyone else in Marble Cove. Certainly, they hadn't seen eye to eye on many issues recently, but if she could do something for him that didn't undermine or violate her pledge to the majority of those in town, she should. She *would*. "So I gather from your response that things aren't going well?"

"Of course things aren't going well. You're the mayor. I'm sure you've heard lots of gory details."

"I've heard a lot of rumors and innuendo, and I read the newspaper article that made allegations but didn't name a source." She figured she might as well not beat around the bush. "Why don't you tell me your side of the story?"

She gestured to one of the wrought-iron-and-wooden benches that graced Main Street at strategic locations. "Let's sit." Without waiting to see what Dennis would do, Beverly seated herself on the wooden bench.

Dennis appeared to hesitate for a moment. Then he threw himself down on the bench, long legs stretched before him, hands balled into fists in the pockets of his light jacket. "Okay. Here's the truth, then." He took a deep breath. "Yes. I did try to bribe a council member. Just one, Jules Benton. I think part of me knew he was too honorable to get sucked into a bribe in the first place. I'm not even sure why I did it." He shrugged flippantly.

"Dennis." Her voice was quiet. "We all make errors in judgment."

"My company is in the tank, Beverly." He looked at the tops of his expensive Italian loafers rather than at her. "I still think Marble Cove's economy would benefit from economic development. The proposals I've made would have revitalized this town. But I bow to the wishes of the majority of the community to keep it simple."

She could tell from his words that "keeping it simple" was not a compliment. "I think you're wrong," she said quietly. "I still think modest economic development combined with more tourism will be successful in helping our economy."

"Well, you're going to get the chance to try," he said, and there was a note of bitterness in his tone that reflected the mayoral race. "Good luck."

"And what will happen to you?"

"I'm selling the company," he said abruptly. "Noah Henry made me an offer yesterday that I literally can't refuse, not if I want to climb out from under this mountain of debt. And then I'm leaving. My uncle runs a construction company outside of Boston, and he's offered me a position with him. Don't worry, I'll just be a crew foreman, so there won't be much chance for me to hatch development plans anywhere on the Northeast Coast."

"I'm glad you have a fallback position," she said sincerely. "Your grandfather is going to miss you."

He shot her one of his patented, cocky Calder smiles. "Oh, I'll be visiting. Don't worry, you're not getting rid of me completely."

"I wish you well. I hope that one of these days you'll find happiness."

"Like you did?" His mouth twisted. "Guess I should offer you congratulations on the big wedding. Only two days away, right?"

"Right." She smiled. "I'll pray for you, Dennis. I'd like to think of you as a friend."

"Works for me." But he looked a little taken aback at her obvious sincerity.

They were silent for a time, simply watching the foot traffic and the vehicles pass. Finally, in the least antagonistic tone she'd heard him use in a long, long time, he said, "I really do hope your wedding is the start of a long and happy life for you. And I—I appreciate your good wishes."

CHAPTER TWENTY-ONE

Shelley had intended to keep all day Thursday and Friday free in case Beverly needed her for last-minute wedding assistance. But when Dan asked her to go with him to speak with Wayne that morning, she didn't feel she could refuse.

As they walked into Stover Electric, Shelley slipped her hand into Dan's and squeezed. He looked down at her, his blue eyes sober—and then he smiled, raising her hand to touch his lips before releasing her.

Wayne looked up sharply when the receptionist ushered Dan and Shelley into his office. His keen eyes took in their expressions, and he slapped down on his desk the sheaf of papers he was holding. "So you're not taking the job."

Dan's mouth fell open, but he managed a response. "No, I'm not. Wayne, you did me a great honor with the confidence you expressed in me. And I will appreciate that for the rest of my life. I hate to miss out on a chance like this, a chance to broaden my skills and all...but my family has roots in Marble Cove. My wife is starting a business, we love our church, we have a lot of extended family around, and my father's health is uncertain right now. We're just not interested in relocating, no matter how attractive the offer."

Dan stopped for breath, and Wayne said, "All right—"

"I'd be grateful if you'd get the IBEW to assign me to someone else local. Although frankly, after working with you and learning the right ways to do things, it will be hard to leave. I can't imagine working for a better, more capable electrician and teacher, as well as someone who's become a friend." Dan's voice broke on the last word, and he thrust out his hand. Shelley could see him squaring his jaw, determined not to do anything as unmanly as cry.

"Well, that's about the best news I think I've had since my wife said yes!" Wayne was smiling, and Wayne Stover *never* smiled.

Shelley could hardly believe her eyes. The best news? Hadn't Wayne been eager for Dan to move on?

"No way," said Wayne, wagging a finger at Dan, "no way is some other electrician getting his grubby little paws on a guy with your skills, especially with the busy summer months just around the corner. No sirree. I'm going to tell the IBEW that I'm sorry, but they are going to have to place their new guys somewhere else this time."

"You—you want me to stay?" Dan seemed unable to take it in. "But I thought you wanted me to go."

"Dan, you're the best apprentice I've ever had." Wayne rubbed his jaw. "Last thing I wanted was for you to leave. But it was a good offer. That job in Portland would be a step up if you really do want to get into big commercial projects. I didn't want to stand in the way of your ambitions if that's what you wanted. It wouldn't have been fair of me to turn down an opportunity like that without letting you decide."

Shelley was rooted to the spot. Deep gratitude filled her, and an even larger sense of the awe she often felt in Wayne's presence. He was one of the most deeply honorable people she'd ever met. *Thank you, God, for putting Wayne Stover in our lives.*

"When the apprenticeship ends," Wayne went on, "I'd like to offer you a job with Stover Electric. I'll be needing to take on a partner sometime in the next year or two because I'm planning to retire a few years down the road. Dan, I'd like you to consider being that partner. I think we could work well together, and I'd be pleased at the idea of handing over the business to someone else who'd take as good care of it as I did."

Dan blinked. "Ayuh."

Shelley laughed and elbowed him. "I believe you've rendered him speechless," she said to Wayne.

The older man grinned. "Looks like it. Well, Dan, what do you say? You willing to consider a partnership in, say, two years?"

Dan blinked again, then nodded and thrust out his hand again as Shelley blinked tears from her eyes. "Ayuh!" he said, and they all laughed.

★ ★ ★

The town council held a special meeting on Thursday afternoon. The only thing on the agenda was a proposal from Noah Henry to preserve the old train station and turn it into a museum. Accompanying that was a second proposal to expand the town's new park into the quarry and designate portions of it as a nature preserve. Even those council members who initially were opposed to his proposal relented when Beverly outlined her plans to apply for grants and work with the community to enhance Noah's generous starting donation.

Beverly recalled what Noah had shared with her friends and her about his grandfather's philanthropic inclinations during the years of his "new" life in Oregon. She thought of his determination to save young Marie Mauer's life. Regardless of what anyone said, she had to believe that Elias had a core of good inside him. He had felt guilty at some level about his actions.

As a unanimous vote of "Aye!" rang out around the conference table, the sound of a distant train whistle pierced the air. Noah looked up sharply, head angled toward the window. No one else reacted.

When he caught her eye, Beverly smiled and gave him a slow wink. She couldn't help but feel that they had just received approval for the council's plan for the old train station.

After the meeting, Noah approached Beverly with an outstretched hand. "Thank you, Mayor Wheeland. Without you and your friends, I don't know if I'd ever have uncovered the truth about my grandfather's past." He looked saddened but stoic.

"Noah," Beverly said, "although your grandfather clearly wasn't a saint during the time he lived in Marble Cove, we know he wasn't a complete villain either. He used some of that money to help Brenna's grandmother. Who knows what other wrongs he may have righted that we'll never know about?"

Noah's face lit in a small smile.

★ ★ ★

When Beverly arrived home that evening, her father met her at the door. "It's Thursday."

She smiled at him, lifting an eyebrow. "I know, Father. It was Thursday when I left the house this morning."

Her father's face didn't show even a flash of amusement. "Your wedding is in two days, and your rehearsal dinner is tomorrow night. So where is your groom?"

Oh, so that was it. She kissed his cheek before she moved past him into the house. "He's on his way."

"It was selfish," her father pronounced. "Taking that job so close to the wedding was just selfish. Jeff isn't the man I thought he was."

Beverly grinned as he thumped into the house behind her, his cane beating an irritated tattoo on the wood floor. "Actually, it was my decision. He was going to pass on it, but..." She paused, trying to explain the feelings she'd had. "I felt that he was called to do that for a reason. There are only so many skilled photographers in good enough shape to sub in on a mountain-climbing trip. And it was an amazing opportunity as well." She put an arm around her father's shoulder. "I've been praying about this, and I refuse to worry." *Much.* She was still human, after all. "Jeff will be here in time for the wedding."

"*Hmph*." Her father still looked disgruntled. "I hope you're right."

He followed her to the kitchen and out onto the porch as she released Scamp from his crate and took him out to play in the yard for a few minutes. "Did I ever tell you I was almost late for your mother's and my wedding?"

"What? No. What happened?" Beverly picked up the slimy ball the puppy had just dropped at her feet. Making a moue of disgust, she gave it a toss and then wiped her hands on a towel she had brought out just for that purpose.

Father chuckled. "Oh boy, that was something. We were supposed to get married at two o'clock in the afternoon. But there'd been a thunderstorm overnight, and the roads were a muddy mess. My best man was a fellow I'd grown up with, and we were both dressed in our good clothes when we took off for the church in my parents' old blue '47 Ford. 'Bout halfway there, we got a flat tire."

"Oh dear." Beverly's eyes rounded. "What did you do?" She was fascinated. She couldn't believe she had never heard this story before.

He started to laugh. "Well, we saw right off we couldn't so much as step out of the car, or we'd be up to our ankles in muck. Nobody was around. It was just a little country track. So we took off our suits and our socks and our good shiny shoes, and we changed that tire in our skivvies."

"Father! I can't believe you did that!" Beverly began to laugh. It was the last thing she'd expected her staid, upright father to confess.

"And then we realized we couldn't get dressed again, because our feet and legs and hands were all muddy."

Beverly tossed the ball for Scamp again. "Don't tell me you drove around in your underwear!"

Her father laughed until tears came to his eyes. "We did. Didn't have a choice. I had one towel in the back, and we used it to clean up as best we could. And then we drove to the church in our skivvies."

She held up a hand, chuckling. "Do not tell me you got out of the car looking like that."

"Didn't have to, for which we were mighty thankful. My friends were waiting, getting a little nervous that the groom hadn't shown up yet. When they realized what happened, one guy ran inside and brought out two choir robes for us to wear long enough to get inside."

Beverly laughed so hard she dropped Scamp's ball. "You went into the church for your wedding in a choir robe. Oh, Father, that's priceless."

"I didn't have it on long," he told her. "Just had to get from the car to the bathroom for a good cleanup. Our friends brought our clothes in, and when the wedding started I was standing at the altar lookin' spiffy. Nobody was the wiser, 'cept for the fellas in the wedding party."

"Oh my goodness." Beverly wiped her eyes with her sleeve, not about to let the soiled towel near her face. "What a great story. Did Mother know?"

"Not until afterward." Her father grinned. "She said it was too bad the photographer wasn't around to get a picture."

After dinner, which consisted of grilled cheese sandwiches and tomato soup, since Mrs. Peabody had been too busy to come by today, Beverly sat down at the kitchen table to manicure and paint her finger- and toenails. Scamp chewed contentedly on a bone at her feet as she considered the things she still needed to do before the wedding hoopla began. Tomorrow they would decorate the Landmark, and tomorrow evening they would rehearse the ceremony and have a clambake on the beach...if the weather cooperated. She was still thankful that Margaret was prepared to step in and open the gallery if rain was forecast.

She wondered where Jeff was now, but she had told him he didn't need to check in, that she would see him at the rehearsal Friday evening. And that, she decided, was all the worry she was going to allow herself. Jeff would be there. He would.

Thinking again of the silly story her father had shared earlier, she realized that for some reason, hearing about his near-late arrival at his own wedding had reassured her. Lots of things could go wrong, and Jeff could still be on time for the wedding.

Chapter Twenty-Two

Beverly pulled into the parking lot of the Landmark Inn shortly after one on Friday. She had taken half the day off, as had Shelley, Diane, and Margaret, in order to prepare for the evening's clambake and to decorate the ballroom, where Beverly and Jeff's reception was being staged.

Early that morning, Margaret had called and confirmed Beverly's weather report: there was no chance of rain that evening, and in fact, the weather would be warmer than normal for Maine. Shelley had already sent Dan, who had also taken the day off, out to the beach to dig a shallow pit in the sand for their clambake, line it with stones and charcoal, and pile wood for the fire. Although she wouldn't actually begin the baking process until later in the day, she needed everything to be set up since time would be so limited.

Allan and Adelaide had been deputized to take all the beach chairs they had been able to find down to the beach, and several friends from church planned to help with the setup. They were even borrowing a couple of large folding tables from the church to hold condiments, side dishes, and desserts.

With Beverly were Celia Patterson and Mrs. Peabody. Margaret, following close behind them in her van, was loaded down with buckets and buckets of flowers that she, Edward Maker, the elderly sisters, and Diane had grown in their gardens and harvested for the big occasion.

"I was afraid my French lilacs weren't going to be ready yet," Celia volunteered as she carefully climbed out of the van, "but thank goodness for that sun! They are going to be absolutely gorgeous."

"I still had some white daffodils going strong, so I brought them." Mrs. Peabody lifted her arm and made a bicep, and Margaret laughed.

Another car pulled into the lot. Beverly's cousin Charlotte, her aunt Helen, and Carolyn all alighted, exchanging hugs with Beverly. "Your cousin is a sweetheart to offer me a ride," Carolyn pronounced.

Charlotte blushed. "It wasn't a bit out of my way."

"Heavens," Helen said. "Look at all these flowers!"

Beverly chuckled. "I suspect we have enough flowers to decorate the entire downtown."

"Only the best for our Beverly," Mrs. Peabody said fondly.

Beverly gave Mrs. Peabody a one-armed hug, carrying the folder full of place cards that identified the food in the other arm. "Thank you. I appreciate you and Celia coming to help."

"We wouldn't have missed it."

The six of them crossed the parking lot and approached the Landmark along the tree-lined sidewalk to the front double doors. The trees sported bright-green shades of new growth, and all along the walkway, impatiens in shades of pink, white, and lavender had been planted.

"*Oooh*, they must have just planted those," Diane said. "Look, Beverly, they're your colors!"

"Never plant impatiens until after Memorial Day," Celia reminded them. "One frost and they're done for."

"It's so wonderful to see this old lady looking gorgeous again," Mrs. Peabody said as they trooped up to the double doors. "It would have been a crime to let this place get as shabby as that poor old train station."

"The council just approved a plan yesterday to turn that 'poor old train station' into a museum, thanks to a donation from Noah Thorpe," Beverly informed them. "It should be in the next paper."

"Oh, that's wonderful news!" Shelley clapped her hands as did Mrs. Peabody.

Inside, the large foyer of the Landmark was cool and elegant. A large round table beneath a central chandelier held a huge vase of fresh lilies. A woman in a well-fitted navy suit with white piping came clicking across the marble tiles in navy pumps with heels high enough to make Beverly wince. Her golden hair was cut in a sleek bell shape that swung along her jaw. "Hello, Beverly. How have you been?"

It was Victoria Manchester. Beverly had spoken with her when she had reserved the space. The two women had seen each other fairly regularly, ever since she'd assisted Victoria with a business plan to restore the faded glory of the old building.

"I'm doing wonderfully. And this place looks lovely. It's hard to believe it's the same inn you inherited, isn't it?"

Victoria smiled. "I know."

"How has business been?" Helen asked.

"Fabulous," Victoria assured her. "Lots of honeymooners, small business gatherings, lots of wedding receptions and graduation parties this month and next. I can't complain." She beckoned to Beverly and the group. "If you want to follow me, I'll take you back to the ballroom and show you what we've set up."

The women obediently followed Victoria through a wide hallway to a set of double doors thrown wide. Inside, the ballroom was a nice-size space, but not so huge that a party of sixty or so would rattle around in it. Three chandeliers dripped glass-faceted teardrops. A buffet table was set against the near wall, and round tables dotted the room. The front of the room had wide glass windows that looked out over the rocky coast to the sea. A small table for the bride and groom had been set up there, with a table not far away for the cake. It would, Beverly thought, make a stunning "cutting the cake" photo with the ocean in the background.

The tables were draped with white tablecloths, and a square pink fabric napkin in the center of each one served as an accent. Each chair was draped in a white cover tied with a pink bow at the back. And in the two front corners of the room, potted palms and dieffenbachia added a lovely touch, draped in white lights that lent a sparkle even in the daytime.

"This is gorgeous!" exclaimed Diane. Immediately, she plunked down the large box she had carried in. Delving into the depths of the box, she came up with a round mirror. "The vases of flowers will go on these in the center of the pink napkin accents."

"Oh, that will be beautiful!" Margaret said.

"If you like, you can drive around and bring the flowers and things in through the doors down there." Victoria indicated a set of exit doors at the end of the hallway outside. "It would be much closer than carrying everything through the front door and all the way down the hall. If there is anything else I can do for you, please let me know. I'll be in my office."

"Thank you." Beverly smiled at the blonde. "This is really going to be a lovely location for our reception."

Margaret vanished immediately behind Victoria. She brought the van around so that they could carry in the flowers. While the other women did that, Celia and Mrs. Peabody set the food placards on the buffet table.

As the women worked to distribute the flowers among the tables, Beverly and Carolyn filled three large vases with flowers that would sit at intervals on the buffet table. Shelley and Margaret set aside a selection to surround the base of the cake and filled another vase for the gift table and one for the baby grand. Diane and Charlotte found a pedestal in a corner and dragged it over to center it behind the bride and groom's table, and Helen added another vase of flowers to accent the space.

"Oh, that looks so pretty," Beverly said. She was fighting butterflies, trying to imagine the space tomorrow filled with their families and friends. Could she really be getting married again?

She hoped she wasn't dreaming. Until Jeff got back, she wouldn't be able to let herself completely relax. The fact that she hadn't heard from him yet was good news, she told herself firmly. He would only call now if there was going to be a problem.

"Hey, I had an idea," Diane said, as Beverly, Margaret, and Shelley stood back with her to take in the whole room. "Noah Henry has been so interested in the town's history, and in how he fits into it. I was thinking last night that maybe we should throw him a party. Sort of a Thorpe family reunion, so that he can see all the people in this town he's related to."

"That's a terrific idea!" Shelley chuckled. "Although you're going to have to hold it outdoors somewhere because I can't imagine there's a space in town large enough for that kind of crowd."

"We could probably have it in a month or so," Diane mused.

"Not while I'm away," Margaret warned, wagging a finger at Diane. "I'm not a Thorpe, but I have no intention of missing a gathering like that. Oh!" She snapped her fingers. "I completely forgot to tell you I got a notification that I definitely have a place in the class."

"That's awesome," Shelley said. "Congratulations. Finally you can stop being anxious."

Margaret laughed. "Finally, I can," she repeated. "And guess what else? I got a really nice note from the artist who's leading the class. He said he found my painting very insightful, and he looks forward to working with me."

"Yay, Margaret!" Beverly raised a fist in the air. "That's wonderful."

"I can hardly believe it," she said. "My dream is finally coming true. I'm going to be a painter in Paris! Maybe only for a few weeks, but it still counts."

"It does indeed," Diane said, grinning. "How's Adelaide feeling as the time draws closer for you to leave?"

Margaret snorted. "Adelaide is Little Miss I-Have-It-All-Under-Control." She smiled, and then suddenly there were tears in her eyes. "You know, Adelaide needed us longer than most children do, and it made me overprotective and far too quick to do too much for her. The past few months, and especially the past few weeks, have made me see that I've been shortchanging her. I figured she was done growing, I suppose, and that couldn't be farther from the truth. It's high time for me to step aside and stop hindering her ability to forge her own path in life."

"You didn't do it on purpose," Diane said. "You've been a wonderful parent."

"Thanks." Margaret sniffed and smiled. "But I've been making a conscious effort to encourage her independence, and so far, she's made every challenge look easy. I'm so proud of her."

"She's an extraordinary young lady," Shelley said fondly. "I was a little surprised myself at how well she did with her ambitious cooking agenda."

"I can't thank you enough for helping her," Margaret told Shelley. "With all the things you have going on, you could very easily have told her you were too busy."

Shelley waved a hand and smiled. "How could I be too busy for Adelaide?"

"How's your father-in-law doing at home?" Margaret asked. "Is it better or worse than when he was in the hospital?"

"Getting better," Shelley said promptly. "I sort of had to browbeat Frances into accepting some help, but she's allowing us all to take turns bringing in meals and helping with laundry and cleaning. Actually, she's far less trouble than I anticipated."

"Or maybe you've just learned how to manage her," Margaret suggested with a grin.

Shelley laughed. "There's some truth in that."

Diane cleared her throat. "The Bauer family is going to miss your influence badly when you move."

"Oh!" Shelley's face lit up as if the sun had risen inside her. "We're not moving! I can't believe I forgot to tell you guys that!"

"What?" Beverly had begun cutting lengths of ribbon to twine among the flowers on the tables. She leaped to her feet and grabbed Shelley, twirling her in a circle. "We're going to be neighbors! I was so upset that I would be moving next door and you'd be moving away."

Shelley hugged her friend hard as Diane and Margaret laughed.

"That's the best wedding gift I could have gotten," Beverly declared as she finally released Shelley.

"What changed?" Diane asked.

"Dan decided he wasn't willing to sacrifice my dream or make the kids start a whole new life. We love Marble Cove. Our family, our church, and you guys are here." She went on to tell them about Wayne's offer of partnership, and all three women beamed.

"Best news ever," Diane declared.

"That's terrific." Beverly looked thrilled, but after a moment her smile wobbled around the edges. "Now if only my groom would show up, that would be the second-best news ever."

"Oh, honey." Diane rose and went to hug Beverly. "Don't lose faith now. You've been a trooper all week. I'd have been a basket case, but you—you've just been such a steadfast example of faith."

"Keep believing," Margaret encouraged her. "Jeff will be here."

Oh, she surely hoped so. Even that morning when she'd prayed she'd felt confident, filled with calm from the Holy Spirit. But as the hours passed and time for the rehearsal drew nearer, her assurance faded away. After all, her wedding was nothing compared to some of the important things people were praying that God would help them with. Who was she to pray for something so trivial?

As if she had read Beverly's mind, Margaret went on. "God has an infinite capacity to attend to all our needs. To Him, one person isn't more important than another, despite their different concerns. He's got your back, Beverly. I sincerely believe that."

A muffled ringtone interrupted her friend. Instantly Beverly leaped to her feet. "That's my phone!"

And as she dug the phone from her bag, she saw Jeff's number displayed on the screen. "It's Jeff," she announced, and his mother, appearing out of nowhere, clapped.

"Hi, sweetheart. I'm on the ground in Boston. I'll see you at the church in a few hours, all right?"

"Oh, that's wonderful." Beverly dropped her head into her hands and began to sob, relief flooding her system.

Diane rose and took the phone as Charlotte and Helen consoled Beverly. "Hey, Jeff. Welcome back."

"Is Beverly okay?"

Diane considered her friend's radiant face as she lifted it from her hands and allowed Shelley to dab away tears. "She's fantastic. Just a little overwhelmed with relief, that's all."

Jeff chuckled. "Yeah. I can imagine. I'm not sure I would have taken this job if I'd known how tight the time frame was going to get. I think I've got some gray hair I didn't have when I left."

"I bet." Diane grinned. "I'm glad you're going to make it."

"Me too. Give my girl my love."

"Gladly! See you soon."

★ ★ ★

Shelley checked her watch. "Timing is everything" wasn't just a trite phrase in cooking, and for this clambake, it was essential. She had run down to the beach and started the fire as soon as they'd returned from decorating the Landmark that afternoon.

The wedding rehearsal was at five. Beverly had assured her it would be short and sweet, so she figured the clams should be ready to eat around six if they went on right at five. At the last minute, she had realized she couldn't be in two places at once to make this clambake work, so she'd tried to hire Brenna to help. Brenna had refused the pay, but she and Noah had volunteered to oversee it.

"You guys are so great. See you in an hour or so!" Shelley gave them a final wave and headed back to the house. Since she wasn't actually in the wedding, she didn't need to arrive early, and Dan had already taken the children over to the church. All she needed was a quick shower, a change of clothing, a little makeup, and she was ready.

As she slipped into the sundress and sweater she had laid out, Shelley reflected that if she was this nervous, Beverly must be a basket case!

★ ★ ★

Beverly had never seen such a welcome sight in her life. The moment she parked the car in the church lot, she spotted Jeff standing on the sidewalk just outside the door. She fairly flew across the space, almost leaping into his arms in a completely unrestrained hug that was exceedingly unmayor-like and even less Beverly-like. Or perhaps it had been in the past. She was, she reflected as she kissed the love of her life, feeling a lot less confined and constrained these days, and she was determined never to go back to her old, constantly uptight self.

"I missed you so much!" she said.

"Not half as much as I missed you." Jeff's blue eyes were serious. "I should never have let you talk me into that trip. It was awesome, but we didn't need the stress."

"Most of the time, I was fine," she told him. "I really was okay with it." She smiled. "Could have done without the weather delays, but look, here you are and everything's fine."

Jeff grinned. "Yes, it is. Let's go practice getting married."

The rehearsal went perfectly, although Emma was a little upset that she wouldn't get flower petals to throw until tomorrow. Shelley, who had arrived a few minutes late because, bless her, she'd been overseeing the clambake, talked earnestly to her child until the mutinous expression on the little face eased, and Emma walked down the aisle with a smile.

It was still only five forty-five when the group disbanded to meet out on the beach.

Beverly couldn't believe her eyes as she and Jeff approached the clambake hand in hand. Large pink and lavender balloons with wedding bells on them had been filled with helium and tied to the corners of the tables. There was even another of Margaret's flower arrangements lending grace to the tables, which were laden with all the things needed to complement the meal and plate after plate of all kinds of desserts. Shelley had completely outdone herself. Beverly made a mental note to send everyone an e-mail afterward with the name of Shelley's business.

Noah, Dan, Leo, and Allan took the lead in removing the tarp from the clams and retrieving all the layers of food. The clams had opened and the potatoes were tender. Everyone participated in pulling back the husks on the ears of corn and getting rid of the silk, and then Shelley brushed the ears with an herb butter mix she'd made. Adelaide followed her, sprinkling each with grated Parmesan.

Jeff wrapped his arms around Beverly, steering her toward the food so that they could be the first to taste the clams. "Let's eat. I'm starving!"

She laughed. "Rehearsing to get married made me hungry too."

An hour later, everyone had eaten and was enjoying the fire the men had built up after the food was removed from the pit. Some people roasted marshmallows and made s'mores. Jeff's best man, his friend Douglas Winston, had brought a guitar and was idly strumming, providing background music. When he started a popular tune that people knew, they sang along.

Beverly left Jeff chatting with a group of men and sidled through the crowd in search of her three closest friends. But before she found them, she came across Jeff's grandfather seated on a rock with Celia Patterson. Celia rose as Beverly approached.

"Keep him company for a moment, dear," she requested. "I'm going to get us some more punch."

Beverly sank down onto the rock with a smile, giving the old man a hug. "How are you doing?" She noticed the thick blanket on the rock was a nice cushion from both chill and the hard surface.

Mr. Maker grinned at her. "Just fine. Got a pretty girl dancing attendance on me, don't I?"

Beverly laughed. "I'm assuming you don't mean me."

"Nope, but I can't complain about you either. My boy's lucky to be getting you."

"And the same for me, getting him," Beverly said. "He's a wonderful man, and I know that a lot of that is thanks to you."

The old man beamed. "He was a good kid, easy to raise, other than a few ornery stunts like all kids. I was lucky to have had him." His smile faded. "Carolyn, she didn't always make the smartest choices, the way I see it. But she loved Jeff, and I think she knew he'd be better off with me than dragging around the world after her."

"It was a loving choice," Beverly agreed. "I know she loves him. It couldn't have been easy."

"You're a peach," Mr. Maker told her. "Carolyn can be a little hard to take from time to time. I was afraid she'd put her foot in her mouth and scare you away. But instead, you've managed to make her think this whole wedding was her idea."

Beverly chuckled. "She's enthusiastic about it, and I'm glad." Celia was returning, and Beverly rose to give the older woman her seat back. "I'll see you two tomorrow."

"Wouldn't miss it for the world!" Celia piped.

Leaving Mr. Maker, she continued on until she had found Shelley, Diane, and Margaret. "Come with me."

The four friends gathered around a nearby boulder, on which Beverly placed a covered picnic basket. From it, she removed three wrapped gifts, handing one to each woman. "I have a gift for Charlotte and for the girls too, but I wanted to give you these separately," she told them, her eyes shining. "When I came to Marble Cove, I was alone, and I was lonely, although I'd never have admitted it at the time. You three took me under your wing and helped me become the person I am today. Thank you." She wiped away a tear. "I hope each of you knows how deeply I esteem you and treasure your friendship."

"Group hug," Diane said, and they all moved together briefly. Then she pulled back. "Let's open these on the count of three. One-two-*three*!"

It only took a moment to uncover the boxes and open them. As they pulled out the gift, Margaret gasped.

Each of them held an eight-by-ten silver frame in which was a photo of the four of them. It had been taken at the light-decorating contest ceremony held at the old train station before Christmas. The four women stood on the steps, arms around each other, beaming into the camera. Across the front, Beverly had hired a calligrapher who had scrolled in silver: "The sisters of my heart."

"Oh." Diane touched the glass with a gentle finger, tracing their smiling faces. "Oh, Beverly, this is . . ." She trailed off.

Beverly nodded, fighting the sob that wanted to escape. "I had one made for myself too. I just wanted each of you to know what a difference you have made in my life. God knew what He was doing when He called each of us to live on Newport Avenue."

Shelley said, "Oh, rats. My mascara's going to run for sure!"

Everyone laughed, using the moment to conquer their emotions, gathering the wrapping paper and boxes as Beverly picked up her basket and went to deliver the rest of the gifts to those helping with the wedding.

It was perfect, Beverly thought as she sought out her groom. She hadn't expected that she'd enjoy a rehearsal dinner on the beach with food baked in a sand pit. But this was a new Beverly with a new life, and it was absolutely perfect for Jeff and her.

CHAPTER TWENTY-THREE

Beverly's wedding day dawned as clear and mild as the day before. After taking Scamp out and having breakfast with her father, she returned to her room for a solid thirty minutes of devotional time. The small knot of anxiety she hadn't realized she'd been carrying around during Jeff's absence had completely dissolved, and she laughed at herself. Here she'd been thinking she was so calm, so accepting!

Still, she had done far better than she would have several years earlier. Back then, she'd have worked herself into a migraine or some kind of gastric distress if her fiancé had gone to climb a mountain a week before the wedding.

At seven thirty, she gave her father a hug when she saw Margaret's van pull up. "Bye, Father. I'll see you at the church. Jeff's best man will pick you up at noon, all right?"

Her father nodded. He hugged her hard. "My dear, dear girl," he said. "Your mother would be so pleased if she could see how happy you look."

"I think she knows." Beverly felt her throat close up. Her mother had been at her last wedding, but *this* marriage was the one Beverly truly wished her mother could be here to celebrate. "See you at the church, Father. I love you."

Then she stepped out the door. The next time she returned to this house, she would be a married woman.

Margaret was driving, and there was room for Beverly to sit in the front passenger seat. As she climbed in, the crowd in the van cheered. And "crowd" was the word. Diane and Shelley occupied the middle row bucket seats, and in the back, Adelaide, Emma, and Hailey giggled and bounced.

"The Cut 'n' Curl train has arrived," Margaret announced.

"Whoo-whoo!" called Hailey, while Adelaide and Emma repeated, "Choo-choo, choo-choo," several times.

"Happy wedding day!" Diane told her.

Beverly smiled, so happy she thought she might just burst. "Thank you. I'm so ready to get this train rolling!"

"Your wish is my command," Margaret said.

Beverly turned to Shelley. "I know I told you last night, but that clambake was the most wonderful rehearsal dinner ever. It was absolutely perfect for us."

"And the food was terrific too," Diane put in. "A truly memorable start to this wedding celebration."

Shelley beamed. "I've done family clambakes for big crowds before, but everything did seem extra-tasty last night, didn't it?"

"It did," Margaret confirmed. "And here we are. Everybody out!"

Carlie's Cut 'n' Curl was only three blocks from Newport Avenue, but the women had decided to drive so that once their "wedding hair" had been done, they would be in no danger from the sometimes unpredictable ocean breezes.

Everyone piled out and trooped into the styling salon, where Carlie, the stylist who regularly worked with Margaret, Adelaide, and Beverly, greeted them with a smile.

"Hello, ladies!" Atop Beverly's head she plunked a circlet of faux pearls with a short veil of net attached. It bore a cardboard cutout of three-inch-high letters that spelled out B-R-I-D-E.

Delighted, Beverly admired herself in the mirror while Diane took a photo with the camera she had slung around her neck.

"Who's first?" Carlie asked. "Shall we start with these young ladies?"

"Me?" Emma asked. "P'eez?"

"Sure." Carlie turned and placed a booster seat on her regular styling chair. Then she turned and swung Emma into the seat. "Mom, what are we doing with this pretty girl?" Carlie asked.

Shelley dug into her bag and came up with a magazine picture she'd clipped. "I thought for both girls the front could be pulled up and back and the rest could be left down and curly like this. Emma's got natural curl. If you make it curlier, it'll hold well. And we made these little combs covered with babies' breath and little pink rosebuds that we could anchor right in front of the hair tie. Will that work?"

Carlie nodded. "Excellent. I think that will work well. I love it when someone comes in with a plan."

As the stylist got to work, Beverly glanced at her watch. "Carolyn, Charlotte, and Aunt Helen were supposed to meet us here." She barely had finished uttering the sentence when the door of the salon opened, and the ladies in question arrived.

★ ★ ★

Shelley got her hair done after the little girls, and Margaret went next. They would deliver the cake and make sure all the flowers and décor at the reception were in place before meeting the rest of the wedding party at the church. Aunt Helen would convey Charlotte, Carolyn, Diane, and Beverly to the church, where they would dress.

"All right," Margaret said, hopping behind the wheel of the van. "Cake time."

Shelley blew out a nervous breath after Dan had come to pick up Adelaide, Hailey and Emma. She'd done a lot of decorating and a lot of baking. She'd consulted with her friend Liza Cramble, who owned the Cakery, to make sure she had every detail of how to make Beverly's cake down pat. But still... she would be very happy and relieved once it was all in place on the table in the ballroom at the Landmark Inn. "I hope this goes okay," she confessed. "I'm a nervous wreck."

"Better you than Beverly," Margaret said. "She seems a lot calmer than I'd expected."

"Jeff's back," Shelley replied. "Having him away was actually a good thing, I think. It made her realize that the only really important thing about this wedding is that they are together."

"Then why are you worried?"

Shelley laughed. "Trust you to hit the nail on the head. It'll be fine."

And it was. As Shelley placed the final flower blossom at the base of the cake an hour later, Margaret stood back and clapped. "It's gorgeous! Beverly's going to be blown away when she sees this."

"Thank you." It had turned out well. Shelley glanced around the room. It was a symphony of pink and lavender on white. Silver chafing dishes and cutlery matched the gleam from the chandeliers, and an ice sculpture of the lighthouse stood atop the baby grand. Through the wide windows, the sea crashed against the rocks and the real lighthouse mirrored its ice image. "Everything looks perfect, doesn't it?"

Margaret nodded. "I can't think of a single thing I would have done differently. Are you ready to go get gussied up?"

Shelley nodded. "Let's go."

Of course, all they had to do was go directly to the church. Beverly had everything all planned out. They had taken their dresses, makeup bags, shoes, and accessories to the church yesterday. If she'd been organizing it, Shelley was pretty certain she'd have left her dress at home and probably forgotten to set up the guest book altogether.

The rest of the women had just arrived at the church when they pulled in, and everyone walked in together.

They took a quick peek into the sanctuary, which was looking good despite the damage it had sustained some months ago. While the restoration hadn't been fully completed, the huge space had already received a new roof, and the windows all had been cleaned and releaded, allowing the afternoon light to stream into the sanctuary as it hadn't done in years.

As Beverly had prearranged, Mrs. Peabody and her sister Celia were waiting for them with sandwiches, fresh fruit, and drinks. The wedding was slated for two, so no one would have time for lunch. The ladies ate and dressed in the choir room, far away from the Sunday school classroom designated for the men. Beverly didn't want to take any chances on having Jeff catch a glimpse of her before the ceremony.

The time dissolved into a series of snapshots.

Diane and Charlotte carefully gathered Beverly's dress and lifted it over her head. As it settled into place, the skirt floated out around her, and the two bridesmaids gently spread out the train.

Shelley discreetly double-knotted Emma's sash so the active little girl's antics wouldn't result in a yard of chiffon trailing across the floor.

Beverly's aunt Helen, stunning in a pretty pale-green suit, tenderly closed the clasp of an heirloom bracelet around Beverly's wrist. It had been given to Helen by Beverly's mother, and she had worn it at her own wedding before passing it on to Beverly.

Jeff's mother, tears in her eyes, placed the sapphire necklace about Beverly's neck and kissed her cheek.

Margaret appeared in the doorway, her arms filled with bridesmaids' and the bride's bouquets.

Beverly stood at the altar for the first of dozens of photographs, surrounded by her bridesmaids and flower girls, her smile wide and beautiful.

Adelaide greeted Shelley and Dan who had just dropped off the kids with Diane. "Sign right here," she directed, pointing at the guest book, before Jeff's cousin Ames escorted them to the very front of the church to sit in Beverly's family section with Beverly's aunt Helen and uncle George, Charlotte's two sons, Margaret, Allan, Mrs. Peabody, and Celia.

The final strains of the prelude concluded, and Shelley's heart leaped into her throat as she realized that Jeff's mother Carolyn had just been seated next to Mr. Maker; the wedding was about to begin!

As the first simple melody of Johann Pachelbel's Canon in D Major began to fill the church, Reverend Locke entered through a side door, followed by Jeff, Aiden, Doug Winston, and Jeff's college roommate Brian. At the same time, Maddie Bancroft slipped into the choir loft, where she would sit until time for her solo. Reverend Locke ascended the two shallow steps to the altar and, with a smile, gave a tiny nod to Beverly's cousin Charlotte in the very back.

Clad in a beautiful white shantung silk dress with a square neckline and high-waisted A-line skirt of lavender, Charlotte slowly began to walk up the aisle. She looked very nervous, but when Shelley winked and gave her a thumbs-up, Charlotte smiled and her shoulders visibly relaxed. As she reached the first two pews, Diane, with a huge smile, also began to come forward. The beaming matron of honor wore a dress similar to Charlotte's but with a peach skirt. Then it was Shelley's turn to be nervous as Hailey started forward. Beverly had decided to have Hailey carry a bouquet like the bridesmaids and to let Emma throw flower petals from a small basket. Hailey's eyes were wide, but she smiled as she walked, and she blew a tiny kiss to Dan and Shelley as she passed them.

Thinking of the difficulties the young girl had faced, and of how she had blossomed during the months she had been in their care, Shelley felt her throat grow tight. *No tears! No tears!* she admonished herself.

And then she saw Emma, as Dan reached forward and twined his fingers through hers.

They had feared the faces all along the aisle might intimidate Emma, although she'd seemed fine at the rehearsal last night.

Their fears had been baseless.

Emma took two steps, stopped, and took a petal from her basket. She tossed it high in the air, watched it flutter to the ground, took two more steps, stopped, and repeated the process. She caught the eye of someone in a pew and smiled coquettishly, waving.

People began to grin. A few giggles were heard. Emma was oblivious, happily making her way oh so slowly up the aisle. The organist, realizing what was happening, repeated a section of the Pachelbel.

Shelley turned and glanced up at Dan. His shoulders were shaking with suppressed mirth. Margaret was wiping tears of laughter from her eyes. Realizing there was absolutely nothing she could do, Shelley shrugged and struggled to contain her own giggles.

It was at that point Diane saved the day. Handing her bouquet to Charlotte, Diane walked down the aisle to Emma. Kneeling, she whispered, "Throw a *whole bunch*. Make the floor look pretty!"

Emma filled a chubby fist with petals, threw them up and all over both herself and Diane. "Wike dis?"

"Yes, that was perfect." Diane grinned at the little girl. "And keep walking while you throw them."

"You want to help?"

"I'd love to." Diane took a small pinch of blossoms and tossed them, and Emma mirrored her movements, picking up her pace. Together, the two of them arrived at the altar, and Diane resumed her place. Hailey held out a hand for Emma, who slipped into her spot right in front of Hailey.

"Oh, thank heavens," breathed Shelley.

Dan leaned forward. "That one is going to give us gray hair," he whispered into her ear.

All conversation ceased then as the organist began the "Trumpet Voluntary" by Jeremiah Clarke that Beverly had chosen as her processional. Everyone rose, facing the back of the church.

★ ★ ★

Beverly's father kissed her on the forehead and offered his arm. "You look beautiful, Beverly."

"I love you, Father." She laid her head against his shoulder very briefly as she took his arm, and then her attention turned to the front of the church.

Jeff waited for her there. He and his attendants wore gray suits with pinstriped jackets. His tie was white, while theirs were the same gray as their suits, and he wore a white rose in his lapel while they wore pink roses. But even if they'd all been dressed identically, she'd have had no trouble finding him.

Love shone from his eyes. His steady confident smile banished the nerves she was fighting, and she let her father slowly lead her up the aisle.

Familiar faces beamed at her. Fred and Cindy Little were there, and Cindy had a crushed tissue in her hand already. Frances Bauer had come with a group of her friends from church. Beverly knew Shelley's sister-in-law was staying with Ralph for a short time and that Frances wouldn't be attending the reception.

Noah Henry and Brenna McTavish sent her cheery smiles and Noah winked. A number of members of the choir from Old First were there, friends she'd made when she'd stepped in as the organist briefly at Easter last year. And there was Jules Benton with one arm around his wife, and Angela, her office receptionist, with a young man Beverly had yet to meet.

Evelyn Waters was wiping tears; Augie Jackson gave her a little wave; Leo Spangler was grinning. As she reached the front of the church, she stopped and gave Jeff's mother a kiss, then reached past her to kiss his grandfather as well.

And then Jeff reached for her hand, and her father relinquished her with a final kiss. He'd seen her marry once before, in a much larger, more formal ceremony. This time, she knew in her heart that the man she was about to offer her pledge to was the one with whom she would spend the rest of her life.

Reverend Locke cleared his throat quietly as the processional crescendoed and drew to a close, and Beverly turned her attention to him.

★ ★ ★

Beverly felt as if someone had filled her with helium, as if she could just fly away into the sky, she was that happy.

She caught a glimpse of herself in the foyer mirror as they lined up to greet their guests after the ceremony, and she knew she looked as lovely as she was ever going to look. Her satin gown should have looked simple, accented only by a crystal-and-pearl design at the top of the high waistline. Instead, she looked impossibly elegant, amazingly perfect. She had opted not to wear a veil, and instead had chosen a bandeau adorned with pink and white rose petals that mirrored the decorative crystal-and-pearl piece on her dress. Her shoulder-length hair was swept up and back and woven into a loose, lovely design of ringlets.

The rest of the wedding party had followed them down the aisle. Quickly, Diane and Charlotte bustled up the modest train on Beverly's gown so she didn't step on it as she moved around.

Jeff leaned forward and touched his lips to her forehead. "Finally," he said. "Married to the most wonderful woman in the world."

She smiled up at him and then touched a hand to the sapphire necklace. "Do you recognize this?" she asked.

Jeff's eyes widened. "That's my mother's, right? From her wedding to my dad—she gave it to you?"

Beverly nodded. "I think I've made the cut."

"I'd say so." He grinned. Then: "Hey, look to your left," he whispered.

Diane stood a few paces away, Leo at her side.

"Hello, gorgeous," Leo said to her. He looked striking in a navy suit, his silvering hair gleaming. "Save a dance for me at the reception?"

Diane's expression warmed and she smiled, taking his arm. "I can't think of anyone I'd rather dance with. How about I save you all of them?"

Leo's gaze deepened. "I'd like nothing better. No," he corrected himself. "I'd *love* nothing better."

Diane blushed, but her gaze was steady on his as she stretched over and touched her lips to his cheek.

Beverly hand tightened on Jeff's. "Any bets on the next wedding we attend?" she whispered back.

Jeff shook his head, smiling. "Not taking that one. I'd lose for sure."

As she greeted all the guests eager to congratulate them, Beverly kept an eye on her friends.

Shelley and Dan and the children came to stand beside Leo and Diane as they waited for the receiving line to end. Margaret, Allan, and Adelaide joined the group. Adelaide had just finished circulating through the crowd, making sure everyone had received birdseed to toss.

The last guests through the receiving line were Noah and Brenna. After giving her a hug and Jeff a hearty handshake, Noah said, "Thank you for inviting me to the wedding. It's my very first one in Marble Cove, but it won't be my last. I've decided to look for a home here."

Beverly gasped. "Noah, that's wonderful!"

The young man smiled. "I have a lot of reasons to stay, you know. After all, who better to oversee the museum renovation?"

Jeff laughed knowingly, looking at Brenna's hand clasped firmly in Noah's. "Yeah, I'm sure that's the biggest reason you want to stay."

Noah merely grinned. Then he gestured toward the doors. "There's your ride." Beverly turned to look. There, parked right outside Old First, was the silver Jaguar Elias Thorpe had purchased not long before he'd left town.

It was nice to see it being used for such a joyous occasion. She could only imagine that for Elias, it had been a status symbol. For Noah, it was a family connection to a man he had loved, a man who seemingly had changed so radically from his Marble Cove days that it was hard to even fathom he'd been the same person. But anyone looking at photos of

Noah and his late grandfather would have little doubt that there was a family connection.

Family was a funny thing, she mused. It played such a role in people's lives in so many ways. Today, she and Jeff were creating a brand-new family to blend with those of which they were already a part. Elias had helped Brenna's grandmother because she was family, according to Noah. Shelley had become a vital member of the Bauer family during Ralph's illness. Adelaide had recently begun to show her family that while she loved them, she could be independent, and Diane...well, Beverly wouldn't be surprised if Diane found herself creating a new family structure of her own in the not-too-distant future.

As for herself, the gifts she had given to her three dearest friends last night had said it all. These treasured relationships she had forged since moving to Marble Cove had made them far more than simply neighbors. In truth, they were her family now, and she part of theirs.

EPILOGUE

Diane awoke early on Monday morning. She was still basking in the glow that came from Beverly's wedding. From the first moment to the last, not a thing had gone wrong. It had been a wonderful day, and one she and her friends would always remember.

It had been a wonderful day in a very personal way as well. She had been very conscious of Leo in the room when her friends had been speaking their vows. Her relationship with Leo had changed since their early days of dating casually. It was richer and deeper now, in part because of some of the experiences they had shared during her illness. It was, she had begun to realize, the sort of relationship she could envision lasting for many years. On impulse, she grabbed her cell phone and texted him good morning before getting on with her day.

As had become her habit, after breaking her fast and walking the dog that had become her treasured companion, she retreated to her office to begin work for the day.

The sun streamed in, highlighting the shades of ocean and shore that she had chosen for the color theme of her little beachside cottage. Through the window, she could see her hydrangea bushes and irises beginning to bloom. It was a peaceful, inspiring setting in which to work.

Pulling her laptop computer toward her, she set her fingers on the keys with a sense of anticipation. Today was The Day. She had been planning her new book for some time now, and finally, she believed she was ready to write.

She smiled at the photo occupying a place of honor on her desk. She, Beverly, Margaret, and Shelley smiled out of the photo, solidly connected to each other and entwined in each others' lives. When she'd come to Marble Cove, she'd hoped to begin a new life. She could never have imagined how much more she would find when she decided to purchase her little cottage on Newport Avenue.

She flexed her fingers and set them on the keys. What was the best way to begin? Ah...of course. She'd been hoping for—

A second chance.

That's what the lighthouse on the bluff meant to her. At least, that's what she hoped it would mean...

About the Author

Best-selling author Anne Marie Rodgers has published nearly four dozen novels since 1992. She has written for four Guideposts series, including *Tales from Grace Chapel Inn, Mystery and the Minister's Wife, Stories from Hope Haven,* for which she wrote the launch book, and *Miracles of Marble Cove.* When she isn't writing, Anne Marie devotes much of her time to animal rescue. Since childhood, she has felt called to help those of God's creatures in need who cannot speak for themselves. Currently, she coordinates the Orphaned Kitten Program in State College, Pennsylvania, where she makes her home, and assists with a variety of other animal rescue efforts, including wildlife rehabilitation and canine rescue. She and her husband share their home with three dogs and three cats. They also served as the intake point for more than one hundred infant kittens in need this year.

Baking with Shelley

Carrot Cake

3 cups carrots, peeled and grated

1½ cups vegetable oil

2 cups sugar

4 eggs

2 cups self-rising flour

2 teaspoons cinnamon

1 teaspoon vanilla

Preheat oven to 350 degrees. Cut parchment paper to fit the bottom of two round cake pans. Spray pans with cooking spray and put parchment paper on the bottom. Prepare carrots; set aside. Combine oil and sugar, and mix until smooth. Add eggs one by one, beating well after each. Add flour; mix well. Stir in cinnamon and vanilla. Stir in grated carrots. Pour batter into pans. Bake for twenty-five to thirty minutes. Let set in pan ten minutes before removing to cooling racks. When cool, cover with cream cheese icing. (Try baking this recipe in cupcake or mini-muffin pans for a delicious fun treat for the kids!)

Cream Cheese Icing

1 eight-ounce package cream cheese, softened
1 stick butter, softened
1 pound confectioners' sugar
1 teaspoon vanilla
½ cup chopped pecans (optional)

Combine cream cheese and butter; mix until creamy. Add confectioners' sugar; mix until smooth. Stir in vanilla and pecans. Spread on cooled cake layers.

FROM THE GUIDEPOSTS ARCHIVES

This story, by Melody Behrs of
Racine, Wisconsin, originally appeared
in the February 2008 issue of *Guideposts*.

Our wedding was unconventional—exactly what Matt and I wanted. We both had failed marriages in our past, so we planned to do something different this time to symbolize our desire that this one would last: a sunrise ceremony on the Wisconsin shore of Lake Michigan, releasing balloons instead of lighting a unity candle, to signify letting go of the past. We even wrote our own vows and put them in a bottle. To share our love with the world, we would cast the bottle into the lake. I included our names, address, and the date of our wedding: Matt and Melody Behrs, Married at the Wind Point Lighthouse, August 18th. "It would be interesting to find out where it turns up," I told Matt.

Matt threw the bottle in, but the wind blew it back toward me. I laughed as it landed at my feet. On his second try, the bottle barely made it into the water. *With our luck, that bottle won't go anywhere,* I thought. After seeming to bob in place for awhile, it drifted away, and I turned toward Matt.

One thing was certain. I was lucky to have found him. We'd been together for five years, and I wanted this marriage to last. In the back of my mind, though, I had doubts that I was cut out for marriage, doubts that we could make it work. I wanted to silence all those negative thoughts.

One day, about a month later, happily settled in my new home with Matt, he went to the mailbox and took out the mail. There was a letter addressed to Matt and Melody, with a return address Matt didn't recognize.

He carried the mail inside, sat down at the kitchen table with the letter and opened it. Our bottle had been found! A couple discovered it while walking their dogs—all the way over on the Michigan side of the Great Lake. But that wasn't all. Matt read the rest out loud to me in disbelief and, as he did, I felt the last of my doubts disappear.

"We were also married on the beach, on this side of the lake," the letter read, "just like you, on August 18—twenty-eight years ago. We wish you both the best."

Dear Reader,

You hold in your hands the final Miracles of Marble Cove book. It has been our distinct pleasure to bring this series to you. We have delighted in dreaming up these stories and working with an amazing team of authors to put them on the page. Melody Carlson, Anne Marie Rodgers, Pam Hanson & Barbara Andrews, Leslie Gould, Dan Walsh, Patti Berg, Susan Page Davis, Camy Tang, and Sunni Jeffers did a remarkable job of collaborating to create the world of Marble Cove and bring our characters to life on the pages of every book.

If you have enjoyed these stories even half as much as we have, then we have done our jobs well. We have grown to know and love Diane, Shelley, Margaret, and Beverly— the four memorable neighbors, friends, and sisters whose stories shaped the series. We've been so inspired by how these women have grown in grace and faith through the adventures they shared and the friendships they forged with one another. And while we're sad to see the series come to an end, we are pleased, honored, and grateful that you have chosen to come along with us on this wonderful journey.

With warmest regards,
Editors of Guideposts

A NOTE FROM THE EDITORS

We hope you enjoyed Miracles of Marble Cove, published by the Books and Inspirational Media Division of Guideposts, a nonprofit organization that touches millions of lives every day through products and services that inspire, encourage, help you grow in your faith, and celebrate God's love.

Thank you for making a difference with your purchase of this book, which helps fund our many outreach programs to military personnel, prisons, hospitals, nursing homes, and educational institutions.

We also create many useful and uplifting online resources. Visit Guideposts.org to read true stories of hope and inspiration, access OurPrayer network, sign up for free newsletters, download free e-books, join our Facebook community, and follow our stimulating blogs.

To learn about other Guideposts publications, including the best-selling devotional *Daily Guideposts*, go to Guideposts .org/Shop, call (800) 932-2145, or write to Guideposts, PO Box 5815, Harlan, Iowa 51593.